The Peckish

Jo Milanne

Jaelo Tales

The Peckish

Copyright © 2024 by Jo Milanne

Paperback ISBN 978-1-7637284-3-1

All rights reserved.

The story, all names, characters, and incidents portrayed in this production are fictitious. No identification is intended or should be inferred with actual persons (living or deceased) or with places and buildings.

Contents

1

CHECK OUT

Isla Tickle knew herself to be an ordinary person of little consequence. Knowing her own limitations, she kicked herself for being
foolishly seduced by the charm and apparent wealth of her first ever
lover, Troy Van Baas.

Before Troy, Isla had only two close encounters with the opposite
sex. Both had been fumbling and inept attempts by the boys, who lived
to regret it.

The first had proffered the age old 'you show me yours and I'll show
you mine' when Isla was twelve and the boy thirteen. Isla got a peek
at his pale dangling piece of mischief and failed to see the attraction.
In turn, she flashed him a view of her scant new pubes with her legs
held tightly together. The boy claimed it unfair as he didn't really see
anything and demanded more. He made the mistake of hounding her.
Isla said if he didn't leave her alone she would tell everyone he had a
crooked willy. Since his item was indeed very slightly askew and the
boy knew it, he slunk off, defeated. Perhaps Isla had given him a phobia
for life. She could only hope.

The way Isla had been brought up might have cowered some but it
served to toughen little Miss Tickle.

Isla's next experience happened at age fourteen during a school excursion bush walk. A fifteen year old boy dragged her off the path saying she had great tits and he'd give her half a roll of fruit jubes for a feel. Isla snarled:

"Feel this."

She kneed him in the balls and took the lollies anyway. The whole roll. He had rolled about in agony while groaning:

"Aargh. Pity about your face...I'd need a paper bag.."

That insult hit home, Isla's round freckled face had yet to become interesting.

Toughing it out, Isla managed to laugh and saunter off without a backward glance.

When Troy Van Baas rocketed into Isla's life, it changed the world as she knew it, elevating her to dreamland for the few short months spent as Troy's girl. Her mundane job, five years as a checkout operator, remained the same, but while ever she had Troy, Isla coped well with her tedious work conditions.

The worst part of work at the supermarket had been the lecherous store manager, Fergus Rudin, a married man who forever tried for a grope. One day, Isla exacted a small revenge on him that led to far reaching consequences, not only for herself.

But Fergus wasn't Isla's only man problem: Troy Van Baas had always seemed too good to be true. And he was. Isla was dumped, offended and heartbroken within one short withering conversation with her lover.

Feeling lonely and disconnected after splitting with her handsome high-flying lover, Isla struggled to pick herself up. A few regular customers got to know the check-out girl, but only by the name Isla on her name tag. The young woman had no family.

Abandoned as a newborn, Isla had been found wrapped in a pillowcase pinned with a scrawled note: *Don't want it. Can't keep it.* The 'it' baby was discovered nestled inside a cardboard grocery carton originally labelled: Tickles 1000 Island Dressing. Part of the printing had been ripped away when the tape was torn off, leaving 'Tickle---000 Isla---Dressing. So the unknown baby girl had been dubbed Isla Tickle with the befitting initials I.T.

Isla had been a screaming colicky baby and neither pretty nor obedient as a child. Passed over for adoption, brought up in institutions, the girl lived with the stigma of being forever unwanted.

In time, the plain child reached puberty when she blossomed into a most attractive young woman, much to everyone's great surprise, not the least her own.

Although Isla Tickle excelled in business studies, welfare authorities found the supermarket job for her and said she should be grateful for it. Happy to break away from the orphanage, Isla rented a small furnished flat that took up most of her modest pay packet. On the upside, her rent included electricity and eventually, an opportunity to save a little money.

Isla's flat, built in under an old couple's house was functional and near enough to the supermarket that she could walk to work. Although permanent rentals were difficult to find in the seaside town, the flat only contained a single bed, a small caravan refrigerator and an even smaller television set that sat atop a chest of drawers in front of the bed. Cooking amenities consisted of a one burner camp stove, originally with two butane canisters supplied but once they were used up Isla must buy her own gas. The one sink was a laundry tub that did for everything. A plastic basin sat within for dish washing. A shower and WC were situated semi outside accessed via a flyscreened patio where Isla hung her washing.

The lack in the little flat narrowed down who wanted it but the spartan conditions did not bother Isla. After living so long in shared dormitories, Isla revelled in her own private space and her feeling of independence.

Happily setting out her few toiletries on a window ledge in the shower room, Isla rejoiced in the convenience of having a bathroom all to herself without ever having to queue. Dispensing with the shower bag for every trip to the bathroom was a greater luxury to Isla than being able to watch television in bed with sole control of the remote.

The homeowners liked their quiet tenant and did not intrude on Isla but to ask small favours now and then. For two months of each year, when the old couple visited relatives in New Zealand, Isla's rent was waived in lieu of feeding their aviary birds and keeping the lawn trimmed. Isla found using their push mower was easy if she did a little every day. Caretaker duties were a boon for Isla who saved as much as possible, slowly building a small nest egg.

Isla walked to and from work for the first three years, often wheeling home a few groceries her old landlords ordered, using their shopping cart. When she mentioned saving for a car, they offered their small ten-year-old sedan cheaply with driving lessons thrown in. The elderly man had been thinking it high time he relinquished his driving license after a couple of near misses. Isla probably spent more time polishing that car than driving it but just having wheels boosted her perception of freedom.

Before Troy, Isla had not socialised except at work, if chats with the other girls and women counted as such. The dull job did not encourage anyone to spend more time with their workmates. Everyone was glad to get away at the end of their shifts to spend time with their own friends and families. Isla made the most of her free time alone.

Swimming in the sea became Isla's favourite pursuit. She loved the buoyancy of water and the physical exercise. She slept more soundly after a strenuous workout against the waves and grew stronger and fitter with the healthful activity.

Isla knew she was missing out on male company but accepted her lack of chance, comparing herself to the many beautiful bikini clad beach belles vying for guys. So it seemed a major miracle when Troy Van Baas took a shine to her and approached her on the beach.

Isla was swept off her feet in a whirlwind romance. Suddenly the sun rose more brightly every day and the bored supermarket employee whipped through working hours with a smile. Being with Troy was all she could think about and if her landlords noticed her absence at nights, they did not say.

Overwhelmed by Troy's good looks and wealthy playboy lifestyle, the lonely young woman fell deeply and incautiously in love. Isla had hungered for affection and soon became addicted to sex with Troy. Her needs were insatiable, multiplied by feeling unloved and unlovable her whole life up to that point.

Isla's euphoric dream turned into a nightmare after Troy let her down cruelly. Partying aboard Troy's yacht amongst elitist guests, Isla became aware of an upcoming gala premier event that had them all agog. Naively,

Isla assumed Troy would take her as his partner. Having nothing suitable to wear, she looked into hiring an outfit from a bridal boutique.

Isla tried on several gowns, with growing excitement and a gung-ho attitude at the expense. Finding the perfect fit, Isla sent Troy a photo online, confident the elegant silky dress complimented her figure and perfectly suited the occasion. His prompt phone call in reply broke her heart:

"Isla. Sorry if you misunderstood. But I can't possibly take *you* to that. You realise my partner has to be a *somebody*. But hey. Never fear, I will be back in your arms tout sweet."

Isla reeled from the affront but quickly reacted to his insult:

"Like hell. You can go fuck yourself Troy." She spat.

Isla would not be dumped like that and had abruptly ended the call. She rarely used coarse language but this time nothing less did it for her.

The taint of being a soft touch couldn't be washed away in the surf, no matter how long Isla spent swimming in the sea. She had been too angry to shed a tear. At first.

Isla had told Troy off to his enormous amazement and disbelief. No woman dared do that to *him*. If she had done it to his face he'd have smashed into her with his fists. Instead, he smashed a few crockery items in futile fury, raving that someday she would regret it. He would make her sorry she was ever born. He entertained himself with thoughts of what he would do to Isla, given the opportunity.

Troy Van Baas was unused to being refused anything and it rankled more coming from someone he considered just a common bit of rough. If not for Isla's voluptuous body he'd never have considered her future potential. The silly bitch. He could have made a small fortune from her and thrown her a pittance that would still be more money than she'd ever seen before. Now he plotted to take Isla down, thinking it was only a matter of time. Tick-Tock.

Isla only understood she had climbed above her station in life and the higher she'd risen, the harder she crash landed. Just why Troy went for a nobody like herself became clear eventually as he had a history of recruiting attractive women to be exploited.

Isla nursed her despondency and been stuck in a rut until she hit on a notion to make her boring supermarket job slightly more bearable. It was a silly plan of matchmaking strangers. Trying to survive after Troy, Isla had been clutching at straws to find some purpose to her life. That was her only excuse and she knew it to be a lame one.

Isla's motivation came about while observing frequent supermarket customers and what they routinely purchased, giving her an insight into their lives. It was easy to judge who lived alone, what pets they had and possibly how much they could afford to spend on groceries.

The notion occurred to Isla that she could spice up her own days by getting some of her lone customers to meet socially. How to do it was the question. Sleepless alone in her bed, Isla concocted plans at night as a way of keeping her sadder thoughts at bay.

Eventually Isla decided to secretly slip little notes into customers' shopping bags at the checkout. If she was careful enough her targets would never know how the notes came to be in their bags. Isla knew no one ever bothered keeping close watch on empty reusable bags hung on their shopping trolleys as they browsed around the aisles, so almost anyone might have slipped a note in while a shopper wasn't looking.

Isla prepared small messages printed on various coloured note paper. She was careful never to use her normal handwriting but rather block print with different slants and styles. The notes were easy to have at the ready in her pinafore pocket. A popular local cafe was chosen as a suggested place for couples to hook up.

There was little joy in matchmaking if Isla couldn't see the couple meet. She had a regular breakfast spot towards a back corner at The Tipsy Turnip, a large open cafe overlooking the sea. Of course, Isla planned for her chosen pair to meet in the cafe during the hours she sat there herself. She could sit for up to an hour doing newspaper puzzles, pretending to think of crossword answers. Tapping a pencil on her chin as if deep in thought, Isla could scan the room without seeming to stare at people.

Isla knew herself to be pathetic for going to such lengths. But she was past caring about that, telling herself *if the shoe fits*.

So, over breakfast at the cafe, Isla disguised herself by wearing heavy rimmed spectacles and the type of headscarf often worn by balding cancer patients or others who had lost their hair. She found people steered clear of possible illness. No one ever asked to share her booth.

Isla's first guinea pig choice at the supermarket was a grey haired man who always wore blue denim jeans and checked shirt. He had to be widowed with a cat. The old guy wore a wedding ring but regularly bought frozen meals for one, mens toiletries and cat food.

Another single with a cat, Isla decided, was the curly haired lady who only ever bought single pieces of fruit, meat packs with only one chop or one small steak, small packets of staple goods and cat food. This lady always wore green shamrock earrings.

These customers brought their own shopping bags which they hung on the trolley hooks while walking around the aisles. So that fitted with Isla's plan.

Both single people shopped at various times but always on pension days so Isla came to her work station prepared. The chosen couple each had notes slipped in with their shopping.

The man was given a pink paper note *'I would love to meet you for coffee at The Tipsy Turnip Cafe. I am there 7am most mornings. I will be wearing green shamrock earrings.'*

The lady had blue notepaper: *'I would love to meet you at The Tipsy Turnip Cafe. I am there most mornings 7am. Can I buy you a coffee?'*

Mission half accomplished; Isla waited on tenterhooks over her cafe breakfast at 7am to see what happened. She knew people often left check-out receipts in their shopping bags, but thought the coloured paper notes would stand out and be read. Isla had to be at work by 8 so couldn't linger too long.

The next day the man appeared but not the lady. He also came the second day at 7am and eureka! So did the lady, luckily still wearing the distinctive green shamrock earrings. The man approached her, and the couple spoke. Isla felt a thrill of achievement.

Unfortunately, Isla couldn't hear the conversation, but it seemed to go well. The couple sat at the same table and chatted over coffee. They left together. Isla watched them take the path to the beach, hopefully they were going for a walk to get to know each other.

Isla wondered what would happen if they each denied slipping the notes. She might be prime suspect if they figured it out. Nothing seemed to come of that, and Isla noted the couple meeting again on other mornings at The Tipsy Turnip. Seeing the friendship blossom, Isla felt good about bringing the single oldies together.

Encouraged, Isla sussed out another pair who might benefit from her meddling: A young woman with a toddler regularly bought cheap meals for one adult, some tinned toddler foods and cereals. Once she was short of money and had to put something back. Isla offered to put in the few dollars but the woman declined, embarrassed. Isla noted the young mother had tattoos and several piercings so perhaps had been better off financially at some point to afford these.

Pairing her off was more difficult. Until Isla noted a middle-aged bloke inked with tatts and wearing an eyebrow ring. He usually came in late smelling of petrol or oil, as if he did some kind of mechanical work. Good if he was employed. He seemed single too, often buying one steak, one tin of Coke, small pasta salad and one bread roll in a paper packet from the bakery counter. He never brought his own shopping bags so his note would have to be slipped into the bread roll packet. Trickier. He might suspect someone in the bakery. As long as not herself it seemed worth the risk.

Notes for the tattooed couple simply read: *'Want to meet? Tipsy Turnip Cafe 7am Saturday? BTW I have tatts and piercings.'*

Isla narrowed the day down hoping the man didn't work Saturdays. They both fell for it. Saturday morning: The woman arrived with her toddler in a pram. The man got up and they fronted each other. The woman waved her note. The man produced his from a pocket. Uh oh. They seemed confused and argued a bit. Shrugging the man laughed and so did she. Phew. They had coffee together and seemed to input information into their mobile phones. Hopefully they exchanged numbers and might meet again although they left separately.

Isla's first match, the older couple, made adjustments to their shopping. The shamrock earring lady included a pink lipstick in her next lot. The man bought a rare box of chocolates and a bunch of fresh flowers. When the tattoo guy bought a pack of two steaks and a large bottle of Coke, plus a toddler toy, Isla felt she should possible be sainted.

Isla teamed up a few others who seemed well matched and who also turned up to meet at The Tipsy Turnip. This made her wonder if most people were starved for a little romance in their lives. Perhaps *starved* was too dramatic a word but they had to be feeling at least peckish, she decided.

Isla was having fun with the peckish. So far so good.

Next, Isla strove to identify another single who might benefit from her matchmaking. A handsome well dressed man blipped Isla's radar as a possible candidate going by his food choices. This man looked to be about Isla's age or a little older. She rather fancied him herself. Perhaps this influenced her failure to find any suitable match for him.

Isla nicknamed the interesting man as Mr. Handsome.   He came in now and then usually at times that might be lunch hour or after work. Isla surmised Mr. Handsome had an office job. The more Isla saw of Mr. Handsome, the more she imagined being with him herself.

Biting the bullet, Isla slipped a note in with Mr. Handsome's shopping. *'I'm single, lonely, I'd like to get to know you. If you are interested, please be at Tipsy Turnip Cafe 7am Saturday.'* If Mr. Handsome turned up, Isla would know he was up for meeting someone.

Saturday came around and Isla wore a nicer than usual outfit. She was ready to whip the headscarf off if necessary and shake out her bouncy short brown hair. Excitement at saving the best for herself caused butterflies in her stomach. Perhaps she would hook up with him soon.

Mr. Handsome did turn up. He looked around the other customers in the cafe but skimmed past Isla sitting disguised in her corner. His gaze fell upon a tall tanned young surfer guy with long blond hair tied back in a pony tail and sitting alone with a cup of coffee. Mr. Handsome bought himself a coffee and sat opposite the slim surfie. They spoke briefly, smiled at each other, exchanged high fives and left together. Bummer. Trust her choice to be gay. Isla was discouraged. Seems she could orchestrate dates for others but not for herself.

Isla decided to give her matchmaking hobby a rest. Back at the supermarket, she wearily donned her pinafore apron in the locker room and returned to man her check-out station, thinking this would be her sad lot for ever.

Isla shrunk at what happened next. Mr. Handsome came into the store with the slim blond surfer guy. Isla tried to ignore them but to her dismay, they apparently knew her by name and introduced themselves:

"Isla Tickle. My name is Aiden Birdwhistle and this is my brother Ethan. We are partners in a private eye agency employed by this supermarket."

"Oh?"

"Following reports that someone has been putting notes in customers' shopping to engineer meetings, we have ascertained you are the culprit."

"Why me?" She gulped. How could they possibly know about her secret hobby?

"We know you are at The Tipsy Turnip Cafe every morning. No one else is there every day."

"So?"

"Come on Isla. Your apron pocket was searched in the locker room. The coloured note paper and felt pens were found by the store manager."

Isla knew the lecherous store manager, Fergus Rudin, would love to bring her down. She couldn't deny it.

"And? It's only spam. Not a crime."

"True. Nevertheless the manager takes a dim view."

Isla knew her heated face must be beetroot red. Maybe she had not committed a terrible crime but felt as if she had. She was sure to be sacked. In horror she imagined her shameful story flashed across newspapers and online media. People knew her by name. She'd be called Isla the creepy voyeur.

Isla abandoned her check-out station and fled to the locker room, deciding she would preempt her dismissal by emailing her resignation, leave town and try to put the whole embarrassing experience behind her. She would never go to The Tipsy Turnip Cafe again.

Aiden Birdwhistle caught up with Isla in the car park where she scurried to her old car prepared to get as far away as possible as quickly as possible, even though she had little in savings and no idea where to go.

"Isla wait."

"What do you want now?"

"Wondering why you didn't team me up with anyone. My brother thinks that's hilarious."

Isla was peeved and had nothing more to lose at that point.

"OK smart arse. I was checking you out myself. I am a check out chick after all. Or was."

"I've been checking you out as well." Mr. Handsome said somewhat shyly.

"Obviously." Isla fired back.

Biting back tears, her chest heaved with held back sobs.

"Come on Isla. I have a proposition you could like. Will you walk with me on the beach? Please? I find it's the best place to think."

Isla knew she was not fit to drive safely in her highly emotional state of upset and abject humiliation. Also her curiosity was tweaked and she rarely backed down from a challenge.

They took the path to the beach. A light drizzle of rain meant they had the sandy shore to themselves. Only a handful of dedicated surfers paddled on boards out beyond the waves in a grey stormy looking sea.

"Here's the thing." Aiden began. "We need to take on another person at our P.I. agency. My brother Ethan and I see your obvious potential in our industry. Would you consider working with us?"

Isla could not believe he wasn't kidding. But she liked that he said 'working with us' not 'working for us'.

"Why me?"

"We know you're good at disguise, can deadpan, are up for a bit of intrigue. And you like to watch. No brainer really."

"Is that all?" Isla asked.

"Also you seem pretty feisty. An advantage at times in our field."

Isla was sceptical. It sounded too easy. She'd run the gauntlet of Troy seeming too good to be true. Her reply weighed heavily with sarcasm.

"You'd want to employ someone like me who did all that sneaky under-handed spam note matchmaking?"

"Firstly, I'd like to tell you how we saw it. Ethan and I both considered your case to be so trivial we couldn't believe the supermarket manager wanted to pursue it. We quoted him well over full price because we actually didn't want the job. When he accepted, well, we can't afford to knock back a bird in the hand."

The brothers had taken an instant dislike to the supermarket manager, Fergus Rudin, on sight. There seemed something not quite right about him, but nothing they could put a finger on. Sometimes it was just a hunch.

"Fergus Rudin has been looking for a way to get back at me for a while." Isla said.

"I guess he's had it in for you. That explains why he paid from his personal bank account and not the supermarkets. We thought it had to be personal. Do you want to tell me about it Isla?"

"Sure I've got nothing to hide. Old Fergus is a groper. He tried it on with me at every opportunity. I dreaded being called to his office. One day his wife, Sylvia, came in and put a few items through my checkout on his staff discount card. So I told her we had the fancy condoms her husband ordered set aside and asked did she want to take them now."

"Were you fibbing to her Isla?"

"Yep. I tried it on to see her reaction. I could tell by her face I had put him deep in it. A shame I had to involve his wife that way. But what the hell, she might as well know what she is married to."

In fact, Mrs. Sylvia Rudin had long known her husband had the hots for that particular employee. She'd noticed the way his eyes followed Isla and how he licked his lips when she bent over. Sylvia declined taking the condoms and hurried out of the store. She didn't know if Isla was having a laugh at her expense by the condom remark. But she had a burning ambition to find out.

Aiden considered the clue given to Rudin's wife. It convinced him even more that Isla would suit working with them at the P.I. Agency. He went on to say how he and Ethan were dumbfounded when Rudin accepted paying the exorbitant fee they quoted.

The P.I. brothers had been itching to purchase some state of the art surveillance equipment. The supermarket job windfall went towards magnetic devices that could attach to vehicles for tracking remotely via their mobile phones.

Often they were hired by husbands or wives to check on their spouses and it boded well that Isla had no qualms about dobbing in a cheater. Although the majority of sleuthing was to catch out compensation fraudsters faking injuries, cases were various and could be quite odd. He admitted spying was a lot easier these days. It was commonplace to see people engrossed by their mobile phones in the street or anywhere. No one could tell for sure if they were taking photos, videoing or merely browsing online.

The Birdwhistle brothers sold the evidence they obtained to their clients and did not get involved with perpetrators. They could follow, watch, and record from hidden devices but avoided confrontation with the quarry. That was up to the people who hired them. The brothers also did not want to be recognised in case future revenge was taken by people they'd caught out. Aiden explained all this to Isla.

"Except in my case." Isla frowned. "You made sure to embarrass me to the fullest."

"Sorry but Mr. Rudin made it conditional that we confronted you at your work station. He seems not a very nice person to work for."

"He might report what I did to the papers." Isla worried.

"I've warned him not to do that. He would be inviting all sorts of repercussions that would reflect badly on the supermarket. After what you've told me about his groping, it must surely occur to him that you could accuse him of sexual harassment."

"True. And I would. But not now or he'll use what I've done to say I'm making that up."

"You're well out of that job Isla. You can't have liked it."

"I never liked it but of course I have to make a living. Alright. So you want a sneaky sheila as extra back up in your business. And I pass with flying colours. Apart from a basic grasp of business studies, that's about all I can offer you anyway." Isla said gruffly, still not over her upset. "I suppose I could give it a trial run. No promises."

Aiden smiled hoping to recruit and befriend the attractive but angry young woman. Since she had shown interest in matchmaking herself to him, he dared to try coaxing Miss Isla Tickle:

"Well not all you could offer. You'd definitely improve the scenery in our office."

"Are you actually flirting with me? After you caught me red-handed and made me walk out on my job? And I just told you what led to all this with Fergus Rudin and his stupid ego?"

Aiden held up his hands in surrender.

"Sorry. I guess that could be taken as flirting. Don't worry. I'm harmless. Just ask Ethan." Aiden smiled. "He says I'm a pushover. Actually he says *pathetic pushover*."

Dropping her hostile stance was easy. Aiden did seem nice. And he was very good looking. Isla saw she could do this. And it was not as if she had other options. His offer seemed genuine so why not try it. She could keep her little flat and would not have to leave town. Relief and wonder surged as she realised she was free at last from her boring supermarket job and grubby groping old Fergus Rudin.

Isla liked Aiden's mild flirting and welcomed his attention. He must know she fancied him a bit from her matchmaking confession. It had been months since she'd split with Troy and there could be lovely bonuses from working closely with Aiden.

"So Isla. Are you up for it?" Aiden asked eyeing her with a friendly twinkle.

"I am." She smiled with more than one meaning in mind.

There was no reason not to accept Birdwhistle's interesting offer and it had all happened so quickly. Aiden took her around to Birdwhistle's office to work out details of her new employment. Housed in a solid two-story brick building that had seen many businesses come and go over the years, including a tobacconist, barber shop, hair salon and real estate agency, the office seemed well equipped. Isla noticed what appeared to be living quarters on the upper floor, its verandah stretched the entire width of the frontage and doubled as the awning over the footpath.

The building sat on the corner of a quiet lane, one block back from the esplanade. The lane crossed the main street and led down to the beach. Opposite Birdwhistle's building, a car park beside a kindergarten and preschool faced the street. Next door to Birdwhistle's, separated by a narrow walkway, an old-fashioned hardware store had bags of firewood stacked in wheelbarrows out on the footpath. Some other small shops and businesses occupied the street but the main shopping centre where Isla had worked was further into the town.

Hotels, motels and takeaway food outlets were mostly along the esplanade, so Birdwhistle's agency occupied the quieter old area of town. A series of connected events led to the private eye business being operated from its current location:

In the past, Aiden Birdwhistle held a promising career as a building inspector until a crane toppled from an upper story, killing one workman and injuring several others on site. Aiden spent two years undergoing painful rehabilitation therapies. His full recovery was finally achieved largely due to his own determination and stouthearted efforts.

Before the accident, Aiden became engaged to a beautiful girl, Jenni McKinstock. Jenni was impatient with Aiden's lengthy recovery, and without his knowledge, took other lovers. Biding her time, she had no intentions of returning the valuable diamond engagement ring. In the interim, Jenni threw crumbs of affection Aiden's way, and he became inordinately grateful for every small favour his cheating fiancé allowed to him. Regaining Jenni's approval became Aiden's driving incentive to recover physical strength after the accident.

Awarded a substantial compensation payout in the wake of his workplace accident enabled Aiden to begin having his dream home built in the hinterland hills, high above the beach, the site commanded a breathtaking sea view. He shied away from putting all his eggs in one basket so also purchased the solid old brick shop building as an investment property.

Thrilled with the modern architect designed show home under construction in the posh suburban heights, Jenni McKinstock finally agreed to marry Aiden.

Jenni took over many decisions for fittings and décor, running up costs well over Aiden's initial building budget, eventually requiring a mortgage. However, at the time Aiden had his head in the clouds believing he had it all, the grand house, the beautiful wife, an emerging private eye business that he began from his home office and the investment property.

Alas, the marriage ended in heartbreak for Aiden, when before long, he discovered firm grounds for divorce. Although Jenni was entitled to half the house and contents, she stood in the way of it being sold. Aiden moved out but maintained the outstanding mortgage repayments.

Originally, Aiden purchased his shop building as a rental investment but an ensuing downturn in the general economy had it sitting empty. Rather than waste the resource, Aiden used it for expanding his private eye venture.   The flat on the second story was the obvious place for Aiden to occupy, in the wake of leaving his unfaithful wife.

Ethan, his younger brother had been getting by on temporary casual jobs that fitted with his surfing lifestyle.

The brothers had lost their parents in a light plane crash just as Ethan entered high school.

The Birdwhistles willed everything to their two children, to be split as they saw fit, but after all was settled their sons did not receive huge inheritances.   Between themselves, they decided Ethan should have their late model car as Aiden already had a good one of his own. Aiden took some old family jewellery as his share of the chattels since the value worked out about the same. All else was sold to cover costs leaving the brothers with a few thousand each in the bank.

Ethan was smart and had been a good student but after the tragedy he couldn't concentrate and failed all his exams. Surfing became Ethan's escape from grief. Although Aiden worried about his brother's future, he was happy when Ethan qualified as a lifeguard and found a bunch of good mates at the surf club.

The economic climate dried up casual work options yet the P.I. business continued to grow and attract plenty of custom. Ethan could barely meet his rent, so Aiden brought his struggling younger sibling into the business after moving Birdwhistle Solutions to the brick shop building.

In the long run, making the investment building Aiden's primary workplace also served to prevent his ex-wife Jenni from claiming any right to it.

The private eye business became so busy, the brothers discussed bringing in a third person to help out. During their last visit to The Tipsy Turnip Cafe they realised their latest target, the check out chick sitting well disguised in the corner, would be ideal.

The brothers were unhappy and uncomfortable with instructions to accuse Isla publicly at her checkout station, seeing it as unfair malice from the store manager. So they agreed on the spot that offering Isla Tickle alternative employment was a perfect solution to the dismissal she was about to face.

At The Tipsy Turnip, Ethan had scanned the cafe and saw no possible match for his brother.

"Looks like your match didn't show up Aiden. Unless it's herself." Ethan had laughed.

"Now that would complicate things." Aiden replied.

"Yep. But we agree she'd be good to take on as our third."

"If she's willing." Aiden replied. He hoped she would be.

They high fived with the plan to set it in motion and confronted Isla at the supermarket check-out counter as tactfully as possible, while still fulfilling the obligation to their client. After which, Aiden wasted no time in catching up with Isla in the car park, to offer her alternative means.

Employing Isla as a consequence would infuriate Fergus Rudin if he knew of it but the brothers saw their scheme as a fitting coup to the man's spite. Isla Tickle was to become the best ever Birdwhistle Solution in both brother's opinions.

The retainer Aiden could offer Isla was less than her supermarket pay but the young woman considered her fortunes to have taken a turn for the better. Never again would she wear a supermarket pinafore or need to fend off sexual harassment in order to stay employed.

Aiden asked if Isla might meet him for dinner ostensibly to discuss her new position and what it entailed. In line with their usual brotherly banter, Ethan joked it was amazing the lengths his brother went to, to get himself a date.

Isla rushed home to iron something nice to wear. This day had been full of ups and downs. The good surprises outweighed the bad. The best part was Isla again felt enabled to look forward to her life ahead instead of miserably marking time.

2

The night of that first work dinner meeting was warm and still, rain had cleared but weather remained humid. Aiden chose an outdoor table on a patio overlooking the sea at one of the better coastal hotel restaurants.

He wore chinos teamed with a neat button down short sleeved shirt. His leather brogues were in keeping with the hotel dress code that banned open footwear. Isla chose to wear a navy blue and white polka spotted sundress that showed just a hint of cleavage. She teamed the dress with a white cotton bolero jacket and silver/grey court shoes.

"Let's order early in case they take a while to prepare it. I could eat a horse." Aiden said.

"I'm happy with fish and chips. Maybe coleslaw on the side." Isla replied.

"I'm having a lager. You?"

"Light beer would be perfect." Isla decided no use pretending she didn't like a drink with dinner. No way was she kissing up to a boss. Life was too short.

Aiden said Ethan was on stake out duty or he might have joined them. Isla was glad it was just the two of them because it felt more like a date than a business meeting. She couldn't stop smiling for being out having dinner with this handsome, well spoken man, for whatever reason.

"What's Ethan staking out?" Isla asked to keep the occasion relevant to work.

"Trying to get photo or video evidence of whoever is letting their dog poop on the client's lawn every night. The home owner knows it's a dog being walked on leash. Not a stray."

"Sounds like a vendetta. I mean, it's so easy to carry dog poop bags and just pick it up."

"Probably be someone too lax and if their pooch likes to do it on that lawn, it makes the toilet walk quicker and easier." Aiden replied.

"So any incriminating evidence Ethan gathers will be what you sell to your clients?"

"That's right. Whichever way the clients care to use it themselves is their own business. Sometimes evidence like that is published on social media. The perpetrator might see it or might be recognised by others who name and shame. Either way it should put a stop to the habit."

"How will Ethan do it?"

"He'll be a couple of doors down. Sitting in a parked vehicle. Ready to zoom in."

"Wondering why the householders don't just install CCTV?"

"They have it over their front door. But too many shrubs between there and the front lawn. So far they've caught just a glimpse of the dog walker but not good enough. They keep a beautiful garden and manicured lawn so it must be really irking having to pick up after that dog every morning."

"Sure would be."

A waiter brought out their drinks and meals and they both took quenching swigs of the amber ale.

"I guess in the private eye business it pays if you like to watch and wait."

"That's about it." Aiden agreed. "The hours can be taxing and the pay is terrible but hey, there is variety and some satisfaction in it. At least everyday is a bit different."

"Not going through the same old routine every day is a big incentive." Isla agreed.

Tea lights in glass containers on the tables made a romantic glow as evening darkened into night and they enjoyed their meals. Isla's eyes glowed with happiness. In a lapse of protocol, Aiden told her she looked pretty, then quickly apologised for being so forward. The truth was, he hadn't been with a woman for some time and felt wholly attracted to this one. It was only a matter of hours since they'd bandied first fraught words together, yet a romantic nuance crept into that business meeting. He wondered how it might have gone if they'd met as the blind date she tried to set up, without all the awkward confrontation that followed.

Isla felt charmed by her Mr. Handsome and welcomed his interest without letting on with more than a blush and lowering of lashes. The pair got along so well it didn't seem as if they'd met under dire circumstance and only that morning. Their good time wasn't to last:

All went well until a bawdy intoxicated woman propped her hip against their table and accosted them with foul abuse, causing an undignified scene. Other diners tutted, shook their heads or looked away pretending not to notice although the onslaught was difficult to ignore. The irate woman held a small grey coloured poodle dog by a diamante collar and lead. The little dog yapped, growled and peed on the floor. Looking crazy with her hair in wild disarray, the intruder's voice grated loud accusations at Aiden. Isla was brought into the tirade as well. Neither Isla nor Aiden spoke. Aiden simply appeared upset and embarrassed.

"He likes to watch you know."

The drunk woman hissed the words closely into Isla's face, like a spitting cat, blasting her with whisky tainted breath. Isla had at times been the brunt of rants by dissatisfied customers and knew it best to remain calm in heated situations. At the supermarket, if rational attempts failed to resolve the complaint, she would say nothing more and press a button under the counter to bring the shop manager, thinking Fergus Rudin might as well do something useful. But now, in the company of her new colleague at the table, all she could do was endure the attack silently, keeping her own dignity intact.

At last a hotel security bouncer escorted the loud mouthed woman off the premises, simply telling her 'no dogs allowed' while thinking to himself *and that includes bitches.*

"I am so sorry Isla." Aiden was clearly mortified.

"What the hell was that?"

"My ex wife. Jenni. I divorced her six months ago but she won't let it go."

"Do you want to leave now?"

"Not really. I'd rather have coffee. She could be waiting outside. Give her time to give up and go away."

"Sure. Well I guess we've both had an embarrassing day." Isla laughed to lighten the mood.

"Are you ok?" Aiden asked.

"I'm tough. She didn't scare me. The little dog was funny."

Aiden breathed a sigh of relief that Isla was taking it so well. His estimation of her worth in his P.I. business went up another notch.

"That toy poodle is her only true love. I gave him to her one Christmas as a tiny black puppy but he silvered out fairly soon. The breeder called him Frou Frou but Jenni renamed him Pitbull. He's the only gift I ever gave Jenni that she didn't have any complaint about."

Jenni, being a material girl, knew good value when she saw it but she also grew to love the macho little dog. Aiden remembered the research he'd put in to find a reputable registered breeder of pedigreed toy poodles. Before applying for a puppy, he visited the premises. The breeder, Francis Funicular, kept only a few of the little dogs and bred only occasionally to keep a youngster coming along as part of her dog showing hobby. Francis also checked out Aiden and his credentials before allowing a pup to him. The double sided business card Aiden took home had the kennel name on one side and 'Francis Funicular ~ Wedding Celebrant' on the other. The large lady told him that doing the weddings augmented her poodle hobby. He surmised despite what seemed a hefty purchase price for the pup, it must take a great deal of input to maintain the breeding stock and raise puppies properly.

"I don't know why Jenni chose the name Pitbull. Maybe because the pup had an unpredictable nature. We never knew if he would lick your hand or bite it. That little poodle has always been feisty for his size. He definitely imagines himself to be a big scary dog."

Isla didn't want to talk about Aiden's ex wife.

"I like dogs." She said hoping to veer the subject to generalisations.

"So do I. What's your favourite?"

"I like all the sighthound breeds best. But I like most dogs on the whole. Someday I hope to have one of my own."

All the while Isla chatted, Aiden explored her expressive face and every shade of emotion she showed. He noticed her nose wrinkled a little when she laughed. A light sprinkling of freckles across her cheeks and nose looked impossibly cute and childlike for her age, he knew from her work application, she was twenty-three. Isla hadn't worn much make-up due to the humid weather, only a touch of mascara and lip gloss. Aiden tried not to dwell on her glossy lips too much but was drawn to do so.

Aware of his interest, Isla played with a silver drop pendant she wore on a chain around her neck, purposely leading his gaze to her cleavage. His lips parted in contemplation of her ample breasts. Isla smiled to herself and waffled on. She felt pretty sure she had his interest. Perhaps it was just a matter of time before the bonuses kicked in with her handsome new work companion.

A light drizzle began again so they moved indoors for coffee. When Aiden ordered chocolate cheesecake for two without asking, she liked the man a lot more. Isla tried to keep the conversation relevant to a work meeting:

"So Aiden. I don't want to pry but why did your ex warn me that you like to watch? I mean surely that's the gist of being a private eye."

"Oh God is that what she said? I didn't catch all that hissing. I hope she didn't spray you with spit."

"Probably did a bit. Anyway it would have been disinfected with whisky. Hopefully."

Aiden groaned and ran fingers through his hair in a distraught gesture of unease. He knew he owed Isla an explanation. But it was complicated:

"You might as well know up front what's behind her comment. She knows I've watched her with other men. Hell. Wait. Let me explain that a bit better: Birdwhistle Solutions was hired by a married woman who wanted to catch her husband out. Footage identified the man but his tryst partner wasn't clear. It was enough for the client anyway. She only wanted proof about her cheating husband. The shock for me was that the other woman looked like my wife. I couldn't prove it but a lot of small things began to add up. I was often away working. That's why I gave Jenni the puppy in the first place. But the poodle's company didn't satisfy my wife. I didn't satisfy her either as it turned out... Oh hell. I'm sorry. Too much information."

Aiden drained his coffee and order another. Isla declined. She didn't want to be awake all night and bleary the next day. She could only lend her ear to Aiden's account although after the drama with his ex wife that night, Isla drew her own conclusions.

"Anyway I can't entirely blame Jenni because I had to leave her alone so much. But I began to suspect she brought men home to our own bed. To my shame, I set up hidden cameras in our bedroom. I hoped to prove my suspicions wrong. Instead, I found Jenni had many conquests. Never the same one twice. I'm not sure if that made it seem better or worse to tell truth. Suffice to say, I felt devastated."

"I'm sorry you had to go through that." Isla replied. She didn't know what else to say.

"She'd put on quite a show wearing the sexy lingerie we'd chosen together on our honeymoon in Paris." Aiden's voice broke on that note and he gulped more coffee.

Aiden again realised he was spouting too much:

"Jesus. Sorry again. Why don't I shut up. I'm sure you don't want or need to hear all that. I do apologise for raving on."

Jenni's attack had undermined his composure and natural reserve. Aiden couldn't believe he was relating the sordid details to this person he had only met that very morning. And she his new recruit as well. He realised he was way out of order. It was just that Isla made a good listener and he found her easy to talk to.

"Strangely, Jenni was always insanely jealous and obviously she thinks we are here on a date tonight, so she's said what she could to put you off me."

Isla could understand being jealous of a man like Aiden. Privately she considered his ex wife a gluttonous trollop who liked to have her cake and eat it too. But it wouldn't do to run this horrible Jenni person down. Aiden obviously carried a lot of baggage over the betrayal and divorce but he might still foster basic loyalty, or at least to the person he thought his wife Jenni had once been.

"It's not always easy to move on." Isla remarked, with her own break-up in mind.

"No. But live and learn and I learnt the hard way. I'd been stuck on someone who made me unhappy, thinking if I could just make her happy, I could be happy. But it doesn't work that way." Aiden repeated logic he'd arrived at long ago.

Isla felt sure if Aiden were hers she wouldn't be looking elsewhere. Dream on. She tried to put it into perspective. They'd only just met and however she looked at it, she was now in his employ.

Eventually they left for the hotel car park and their separate cars. Aiden saw Isla safely to hers. They were both aware that this would be the time for a goodnight kiss if they were really on a date. Isla paused as they hadn't discussed all the business intended due to Jenni's rude interruption on their evening.

Aiden tried to quell his desire to kiss Isla. He hadn't been intimate with a woman since his divorce and knew what he was missing. He noticed Isla bite her bottom lip and felt this could signify she felt as he did. His hands twitched in indecision wanting to touch her but afraid of making that move, knowing it was way too soon.

"So when do you want me?" Isla asked.

"What?" Aiden felt momentary confusion. Had she read his mind?

"For work?" Isla clarified.

Aiden shook his head to clear it of what had instantly filled his thoughts.

"Oh. Uh. Sorry I was miles away. Just rock up by 9 tomorrow Isla. You can park around the back. The car park entrance is off the side lane. I'll have the back door open by 8. And thanks for being so understanding about tonight."

"No worries. See you tomorrow morning."

They parted with a brief handshake. Isla went to her bed hugging the wonderful events of the day to her heart. Aiden went to his, arousal over his non-date with Isla squashed by his ex wife's attack. He had loved Jenni once but now saw his ex in a far different light.

Maybe Ethan was right and he was just a pathetic pushover. Aiden decided to tread carefully before acting impulsively with Isla. He should learn by his own mistakes.

Dream on. He thought. Isla was nothing like Jenni.

3

FIRST DAY P.I.

I sla rocked up at 8am the following morning. An hour earlier than required. She didn't mind appearing overly enthusiastic and Aiden was already there, as he said he would be.

"Good morning Isla. Nice to see you."

"Good morning to you Aiden. You must be an early riser too." She smiled.

"I haven't far to travel. Just down the staircase in fact."

"Oh you live above? That's handy."

"Jenni is still staying in our house." He answered shortly.

"Where do I start?"

"First up. Turn the closed sign around and unlock the front door. Thanks."

Aiden smiled as he answered. For the first time, Isla noticed an unobtrusive business title printed on the front window stating the business name to be Birdwhistle Solutions. BS. Bull Shite. She got the implication and felt it was probably intentional. The brothers made a little joke on themselves. There was another notice with a snarling dog face, stating guard dogs on the premises.

Aiden tried to remain cool though he'd been overly keen to see Isla again. Her presence heightened his imagination just as it had the night before.

Her conservative outfit did not hide the contours of her hips and breasts, both of which intrigued Aiden. He wondered what she'd be like to touch. Isla waited to be shown where to sit and what to do next.

"So where do you want me?" She asked.

Aiden's thoughts went unbidden straight to his king sized bed upstairs. Once again, he had to gather his act together. *Jesus.* He thought. *What is wrong with me?*

"Uh. I usually sit here with my laptop. Ethan takes the reception area most of the time. But nothing is set in stone. We're interchangeable. Take the seat in front of the desktop computer if you like Isla. We're often out of the office of course. You'll probably use that computer the most. Clients are only seen by appointment. It isn't the sort of place that invites walk in custom but it sometimes happens."

"I see you have a sign on the door stating guard dogs on the premises. Are they savage?"

Aiden told her no actual dogs existed but the burglar alarm sounded like a couple of big dogs barking. They had it in case of any break in attempts. Though no money was kept in the office, some might seek access to files or try to steal equipment.

Aiden showed Isla where hard copies of files were locked in metal filing cabinets. They also kept main details on their computers. He opened a drawer to indicate it was full of chunky pages of paperwork in manilla folders. Isla had a quick overall scan but couldn't figure out the filing system. It did not appear to be alphabetic or numeric.

"Is it filed chronologically?" She asked with perplexed interest.

"No. I have to admit there isn't any rhyme or reason to it. We just shove it in anywhere and shuffle through it when necessary." Aiden looked sheepish.

"So...do you want me to sort it somehow? Alphabetically would be easiest."

"That would be great." Aiden liked her initiative.

He told himself she was not just a pretty face. And a great body. He gave his wrist a mental slap afraid he was becoming a dirty old man at twenty-seven years old.

Just then Ethan turned up. He shared a crowded beach house with four like minded surfer guys. Their numbers increased when more surfing mates from out of town dossed with them on weekends. There was hardly a gap of space on the living room floor amid all the sleeping bags between Friday nights and Sundays. No Girls in the house became the strict rule, following a few arguments, breakages and one fist fight.   So in Ethan's shared rental, surfing was now the only agenda apart from eating, drinking beer and watching sport on TV.

Ethan was pulling his damp long blond hair into a pony tail as he entered the office.

"Hiya Isla. Welcome to the old BS office."

"I wondered about the possible meaning in that." She smiled.

"Yep. Your instincts are spot on." He laughed. "But we have to laugh at ourselves hey Aiden? "

"And we do have a laugh. Isla has already sussed that neither of us was ever cut out for office work." Aiden agreed. "Now Ethan what did you get from last night?"

"Big guy. Big dog. Lots of clear facials and caught the dog taking a big dump. The clients were happy."

"Alright. Another one bites the dust."

"What sort of dog?" Isla wanted to know.

"Bitsa. By the looks but I'm no dog expert." Ethan replied.

Isla showed interest in how the matter could be resolved.

"I wonder if they'll find out who is doing it. If nobody recognises them on social media, kennel club groups might help although they deal with purebreds. Maybe there are backyard breeder groups online as well. Do you give any clues to the clients on best way to go about identifying the culprit?"

"We suggest using social media. But the breeder groups might be useful. I didn't think of that. I'll follow it up if they have no luck elsewhere."

Ethan began an online search finding a couple of local *Puppy For Sale* sites that dealt with non-pedigreed dogs.

"Some of these have hundreds of pups on offer. They must be puppy farmers."

"They do exist unfortunately." Isla replied.

Aiden made coffee for them all in the tiny kitchenette hidden behind a screen. There was a sink, small refrigerator and some bench space with an electric kettle and a toaster. An overhead cupboard held crockery and a rack had a mix of cutlery. He belatedly remembered to let Isla know she could leave any snacks or whatever in the refrigerator there.

Isla had always taken a cut lunch to work although she hadn't on this first day. Later she took the cups in to wash them up and inspected inside the 'fridge. Apart from a carton of milk that was right on the use-by date, the refrigerator was empty. She decided to replenish the milk and bring in some extra fruit and biscuits for shared snacks with her cut lunch the next day.

"The surf was great this morning." Ethan enthused. "If there's nothing on this arvo I wouldn't mind going out to catch another wave."

"Lets see." Aiden checked his laptop. "Tonight there's a stake out if you want to do that and take the afternoon off beforehand. But don't overdo it. No use falling asleep."

"Sweet." Ethan said. "I'm happy doing tonights gig and taking the board out again now."

"OK. Isla, we can do this mornings hit out. Means we have to be hanging around a park trying to catch a compo faker."

"Wow. Great. Let me know what to do."

"Take this mobile phone. Make sure you know how to video with it. No one else will call you on this number. So if there is a call or message it will be me. OK?"

"OK Aiden."

They turned the door sign back to closed as the office would be unmanned. Aiden said they didn't particularly need disguises but he gave Isla a floppy cloth hat to wear. She had her own sunglasses. All she had to do was sit on a park bench pretending to check her phone or read a book and video the required person if Aiden rang with a clue to what she was wearing and what she looked like.

Aiden knew the target's car number plate and would be staking out the cars parked nearby. Hopefully the offender would jog energetically along giving doubt to her supposed debilitating injuries. Evidence would go to the employer. Aiden had dressed as any other jogger so he wouldn't stand out.

Initial excitement morphed into complete boredom after an hour or so as Isla sat on a park bench beside the walking path overlooking a lily-pond lake. She wished she'd brought her current crime novel *The Bruiser*, but it was at home on her bedside table. Isla checked the mobile phone often to make sure it was operating properly, and she hadn't missed a call from Aiden. Next time she'd choose a bench closer to the public toilet. The coffee she'd had earlier was now a burden. At last Aiden jogged up to her. He was sweating and puffing a bit.

"Sorry. Late change of plan. Hers not mine. She took a different route to what I'd been led to expect. I had to run after her in a hurry. I've been following but couldn't get any clear footage. She runs a lot faster than I can. Anyway she's got hair in two long plaits and is wearing an orange t-shirt and black shorts. So if she comes back this way...."

"I get it. But Aiden I need a loo break first." Isla felt embarrassed to tell him.

"Sure. I'll sit here until you get back. Forgot to warn you it's best to sit near the amenities if possible."

"It's a learning curve." Isla threw over her shoulder as she hurried away.

Aiden felt remiss in his duty to train and inform his new recruit. He even forgot to tell her she could use the 'fridge until this morning. Isla's effect on his senses caused his lapses and he knew it. Normally he prided himself on crossing all the Ts and dotting all the Is.

Isla returned to her bench and sat beside Aiden. Nothing had happened in her absence. They talked and watched mothers pushing prams along the path, dog walkers, other joggers and senior people feeding ducks that swam amongst the reeds in the lake.

During their wait and conversation, Isla and Aiden savoured every detail of each other in snapshot glances. Isla liked Aiden's dark blue eyes and the smoky depths that betrayed his inner thoughts. She liked how his interest in her made him blush boyishly. That was absolutely the best. He was a bit shy and unsure of himself so she felt no risk with him. After Isla's experience with Fergus Rudin and her racy flamboyant boyfriend, Troy Van Baas, she needed to feel safe with any potential new man.

Aiden liked Isla's cheeky smile and her sparkly brown eyes, so reflective of her moods. He even liked that her short brown wavy hair had naturally sun bleached tips. There was nothing false about her. The few freckles over her nose were lightly repeated above the deep cleavage between her rounded breasts. He was fascinated when her breasts bounced a bit when she laughed. Stop! He gave himself a mental smack on the face. He must try to control himself. Isla would think he was a lech if she caught him ogling. He mustn't let on he felt such an intense attraction to his new employee.

When the orange and black clad girl ran into view they almost missed it. Both hurriedly aimed their mobiles in her direction and videoed as she came closer. The path went right by their bench. Suddenly Aiden grabbed Isla in an embrace as if they were sweethearts. The target jogged on by without giving them a glance.

"Hey. Why did you do that?" Isla was taken by complete surprise.

"Sorry. I realised it looked suspicious with us both aiming our phones her way. I did a quick cover up." Aiden said.

Saying so was almost another cover up.

"Now I'm all hot and bothered." Isla made a joke of it, fanning her face, to hide her true feelings. She'd have liked to have the moment go on and on. He felt so good.

Aiden was definitely all hot and bothered. He had to ask himself if his clumsy move was really necessary. He wasn't sure himself. But holding Isla close felt wonderful.

"Thanks for being a good sport about it." He laughed along with her.

They went back to the office to check the footage. While Aiden edited the videos and wrote up the detailed report, Isla worked on the filing system. It was a mess and there were several deep drawers to clear.

The mornings work gave plenty of evidence proving the orange and black clad person was definitely fit to run with no sign of any limp. Aiden provided a written report on the length of time spent observing and the distance the woman ran. It was a good case conclusion that paid well. That took them up to lunch time.

Aiden had fresh bread, ham and tomato upstairs in his flat and wanted to shout Isla lunch. But he worried over the wisdom of taking her upstairs. This thing he had for her was moving too fast. He should try to curb his romantic appetite and not to be the hapless pushover Ethan said him to be.

"Alright if I order pizza?" Isla asked eventually. She was feeling peckish.

"Sure....or I've got lunch stuff upstairs if you want to share?" Aiden kicked himself for being a pathetic pushover. His resolution to go slowly with Isla hadn't lasted long.

"That is kind of you." Isla smiled. "Tomorrow I'll bring a cut lunch like I have always done at the supermarket. Just I didn't know the deal here and wanted to be early."

Aiden locked the office door, put the *Closed For Lunch* sign out and led Isla up the staircase to his bachelor pad above the office. He opened wide the bi-fold doors to the verandah to let in the sea breeze. The view over the street and low roofed buildings opposite, spanned to a vista where the dark line of ocean met the lighter blue of sky on the horizon.

"Wow. This is so nice Aiden. Even a sea view! And it's a lovely breeze up here."

"It's not too bad." he said.

Aiden's thoughts went to his luxury dream home in the suburban heights. The basic flat he now lived in wasn't air-conditioned and not nearly as comfortable or up to date as his marital home.

Jenni held up sale of their joint property with one excuse after another and Aiden's pang of annoyance felt like a sword in his side. According to their divorce agreement the home was meant to be sold and proceeds split evenly between them. Not risking foreclosure, Aiden continued to pay the mortgage while Jenni was in residence paying nothing. He avoided any confrontation but knew he should face his ex-wife's volatile temper or seek legal advice before too long.

Isla chatted on as Aiden made sandwiches. He had juice, tea or coffee. Isla opted for tea. They sat in the open plan kitchen/dining/living area. A hallway led to other rooms.

"Bathroom is down the hall. If you need it." Aiden mentioned.

"Thanks. I do need to wash my hands."

Isla wandered down the hall catching a glimpse of an enormous bed through an open doorway on her way to the bathroom. Everything was neat and clean. Isla guiltily remembered not making her own bed in her rush to be early that morning.

"You're so lucky having this place. Mine is on the ground floor and not nearly as good as this. But it is close to everything at least." Isla rabbited on.

Aiden couldn't help compare Isla's take on what was a nice place to his ex's complaints over every feature if it wasn't the latest thing. He placed a small tray of condiments on the table. Isla wasn't shy about helping herself to mustard as she opened her sandwich and slathered a generous lick on. Aiden also liked that about her, she had no coyness or side to her personality.

"Wow. Great sandwich." Isla winked and nodded as she chewed.

"Thanks. Glad you like it." Aiden replied, smiling and pleased with her comment.

Once again he drew on what Jenni would think of the slab sandwiches for lunch. His ex would want sushi or flamed grilled barramundi with crisp salads that included a variety of vegetables julienned just so, yet find at least one thing to complain about in any meal. If Aiden made the meal himself, woe betide if he allowed different foods to touch on her plate.

Jenni never cooked although their kitchen had to be state of the art. Suffice to say Aiden enjoyed seeing Isla chow down with apparent relish on his slapped together ham and tomato sangers.

Isla would have liked a short kip after eating but considered it a bit too casual with her boss and on this her first day working with him. That changed when Aiden clicked the TV on saying he usually caught any news updates at lunchtime before going back to work.

Aiden stretched out on one of the sofas with a cushion behind his head. He threw another cushion across the room. Isla caught it and took his lead, stretching out on the matching sofa opposite. The news was predictable. Wars. Political upheavals. Royal dramas. Youth crime mostly car theft and joyriding. As the news hour wound up with a weather report, Aiden stretched and sat up.

"No rest for the wicked." He smiled suddenly aware that Isla had nodded off. He tiptoed to the kitchen and clattered about rinsing the plates, pretending he hadn't noticed.

"Oh my god. Sorry. Did I fall asleep?" Isla came awake with a start.

"I don't know. Did you?" Aiden fibbed.

Isla went back to the bathroom and splashed her face with cold water. She was sure he had to have noticed her lapse and hoped she hadn't snored. Or worse, what if she'd farted! Maybe she should have gone lighter on the mustard on an empty stomach. What a first day at work! Aiden was so lovely pretending not to notice. He was a such sweet guy.

During their talks at the park, he'd mentioned his ex wife had been a fashion model when they'd first met. In Isla's mind, that fact put Aiden definitely out of her league. But she could work beside him and at least enjoy some harmless flirtations. She was aware he liked her at least physically and she might build on that.

Abruptly, a crash and deep loud barking interrupted the separate thoughts of the pair. The burglar alarm had been activated. Aiden took the stairs two at a time with Isla hot on his heels.

Someone had smashed a brick through the plate glass shopfront window. A note tied to the brick with string, had heavy black block letters saying:

WHAT A SLUT. BONKING THE BOSS IN THE LUNCH BREAK.

"It must have been Jenni." Aiden supposed with a slump of his shoulders.

Although it surprised him that his ex would sink to this type of deed. Creating a public scene making herself the centre of attention was more Jenni's style. Aiden secured the note in his desk drawer.

"I guess anyone spying from across the road could see us through the open patio doors." Isla said. "Not that we did anything wrong." She quickly added.

"Jenni would make of it what she imagined. And judge us by her own morals." Aiden replied in disgust.

"What do we do about it now?" Isla wanted to rant that it was a crime and he should involve the police.

"I'll have to pay her a visit tonight. This is going too far." Aiden sighed.

Isla was disappointed. It seemed Aiden was playing right into the ex's hands by visiting her.

"The note directly insults me Aiden. I would rather report it." Isla spoke up for herself.

"Yes. I see that. Alright. I will report it as an attempted break in...but do you really want that note shown to police Isla?"

"Yes I do want it shown Aiden. Sorry but I have no reason to protect your ex and this is the second time in less than twenty-four hours she has aimed an attack at me."

Aiden felt sick.

"If it was Jenni. There's no proof. This building isn't covered by CCTV unfortunately. I even thought the burglar alarm was a bit over the top to be honest. Until today. But I would think carefully about making that note known. It isn't that I want to protect Jenni. If she did it, she should be punished."

"Why else would you want to keep the note secret Aiden?" Isla asked quietly.

"Only that the local plods are Neanderthals. They will give you a hard time and so will the media. The local newspaper is always looking for something and they get reports straight from the police station. Once they get wind of a sexy motive they'll use it to sensationalise the story. I want to protect you from unfair judgements Isla."

"So they'll reckon I earned it. No one will believe it didn't happen. And you won't want a slut working for you. Bad for business I imagine. So seems this job depends on not showing the note." Isla summarised. Her resentment of Aiden's ex-wife fed her angst.

Aiden could see Jenni winning this round, if she did it. Her actions might cause Isla to walk out on the job and he didn't want to lose her. He laid it on the line.

"OK Isla. Look I wouldn't blame you for walking out. But please don't do that. I want you to stay. If Jenni did it she wins if you leave. It's what she would want to happen. But I'll leave it up to you about the note. The police should get here this afternoon sometime. They wouldn't rush it. So just give it some thought. That's all I ask."

Now Isla was in a quandary. She thought the note should be reported. On the other hand she didn't want Jenni to win. She also didn't want to be unemployed.

Isla had capitulated before the police arrived. She decided to follow Aiden's advice and keep the note in the locked drawer for now. If her name was made public associated with the note, Aiden's ex would have a win and her old enemy Fergus Rudin from the supermarket would piddle himself laughing.

In the meantime the window had to be boarded up. Aiden called on the convenient hardware store next door to supply materials and tradies to do a quick fix. They ably secured the premises although it made inside the office dark enough to need all the lights turned on.

Isla went on with sorting the filing cabinets while Aiden drew up a list of upcoming surveillance tasks. When Ethan turned up he gaped at the window boarded up and a few stray remnants of glass strewn about. The council often mowed the centre nature strip island in the road and he made his deduction from it.

"What happened? Did it cop a stone thrown up from a mower?"

"Nope. Brick through the window."

"Holy crap. Where were you?"

"Upstairs with Isla. Having lunch. Then we heard the crash and the alarm was set off."

"Uh Huh. Lucky you were both upstairs. Together. Guess insurance covers it?"

"Supposed to. I'm on it. Are you set for tonight?"

"Sure. Can I take a girl? It might be a long wait."

"Against the rules little brother."

"But you...." Ethan began to debate the issue.

"Isla is one of us." Aiden reminded him.

Ethan's mission consisted of gaining proof that someone moonlighted as a cab driver. It was a boring assignment, and he had sympathy for the guy just trying to make ends meet, albeit against the rules of the man's government daytime employment.

"Thing is. My girl would be like a prop. I mean, it looks suss otherwise if I'm hanging about at cab ranks and not taking a cab or sitting in a parked car just watching. With a girl there I can pretend to be loitering over saying goodnight to her. Like in a clinch."

"All just pretence Ethan?"

"I can be very convincing." Ethan replied.

"OK. Suppose so. This once. As long as you get it done. But make sure the girl doesn't blow it."

"Um...I'll try to control her. But she loves to..." Ethan grinned.

"Shut up Ethan. Just go. Get out of here." Aiden waved him away.

Isla had to laugh at the brotherly interaction between the Birdwhistle Boys.

"Bloody little brothers. Do you have any siblings Isla?"

"No. Wish I did but I was brought up in an orphanage. No known family."

"That must have been hard, being raised in that way." Aiden ventured.

"I didn't know any different." Isla shrugged.

"Ethan is my only family now. We lost our parents eight years ago. Plane crash."

"Oh. You poor boys."

Isla felt real compassion for the brothers and Aiden followed that loss with his horrid Jenni episodes. Being alone at least spared Isla from family losses, yet she would still choose to have known her blood relatives.

Isla left the building by 5pm. Despite the brick and the demeaning note, she was happy with her first day in the new job.

With a couple of hours of daylight remaining, Aiden Birdwhistle locked up and drove to his large suburban house, not looking forward to confronting his difficult ex-wife, Jenni McKinstock.

4

AIDEN'S EX

Aiden pulled into the wide paved driveway of his house that no longer felt like his home. The landscaped front garden had no lawn apart from on the footpath. An elderly neighbour on a rider mower, stopped the machine and spoke to Aiden, saying he had been keeping up the mowing for the sake of the street image, implying Aiden had been slack. Red-faced Aiden apologised and offered payment that was shrugged off.

Humiliated by the encounter, Aiden knocked on his own front door, irked with himself that he didn't just use his key. Ethan's opinion about being a pathetic pushover rang in his ears. Jenni seemed to be out, so Aiden did use his own key to enter the house, finding the place smelt horribly of stale cigarettes, yet Jenni was not a smoker. A full ashtray overflowed on the glass coffee table in the lounge room. The glass surface that had always been clear and gleaming was now stained and marked. Obviously, Jenni had been doing a lot of entertaining.

Aiden went into the luxury granite benched kitchen. Every surface was littered with gunk, packets of opened foodstuffs and dirty cups. A few cups had cigarette butts floating in the dregs. Despite the expensive dishwasher, the sink was full of unwashed glasses and crockery. In a reflex reaction born of his private eye career, Aiden began videoing the dirty mess for proof in case it was needed. Aiden agonised that he would have to take the house off the market until it could be cleaned up and made to look respectable. Jenni was delaying selling in every way possible and would do so forever while Aiden paid the mortgage. He wondered what she now did for money as Jenni had never worked during their marriage. He called out Jenni's name, in case she had been in the shower or sleeping. No answer. He went upstairs for a quick inspection of the bedrooms, dreading to enter the scene of his ex-wife's many and varied adulterous exploits. He had the hidden camera recordings of all that in his flat and been guilty of watching repeatedly for his own reasons of anguish and sexual titillation. He felt reduced by doing so and had sunk low in his own estimation.

Aiden had never confided to Ethan exactly what Jenni got up to causing the divorce. No one else had seen the videos but Jenni knew he had them. Presenting the proof preceded a huge row between them. Jenni had laughed making snide unwarranted remarks about Aiden's manhood. Aiden had gagged back vomit at her caustic and careless response, before packing a bag and walking out to the tune of more of his wife's vitriol.

The first nights spent in the flat above the office, he had cried himself to sleep on a sofa and felt like ending his own life. If not for his brother he might have. But he couldn't do that to Ethan, leaving him all alone.

On this visit to confront Jenni, Aiden found the master bedroom empty, the bed rumpled, sheets grey and wrinkled. It appeared to have not been freshened for weeks. Aiden cursed ever loving Jenni and cursed even more that he married her. He'd been dazzled by her glamour and seduced by her sexual favours after he'd recovered sufficiently from his workplace accident. Too late, he realised her true nature. Jenni was slovenly, unfaithful, greedy and grasping.

A daily cleaning service had maintained the house in pristine condition before Aiden moved out. He expected Jenni to take over that account while she was living in the place, but it was apparent the cleaners had stopped coming. As Aiden surveyed the shambles of his house with growing repugnance, he heard the front door slam. The cause of his upset was home. His car in the driveway gave his presence away.

"Aiden. Where are you." Jenni yelled.

"Upstairs. Although it doesn't smell any better up here. The whole place is an utter pigsty."

"You stopped paying the maid service Aiden. Now you blame me?"

Jenni met him at the bottom of the staircase. She put her little poodle down ignoring it as he promptly lifted a leg on the antique hallstand in a long stream of relief. The dog had obviously been dying to pee.

Aiden felt so angry he at once understood justifiable homicide. He accused his ex of deliberately undermining his efforts to sell the place. Unfazed, Jenni smiled smoothly saying they might come to some arrangement.

She'd been to the gym. The poodle probably spent the time languishing in her car. Aiden thought it a great pity the dog hadn't relieved himself in her Audi. Jenni dumped her swimming bag on the hallway carpet, a slight chlorine smell mingled with the smell of dog piss. Aiden made no reply. He felt he had never known this dirty witch but waited ashen faced for her next trick.

"Oh, Aiden honey. You look so cute all trembling mad like that." Jenni crooned.

Jenni pulled undone the ties of her wraparound dress and it fell open. She wore no underwear. Her body was as fit and tanned as money could buy and she knew what effect the sight of it had on Aiden. He felt his pulse quicken despite his contempt.

"How about it honey? One for the road?" Jenni crooned.

"Stop it. That won't work on me anymore."

Aiden pushed by her and went to sit on a lounge chair, strategically placing a throw cushion on his lap to hide his unwitting erection. Jenni sniggered knowingly and draped herself suggestively on the sofa opposite placing a well manicured finger in her mouth before crooking it in invitation for him to join her. He forced himself to recall all the other men she had been with during their marriage. Reminded of her sexual displays didn't help. He had to fight against his own growing lust.

"You know you want to." Jenni wheedled.

She kneaded the mushroom tips of her pointed breasts and moaned in pleasure, letting her legs fall apart as she watched him. Unable to look away, Aiden shot his lot under the throw cushion. Otherwise, he might have taken her hard and fast. His own neediness saved him, but he had to struggle to gather his wits.

"Can you tone down your comical femme fatale act long enough to talk sense?" He asked quietly.

Comical! Jenni was immediately angry her effort hadn't moved him. Or had it?

"Your hair trigger let you down again Aiden honey? Story of our marriage. Sad story."

Aiden ignored her taunts, yet they undermined his confidence and self-worth as always. He told her the house had to be sold as per their legal agreement. If she continued to sabotage that, he would seek legal recourse. Adding that he had taken video of the way she had trashed the place to be compared with the originals given to real estate agents. He assured her she would be up for all the legal fees since he had the proof positive.

"Fine. I'll move out tomorrow if you give me the videos you have of me."

"You mean the adulterous ones of course. Why do you want them?"

"Why do you? Suppose you're getting off on watching me enjoy myself."

"No." He lied.

"You can't keep my intellectual property." Jenni told him.

"The content is far from intellectual. More like very poor R rated rubbish."

Aiden laughed bitterly. The tart had no idea what intellectual property meant. But he supposed if he gave her copies of the sex videos, she wouldn't know he kept the originals.

"Let me get this clear Jenni. All you want is the video proof of your adultery and you'll move out and relinquish your house keys. Never to return here."

"Sure. And no keeping copies I want the originals." She said.

All the while Jenni smiled craftily to herself because she already had copies of her house keys made in case something like this happened. She congratulated herself on her smart thinking. They conned each other. Aiden would keep copies of the sex videos too but considered Jenni too dumb to realise her once trusting pushover of a husband would do that.

Aiden went back to his flat, ran off copies of the sex tapes onto a spare flash drive and returned to his big house before 9 that night. Jenni checked the footage on her laptop and handed Aiden her original set of house keys.

"You better be completely moved out by tomorrow evening." He told her.

"That doesn't give me much time. I might still have clothes in the dryer." She hedged.

"Whatever I find of yours still here will be binned. And by the way you'd better not try the public fish wife act on me again. Next time you'll be sued. Believe it Jenni. I will do it."

"Ooh. Suddenly grown balls. Pity it took you so long."

Aiden looked at the woman he once adored with undisguised loathing.

"I never want to see you again." He said realising he meant it absolutely.

"Then don't go buying any adult movies. I'm about to become a star." she preened.

Nothing Jenni did surprised Aiden anymore.

"You're using your adulterous videos as audition material?"

"I had my physical screen test today and they liked me enough to take me to lunch on a luxury yacht. The artistic director says he can make me appear even more beautiful on the big screen. They asked if I had any video samples to back up my audition. Thanks to your shitty sneakiness I have some." Jenni smirked.

Aiden realised her day had been taken up with the movie audition, then lunch on a yacht, then the gym. He'd never seriously thought Jenni had thrown that brick through the agency window. Now he was sure she'd been too busy all day to have done it, someone else must have it in for Isla. Fergus Rudin became prime suspect. Since he was an unfit overweight man incapable of an agile getaway, he would more than likely pay someone else to do it for him. Rudin's low standard of ethics fed into this speculation. Learning Birdwhistles picked Isla up after he'd paid them to bring her down, gave Rudin strong motives to harm the business and the girl.

Aiden went home to his lonely bed in his ordinary but nevertheless clean flat to reflect on the day.

5

ISLA'S SECOND DAY

Isla was determined to arrive at 8am again so her first day wouldn't seem like a flash in the pan effort. She had made egg and lettuce sandwiches for her lunch, more than enough to share if it came to that. Isla's previous workplace supermarket was the nearest early opening outlet to pick up fresh milk and groceries but that probably meant seeing her old boss, a challenge she would face rather than avoid. Although Isla dreaded seeing Fergus Rudin she also didn't want him to imagine she was afraid of him. In fact she'd have fun letting him know she felt great.

Isla strode around the supermarket aisles confidently, knowing if Rudin was in his office he'd be watching her on his CCTV monitors. Sure enough as she checked out her groceries, the bullying store manager appeared.

"Don't even think about using your staff discount Isla Tickle. It's been cancelled."

Rudin shouted loudly for the benefit of anyone within earshot. The mousy little checkout girl on duty looked afraid and apologetic until Isla got the last laugh on Rudin with a parting shot in her loudest voice:

"And don't you go trying it on with the other females working here Rudin. Listen up girls she yelled, I have your backs. Message me on Facebook if you have any problems with this horny old pot bellied git."

A giggling came from behind the shelves and the girl on checkout duty gave Isla a huge grin when her boss wasn't looking. Isla left the store thinking her day couldn't get any better.

Aiden welcomed Isla for her second day in his office, noting the bag of groceries she took to the fridge. She told him it was just some fresh milk for the coffee and a few snacks if anyone felt peckish. She had brought in a big biscuit tin from home and stored two packets each of lemon creams and ginger nuts in it. Bags of apples and oranges were stowed in the fridge beside her lunch box.

"I've got egg and lettuce on wholemeal for lunch. Plenty to share."

"I'll make coffee. I wouldn't mind a sandwich now if that's ok. I missed breakfast. Had a sleepless night." Aiden said. He had been upset after his dealings with Jenni the night before.

"Oh? Are you ok?"

"I'll get over it."

Aiden smiled thinking Isla was like a breath of fresh air after Jenni. Isla didn't question him further. She had a good idea his ex-wife would be a factor and strove to get on with business at hand.

"First up, do you want me to get onto a couple of glaziers to quote for the insurance? Let me know who you use so I can have them send an assessor or at least a form. I'm not sure what they do but it will be something like that."

"Could you? That would be a load off for me."

Aiden blessed having hired Isla. Isla talked as she set the lunch box on a desk and found a couple of plates and paper towels.

"I had a duel with Fergus Rudin this morning. Ha ha. He was spitting chips when I left the supermarket."

"Really? I was tossing the idea around that he might be behind the brick and the note. Or at least paid someone to do it for him." Aiden told her.

"It occurred to me as well when I was thinking about it last night. We're on the same page with that Aiden. Hells bells. Now horny old Fergus will have even more reason to hate me."

Isla told him how it had gone down with her grocery shopping that morning. Aiden had to laugh and wished he'd been there to see it.

Ethan walked in, went straight for the coffee and exclaimed over the big tin of biscuits. Isla invited him to share the sandwiches and before too long, there were only a few crumbs left in the lunch box.

"So little brother. How did it go last night?"

"She was awesome." Ethan sighed dreamy eyed.

"I meant the stake out."

"No go. Sorry. I'll try again tonight."

"Without the girlfriend this time Ethan."

"Yeah. Alright. She was a bit of a distraction."

Ethan looked sheepish. He shouldn't have let it happen in his car while on duty but getting together with a girl was impossible in the crowded house he shared. Before his brother's divorce, Ethan could always sneak a girl up to the flat at night. Now that Aiden lived there, that perk was denied him. Still, he thought, poor old Aiden had to live somewhere and he was well rid of Jenni.

Ethan had never liked his sister-in-law and been sure she made sneaky passes at him when he was younger. Although his teenage hormones had been raging and her interest flattered him, he despised Jenni's disloyalty to his brother. Not that he could ever tell Aiden. He teased his brother for being a pushover mainly because he hoped Aiden would take a firmer hand with Jenni, he could see she walked all over him. So Ethan was elated and relieved when Aiden announced he was getting divorced. The younger brother knew something dire must have forced the decision and had an idea it would be infidelity on Jenni's part but didn't question Aiden on that sensitive issue.

Now, Ethan went to the computer to check on new business and found a couple of emailed enquiries. One was from a farmer who thought one of his quiet dairy cows was getting milked out at night. His daughter had written the email saying her father was too old to sit up for hours himself and whoever it was probably watched the house anyway. She couldn't do it herself because she had a baby and her husband worked night shifts. The other lead was from a woman wanting her husband's night time outings checked on.

"The cow one sounds right up your alley Ethan."

"Can I take…"

"No. Stealth will be paramount. You might have to creep around behind a herd of cows. But don't confront anyone. Just follow them and try to see where they live. If possible."

"Sounds fun." Isla put in, thinking she'd like to be doing that one herself.

"This is taking BS to a whole new level." Ethan moaned. "I'll be literally stepping in it."

"You'll be OK. I'll tell the clients you can begin tonight and I'll do the cab driver sting myself." Aiden said.

Isla took charge of the filing since sorting it had become her project:

"I'll print these emails out for filing. Oh my god! This other one is from a Sylvia Rudin. Unless anyone else goes by that name she's Fergus Rudin's wife."

Aiden read through it. He noted it had been sent from a free generic account. The return email address gave no clue. No phone number given, which wasn't unusual. Clients never wanted to field calls as the timing and their location could be tricky. Aiden emailed a reply saying he would be happy to discuss her case and suggested a few appointment dates that might suit her. The woman answered immediately, taking the soonest date which was for the next day at 9am.

"Maybe she took my condom dig seriously and that's spurred her to check on Fergus. Hell Aiden. I'd better make myself scarce when Mrs. Rudin comes in."

"True. Better if she doesn't connect you with us. For now anyway." Aiden agreed.

Lunchtime came around and Isla had no sandwiches. Aiden suggested walking down to the beach and grabbing hot dogs from a stall there. Ethan asked for the afternoon off for a snooze since he would be out all night with the cows. Granted. Aiden looked forward to a lunch break alone with Isla and she had no complaints about it either.

Isla ordered her hot dog on a grilled cheese roll. When asked if she wanted fried onions with it, she replied: "Sure do thanks. I don't expect to be kissing anyone today."

Aiden ordered his the same. He didn't expect to be kissing anyone that day either. He wasn't likely to be kissing Jenni goodbye when he went to inspect the house that evening.

It was a beautiful day, blue sky, sun shining, waves lazily shooshing as they lapped the shore. A frothy surf slid over a myriad of shells shining on the tide line and three little sandpipers probed the wet sand near waters edge. Aiden commented it was a pity they couldn't sit on the beach as they had no towels. Isla gave him an odd look. They both wore jeans and the sand was dry. She wanted to sit on the beach.

"The sand will brush off." She said. "Come on Aiden. Be a devil." She laughed.

Isla was always surprising him. He really enjoyed her company. She was balm to his ongoing problems with Jenni. They both sank to the clean white sand and sat cross legged. Isla took a huge bite out of her hot dog and made appreciative noises that nudged at Aiden's inner thoughts. He imagined she might make similar sounds of pleasure in other situations.

"Ah. This is sooo good." Isla enthused wiping a dribble of sauce off her chin with a finger, then licking it off. Aiden was mesmerised.

Isla still couldn't believe the change of fortune from her boring supermarket past. Here she was, sitting on the beach with a delicious hot dog beside her lovely new boss. Aiden wished for a convenient throw cushion as he observed and listened to her enjoy that hot dog. He had to make do with the hot dog packet.

"Be great to go for a quick dip while the weather holds and I've got my togs bag in the car.." Isla said. "Are you up for it Aiden. How about it?"

"Now that sounds like a dare."

He smiled. He was definitely up for anything with Isla. There was nothing too urgent to be done at the office. Extending the lunch hour a bit was far more tempting. Isla changed in the office bathroom and Aiden reappeared from his flat in board shorts with a towel over his shoulder. Isla assessed his toned body in one quick scan. She liked the way his chest hair ran in a line to below his navel. In her imagination she pictured how it would grow all the way down.

Isla wore a modest white one piece swim suit with Hawaiian board shorts over the bottom half. Aiden saw at once that her breasts were even fuller and rounder than he envisaged.

"Haven't you got a towel?" He asked.

"Don't need one. Just be more to carry." Isla replied.

Aiden remembered all the paraphernalia it took to get Jenni onto the beach. The big bag, lotions, towels, cushions, beach umbrella, esky. Not that Jenni ever entered the sea. Too salty. Too sandy. A beach excursion was all about posing in a brief bikini.

They hurried back to the beach feeling rather like truants stealing free time out of school. Puffs of breeze off the water, cool and briny, invigorated Isla to rub her bare arms. She felt her nipples harden in the fresh air and was sure the effect would not be lost on Aiden without even looking at him.

"Are you cold?" He asked.

"No. I'm just pleased to see you." She joked the old one liner, her dark eyes merry.

Aiden blushed. It wasn't what he meant but guessed she'd caught him checking out her assets. Isla ran into the surf, while gleefully yelling a challenge:

"Last one in is a rotten egg."

Aiden was thankful to hit the cold water before his state of arousal became conspicuous. They splashed about like children. Aiden decided Isla looked even better wet. Her rosy nipple colour was faintly discernible through the wet fabric of her white swim suit. He liked the way her board shorts clung to her rounded bottom as she dove under a wave. She was so well rounded in so many ways. Isla liked the way Aiden's board shorts outlined his firm buttocks as well and the way he was laughing and having fun. She began to think of him as Mr. Sweet Cheeks.

They emerged from the sea to lay in the sun for a few minutes before rinsing off under a cold public shower beside the surf club building. Aiden couldn't drag his eyes away as Isla ran busy hands over her body and through her short brown hair to get all the salt water out.

"What are you looking at?" She teased.

"Um. Just um…w-wondering why you wear the board shorts over the swim suit."

Caught looking, he improvised what he hoped justified his ogling.

"You know what a Brazilian is?" Isla asked.

"Yes. I am familiar with the style." It was one of Jenni's high maintenance procedures.

"Well I don't have one. And I'm a natural brunette."

Aiden's face turned scarlet. Isla laughed out loud. She enjoyed shocking him. He was so easy. It was so much better orchestrating her own flirtations than setting it up for others, as she'd done at the supermarket. Aiden wasn't sure what else he was getting himself into, only certain he was on the edge of a very slippery slope.

6

STAKE OUTS

That night, with Ethan out chasing the phantom milker, Aiden had to do the moonlighting cab driver stake out. He was armed with a photo likeness and description of the man given by his government employer.

Before the stake out, Aiden checked that Jenni had vacated their marital home. The house still stank. Jenni hadn't even tried to clean up. He found a garbage bag and emptied the ashtray into it along with what else was on the coffee table, regardless of whether it was washable and reusable. Walking about the living room picking up rubbish his anger grew seeing cigarette burns in the expensive lounge suites. In a fit of pique, he ran upstairs to the master bedroom and stripped the stained sheets off the bed in a fury of disgust.

Aiden took the bed sheets to the kitchen, spread them on the floor and scooped everything off the littered bench tops onto them. Dumping it all in the wheelie bins did little to calm his mood. At least the bins had been empty since Jenni had never bothered to take the trash out. Back in the kitchen, Aiden checked the dishwasher. It was full and had a bad smell. He turned up the water temperature and set it to run through a full cycle. It would take another cycle to clear the sink of dirty crockery. After the worst was disposed of, he would get onto his trusted cleaning service to restore some semblance of cleanliness to the place before putting it back on the market. The house had to be well presented to gain best price.

Jenni had always had someone to pick up after her but Aiden couldn't understand anyone living in such squalor instead of doing something about it.

Insult was added to injury when he found his ex had taken all the best silverware and glassware. Aiden realised Jenni probably kept copies of her house keys. He would have liked to change all the locks before Jenni got away with the furnishings and appliances but technically the house contents were half hers and he didn't want to push her spiteful temper.

Glad his ex had moved out at long last, Aiden got onto the cleaning company to begin making inroads on restoring cleanliness and order to the house.

Since the interview with Mrs. Sylvia Rudin was at 9am the following morning, Isla would be going in late. So, she asked if she might help with that nights stake out. He had a fleeting pang of guilt after telling Ethan not to bring a girl due to the distraction. Isla's presence was excusable although Aiden also knew she distracted the hell out of himself.

Aiden was talked into letting Isla go on the mission, realising truly they could cover twice the ground with two on the case. Armed with photos and descriptions of the cab driver, who would not be using his real name, they planned to check cab ranks from north to south and meet in the middle. Aiden trusted Isla would play it by ear without too much trouble.

Isla did have her own plan. Putting on a girly act, she spoke to a few cab drivers saying she was looking for her uncle because he was needed urgently at home. Before long, another driver recognised the man in her photo and directed her to a shopping mall cab rank. Isla went straight to the rank where a long line of taxis had idle drivers leaning on their vehicles, chatting and drinking takeaway coffees.

Isla spotted the man they sought, his cab was second in line on the rank. Pretending to text, she managed to click several photos including the taxi I.D. She waited supposedly engrossed in her phone until his was the next cab on the rank. Then she wandered over and hired it asking to go to the prearranged meeting place with Aiden. On the way she phoned Aiden from the back seat of the taxi.

"Hiya Sweet Cheeks. It's me. I am on my way with that thing you wanted. Meet you where we said. Ok? See you in a bit."

Aiden was gobsmacked. His untrained newby had delivered within two hours of beginning her first stake out alone. He made it to the prearranged meeting place in record time. The moonlighter had no idea he'd been nabbed and would never connect it to the ditzy young woman fare who was obviously meeting a boyfriend.

The time was not yet 9.30pm. Aiden suggested they go for a late supper at a pizza restaurant. He hoped to learn more of Isla's personal life. Despite her matchmaking attempt with him, he felt certain she must have other possible boyfriends lurking in the background and needed to know before he let himself dream on.

Aiden didn't want to ask outright if Isla had a boyfriend so skirted around it:

"Onions for lunch, garlic for supper. Lucky I don't have anyone to kiss goodnight. Ha ha."

"Me neither." Isla said shortly.

Isla wanted to say she'd kiss him goodnight but judged that to be a tad forward with a new boss and on only her second day. Aiden ventured further.

"No boyfriend?"

"Having a break. I was stung by the last one." She admitted.

"Any time you need to unburden, I'm all ears."

Aiden tried for a kindly uncle type smile. Isla had nothing to lose by telling Aiden her ex dumped her for someone more suitable.

"Turned out I embarrassed him. Troy had lofty ambitions. He needed a better class of sheila to wear on his arm. Better than a check out chick who says all the wrong things in front of his elite crowd." Isla said it matter-of-factly.

Aiden got that it cut her deeply. He also got a hit of elation that Isla was currently unattached.

"So. Aren't we a pair of sad sacks." He laughed. Trying for a light hearted approach yet underlining his own single status.

"I'm not that sad. Anymore. Only wish I had dumped Troy before he dumped me."

"His loss." Aiden remarked hoping it might eventually be his gain.

"Thanks Aiden. For everything. Today has been really great. All of it."

Aiden dared to ask about her cheeky phone call from the cab.

"Um. Just wondering why you called me Sweet Cheeks on the phone."

"Thought it prudent not to use your name Aiden. You know, the whole undercover thing."

"Right. You just came up with a nickname on the spur of the moment? Clever."

Isla thought it also prudent not to let on she'd been thinking of him as Sweet Cheeks ever since seeing him in clingy wet board shorts. Aiden drove her home. Isla dived from his car before acting on an impulse to kiss him goodnight. Aiden would have liked to linger in the car with Isla but he knew it might seem inappropriate. He hoped not to scaring her off with his cat and mouse chase. She'd suffered unwanted attentions from Fergus Rudin so he must take extra care not to seem that way inclined.

Having been reminded of her humiliation with Troy, Isla went to her bed cursing that Aiden also seemed out of her league. There were many reasons stacked against her own self worth: His manner was refined, he owned his own business and had been wed to a gorgeous fashion model, even if she was obviously a super bitch. Isla assessed herself as a former check out chick dumped for her common background and unruly personality. She recalled telling Troy to go fuck himself. How's that for lower class she told herself, yet she'd do that again in a heartbeat.

Isla's former boyfriend, Troy Van Baas, believed it perfectly reasonable to prefer a more sophisticated companion to further his career and social ambitions. Assuring Isla he would still be with her whenever he had time, was akin to throwing her a bone. Isla knew that meant his bone. She also knew Troy would have plenty of others vying for that honour and realised too late what a mug she had been for allowing herself to be bedazzled by him.

7

MOVIE BUFFS

Waiting for his 9am appointment with Mrs. Sylvia Rudin, Aiden cleared his desk and wiped the surfaces with lemon furniture polish. It paid to give respectable first impressions although the front window remained boarded up which didn't look good. He hoped glaziers would arrive to fix it soon, Isla had set wheels in motion but the glass repair tradesmen and insurance brokers refused to be hurried.

Sylvia Rudin arrived on time. She got straight to the point:

"I want my husband Fergus followed to find out where he goes and who he is with on his frequent nights out."

"We can help with that Mrs. Rudin. Please know whatever you tell us and whatever we find will be strictly confidential."

"Firstly, I need to know how much it will cost. I have limited funds and cannot ask my husband for more money. I do not have my own income. But with three children under the age of five at home.... You understand."

Aiden quoted a less than half price figure. He really wanted this account. It would be so good to catch Isla's old boss out.

"And you pay nothing if we don't get a reasonable result." Aiden told her kindly.

"Thank you. So. Where do I begin? What do you need to know?"

"It will be helpful to have a recent photo of your husband and a description of his car and its number plate."

Fergus's wife already had the information in her handbag adding that he usually went out for a few hours between 7 and 10 after the evening meal. She refused coffee saying she must rush home as an old neighbour was watching the children.

Aiden decided to give the Rudin account his dedicated attention beginning that very night. He phoned Isla saying Sylvia Rudin had left so she could come in anytime now.

Isla shopped again at her old supermarket, rubbing it in on creepy Fergus that she planned to continue being in his face. She bought fresh milk again and the makings for sandwiches to be made in the office kitchenette.

"Hello Aiden. How did it go?"

"As expected. She wants Fergus followed to see where he goes at night."

Before that discussion went further, Ethan arrived full of news. He'd identified the phantom milker the previous night and drew out the story for dramatic effect:

"So I got there on twilight. The old farmer showed me where the cows would be. He had them confined to a few acres with a low electric wire. There was a little stand of trees nearby and I found one with a fork I could prop myself into. Then I just waited until dark."

"And you saw the offender and got video?"

"I did. Caught the culprit in the act. I quietly phoned the farmer to tell him it was happening as I spoke. The old guy came out with a rifle and shot the thief stone dead."

"What! No!"

His brother and Isla were shocked. Ethan enjoyed his moment in the limelight. He grinned.

"It was a big fat pink pig. It ducked its back under the electric wire like a limbo dancer so knew how to avoid a jolt. It tried a different cow and copped a kick before finding the old quiet one that he sucked dry."

The farmer said the pig had gotten loose long ago from a neighbour's place. They'd given up looking for it. He planned to turn it into ham, bacon and pork chops because it owed him.

"So a pig was the phantom milk thief. No wonder it was fat. All that Jersey cream."

"Yep. I even helped the farmer drag it back to his barn and hang it up. Gruesome."

"You did well little brother." Aiden meant it.

Isla enjoyed that it was never a dull moment at Birdwhistle Solutions. She went to make coffee for them all while the brothers relived their recent successes.

"Who wants a sandwich? Ham, cheese, tomato?" Isla needn't ask twice.

Aiden went up to his flat to fetch the Dijon mustard. He knew it was Isla's favourite.

Ethan and Isla were given that night off while Aiden followed Fergus Rudin.

Parked down the street from the Rudin family home, he waited. On cue, Fergus drove out at 7pm. Aiden followed at a distance and drove on by when Fergus stopped and parked in a quiet street. Several other cars were parked along the roadway. Aiden slowed and did a U-turn seeing Fergus walk up to the front door of a large house.

The place was a veritable mansion with an imposing facade and heavy studded front door. Aiden drove quietly by. He would repeat the exercise on other nights to see if this was Rudin's regular destination.

Isla was interested in the findings relating to Fergus Rudin. Aiden told her as much as he knew but said the vigil was ongoing. As a precaution, he would use Ethan's car on alternative nights but would go alone.

Subsequent nights drew blanks with no outing. Then on the fourth night Fergus ventured forth once more. Aiden cruised behind him at a distance. The chase led to the same mansion. This destination was confirmed as Fergus's regular visiting place after a few more excursions. Each time, what seemed an unusual number of other vehicles were parked along the street near the place.

Other homes along that tree lined avenue were privately situated back from the road and hidden by high fences and shrubbery. Aiden deemed that the substantial residences would surely have garage accommodation behind their closed gates and not park their cars out on the roadside.

Aiden puzzled over how to find what went on in that house but decided it could possibly be illegal gambling. He parked under deeper darkness of a spreading tree canopy and watched men come and go. Most wore dark clothing and caps pulled down. Obviously none wanted to be recognised. Aiden could obtain footage but with no definite identities.

Getting nowhere, Aiden had to take a risk. He stepped out of his car and waylaid one of the men hurrying away along the footpath.

"Wait mate. Just want to know if I'm at the right house where the action is."

"You are." The man replied gruffly pulling his cap down further.

"There's a fifty in it for you. Tell me how to get in on it."

"Just knock. Cash only. Password is in an ad for racy PW dirt bikes. The local paper."

The man grabbed the fifty and scuttled off. Aiden thought he'd probably never see anything for the money but checked the local daily newspaper early next morning. There were a few ads for PW dirt bikes. One description had Racy PW dirt bike. The only possible password might be the colour given as turquoise. He found a couple of older copies of the newspaper and checked ads for Racy PW dirt bike. The ads gave different colours on different days convincing him that the colours were the daily passwords. He guessed turquoise was tonights password, but he wouldn't attend if Fergus was going, not wishing to run into him.

Aiden once again staked out the Rudin family home. Fergus did not go out, so Aiden fronted the mansion in the night. He knocked. An intercom crackled but no voice spoke. Aiden took the bull by the horns and said 'turquoise'. He was admitted by a huge bulldog of a man who held out his paw for money. Aiden put down a fifty. Getting no response, he put down another fifty. Same non response. He was out by two hundred by the time the ape let him pass.

Another beefy bouncer met him in the grand hallway and led him to a room where several chairs were set out like a home movie lounge. Instead of a movie screen he faced a blank glass window. Aiden sat sweating for another fifteen minutes in darkness until seven more men had entered and sat down quietly.

Music began as the glass window lit up. The scene revealed a bedroom. As Aiden suspected, the glass window was a two-way mirror. Three naked players, two muscular young men and one trim bodied woman, romped in and jumped onto the bed together. They all wore masks that hid their faces.

The hot action began with every type of sexual feat exploited. Aiden became uncomfortably aware of men around him grunting and the slick slapping sounds of their wanking. To his self-disgust, he ached to do the same but resisted the urge. At the end of the show the audience was ushered out quietly in intervals of one at a time.

Aiden couldn't wait to get out of there for a couple of reasons. The most urgent was to get home and masturbate under a warm shower. He knew memories of the experience would excite his lust forever. It was just as Jenni's sex tapes did, to his shame.

After Aiden exhausted himself, he fell into a deep sleep, naked on top of his bed covers. At some time in the early hours before dawn, he awoke with a start and a sudden conviction: The woman performing in the brothel show had surely been his ex-wife, Jenni!

The irony of her big screen debut being a smutty sex show in a brothel situation was not lost on her ex-husband. Bitterly he concluded she would be earning her keep at last. Albeit by servicing a whole roomful of men at the one and same time.

Aiden let Isla know Fergus Rudin had been visiting a brothel. He did not elaborate on the sex show. He didn't want to reveal to either Ethan or Isla that he had attended that type of event or that his ex wife Jenni had been one of the stars.

Since Aiden had not obtained any proof of Rudin's attendance to show Sylvia, he agonised over going back to the brothel the following week. If he managed to attend at the same time as Fergus Rudin it would be impossible to obtain video inside the premises anyway. There was surely a reason for the thuggish goons as security guards. To try was to risk getting a bashing or worse. Aiden knew himself to be more of a lover than a fighter.

At best, video of Fergus walking up to the front door of the mansion and gaining admittance might be possible. He decided that would be better than nothing and at least it would be something to give to Sylvia Rudin. Aiden duly went back the next time Fergus went out. He parked a long way up the street and walked back, his mobile phone on mute but poised ready to video. His nerves jangled knowing there could be thugs posted to observe and trounce anyone lurking about.

However, without further incident, Fergus was captured on video going into the mansion brothel. The image would be rather dark and shaky, but Fergus's identity should be easily recognisable to his wife. Her main brief had been to find out where he went at nights and that was fulfilled. Aiden sped home, loaded the footage on computer and clarified it with enhancing technology. He felt sorry for Mrs. Rudin but as Isla had said, better she knew what her husband was up to.

The problem for Aiden was, he yearned to go back to the brothel for another viewing. Being so close and knowing what he might see behind those closed doors teased him. He told himself it was to ensure the woman really had been Jenni. It could conceivably be someone who resembled her. He talked himself into going back without too much trouble.

Grabbing a local daily paper, Aiden saw the colour on the latest dirt bike ad was black opal. He cashed up at an ATM. That night, agog with excitement to be going back to the porn show, he didn't care whether Fergus was present or not.

Aiden gained entrance using the black opal password. He was required to pay a lot more this time. The ape on the door leered knowing yet another sucker had been hooked on the live sex shows. Entrance fees grew in line with growing addictions. The doorman kept it all in his head and never forgot a face or what they had paid last time. Some long-timers were forking over four figure sums but they still attended regularly. God knows how they came up with the cash but that was their problem.

As before, Aiden was shown to the viewing room. He waited in darkness, palms sweating. Several other men drifted quietly in one at a time. At last the music heralded the start of the show.

This time two women sashayed into the room and lounged on the bed. They wore nothing but glittering bejewelled cat masks and red nail polish. One was a very tall ebony skinned female. Aiden surmised the dark beauty to be of African descent due to her extreme height. He was sure Jenni was the other although she wore a long white wig and the sequined cat mask disguised her face. But he knew her body well. Except for being so hypnotised by what went on the first time, he'd have recognised his ex wife immediately.

The women began slowly kissing and fondling before sliding a toy box out from under the bed. The women displayed each sex toy like sales girls promoting products. Aiden saw that the light show on the wall flashed prices as each device was held up for viewing. He guessed purchases must be made via the doorman. After the sales pitch, the players demonstrated intended purposes of each toy in erotic games.

Aiden had worn two pairs of cotton underpants anticipating his loss of self-control. This time, the show so engrossed him, he hardly noticed the other men in the room panting, grunting and pleasuring themselves. It hadn't taken long for him to become one of them, lost in the group orgy of lust.

At the height of sensation, a disturbance erupted outside the viewing room, sounding like someone being forcibly bounced off the premises. A savage fight was underway. The walls shook as heavy thumps slammed hard against them. In the dim light from the two-way window, the men in the viewing room exchanged alarmed looks, thinking it was a raid or worse. Zips were speedily pulled up, sticky hands wiped, and handkerchiefs stuffed into pockets.

Aiden saw that most of the men were older. Only one was about his own age, a good looking dude with fair hair that flopped over one eye in a hip hairstyle. One of the older men indicated to the others to remain silent. No one disagreed. They all waited tensely.

What followed next in the bedroom scene had them gasping again, in fright rather than in lust. Three extremely tall athletic black men barged in and roughly grabbed the dark woman. One of the men held a bloodied long bladed knife close beside his leg. Jenni screamed, leapt from the bed and cowered into a corner of the room. Her mask and wig fell askew. The dark intruders ignored Jenni, but the tall woman was dragged away kicking and struggling with a big hand clamped hard over her mouth.

The kidnapping rescue or whatever it had been was all over within minutes. The men in the viewing room waited another five minutes, expecting the brothel goons to enter the bedroom. No one appeared.

Jenni still cringed in the corner sobbing. When she pulled a sheet off the bed, to wrap around herself, a large brown dildo to fell to the floor with a clunk that set it off vibrating again. As it chattered across the floor, Jenni's sobs turned to manic laughter. Some of the old men whispered saying she had become hysterical.

Knowing his ex-wife's warped sense of humour, Aiden wasn't at all surprised that the device juddering across the floor struck Jenni's funny bone. The guy with the hip peek a boo hairstyle also found it hilarious. He held his arms about his body trying to chortle quietly while tears of mirth gathered in his eyes. The laughter was contagious. Some other men began to see the comedy of it. Even Aiden had to suppress a desire to chuckle along with the rest. The porn show music had kept playing as if this was part of the show. But it was not.

After a while, the theatre buffs decided to hightail it. Cautiously the door was cracked open. It opened inwards. The body of the burly door-keeper blocked the entrance. His eyes stared in surprise from a face mottled in a mix of purplish hues. His throat had been slashed from ear to ear in a macabre drooling crimson grin. Nearby another bouncer shared the joke with him in a similar mode, slumped against the wall in a spreading pool of dark red gore. No one was laughing anymore.

The young blond guy elbowed others aside and was first out, hurdling the body and running like blazes. The older men followed almost jamming together in the doorway in their haste to depart. One paused momentarily to extract a thick wad of cash from the doorkeeper's pocket, then ran like the devil chased him.

Aiden procrastinated long enough to consider the implications of being found there. He paid serious credence to the old adage that discretion was the better part of valour. Except, in a split-second decision, he knew he had to get Jenni out despite what he thought of her.

He paused staring at the bloodied bodies in the hallway in shocked disbelief. When the porn show music built to a final crescendo, it stirred him to make a move. Thinking over it later, he realised it was strange how his mind processed the drama. In the midst of the horror, he vaguely regretted having missed some glorious culmination, had the show gone on. He'd been hit a cool five hundred bucks for it so it might have been spectacular.

The music stopped. Aiden looked back through the two-way mirror and saw the room was now empty. Jenni's long white wig and glistening cat mask lay on the bed. Jenni had managed a hasty retreat to who knows where. Aiden knew she was good at looking after number one but he felt compelled to get her away from this house of horrors. He would have done the same for anyone in the same situation.

Aiden stepped over and around the grisly dead and walked further up the grand hallway calling Jenni's name. No answer. The door of the display bedroom did not open into this hall. He called Jenni's name louder and knocked on the wall. The place was completely silent and full of evil portent.

A creeping prickling of his scalp had Aiden stride swiftly from the mansion and run to his car parked further up the street. All the others had gone leaving the street quietly deserted.

Aiden knew himself for a coward for leaving Jenni without a more thorough search of the house. But he knew she survived the attack; the tall black men hadn't given her a second glance. He told himself that Jenni chose her lifestyle and must bear the consequences. That was his only justification. In the back of his mind he also hoped this might teach her a lesson.

Sirens were heard in the distance as Aiden made his escape. Perhaps they were for some other drama unless someone had already called 000. So they had, as a late breaking news report indicated the mansion as the location of a double murder.

TV footage showed the respectable frontage of that distinctive lodge. Aiden guessed there would be scores of men thanking their lucky stars not to have attended on that particular night. Perhaps Fergus Rudin was one of them.

No mention of anyone else being inside the house came on the news. Police would surely have discovered the peep show set up but only disclosed publicly that the investigation was ongoing. Once media got hold of all the facts it would escalate into a huge sensation.

Householders interviewed for TV news said theirs was a quiet street where people kept to themselves. They were shocked for this to happen in their nice upper class neighbourhood. Apparently not even close neighbours knew what regularly went on in that mansion. The killings seemed to be considered a home invasion by the general public living in the near vicinity. Some people even left bouquets of flowers, religious symbols and sympathy cards at the scene.

Within one day of the double murder news, yet another murder stole the headlines. The mutilated body of a woman was discovered by a dog walker. It lay partly covered by branches, in bushland some miles away. The victim was described as being of Sudanese appearance and wearing nothing except for red nail varnish. If any connection to the mansion brothel was suspected, it was not publicised.

Aiden broke into a cold sweat knowing he'd dodged a bullet. Now when he thought of his lust over the live porn shows it sickened him. He thought of Isla being so wholesome and natural in contrast to what he had sunk to. Aiden admitted to himself that the former matchmaking check out chick was indeed too good for him.

The cleaners contacted Aiden to say they'd done their best with improving the sorry state of his big house. The firm specialised in presenting homes in pristine condition for sale. Aiden's house had been so neglected it took more than one day. On the second day they reported that someone had been inside and undid a lot of their careful detailing. It was nothing too bad. But the sparkling shower glass in one of the bathrooms was spattered with soapy droplets and towels were dampened, obviously used. The polished kitchen floor showed a few small drops of spills as well. The cleaning firm manager said she was just letting Aiden know in case he thought they'd been lax in their duty, because they had left it in pristine condition.

Aiden was furious. It had to be Jenni. He certainly did not want to see or argue with her so he put it off. He thanked the cleaning personnel for their diligence and paid them up to date, saying to leave it with him and he would engage them again when he could.

In the meantime, evidence of Fergus Rudin's transgression was presented to Sylvia Rudin. She was told her husband had been seen on several occasions frequenting the house shown on his video. Aiden gently advised the woman that the mansion was a known brothel.

The fact that her husband attended the brothel, was tempered by hearing he was unlikely to return there as it had been the site of the double murders reported on recent TV news. Sylvia revised her belief that Fergus still chased Isla, his former check out girl.

Privately, Aiden hoped Fergus's wife might go to police and indicate her husband's connection with the brothel. That was her call. Aiden had done his job and wanted nothing more to do with that mansion of mayhem.

8

THE KISS OFF

After the brothel mansion episodes, Aiden became subdued and introverted. Concerned, Isla mentioned her thoughts to Ethan who told her his brother had leftover baggage from his divorce that weighed heavily on him a lot of the time. Out of tact and loyalty to Aiden, Ethan did not discredit Jenni, but it was on the tip of his tongue to do so.

Isla strove to cheer Aiden up. The weather had remained pleasant so she suggested they go for another swim in the sea. He wasn't keen and used the excuse of catching up on work.

"How about Sunday then Aiden. Day of rest."

"I don't know."

"Have I done something wrong? Is this the big kiss off Aiden?"

Aiden hastened to reassure Isla:

"NO. No of course not. You've been great. Your are great. Best thing I've ever done was convincing you to come here."

Aiden knew himself to be sliding into deep depression. He felt he would never be rid of Jenni nor be able to overcome how he'd been dragged down to her level. Half waking with yearnings, alone at night, he knew he could never unsee the sex scenes he had witnessed. They were seared into his brain, pervading and spilling over into erotic thoughts of Isla. He dreaded to think what Isla would think of him if she knew.

Isla's kind attempts to cheer him up only enforced his sense that she was far too good for him. Isla did not give up easily:

"I can't believe I've done nothing wrong unless you come swimming again."

Aiden had to relent for fear of hurting her feelings. None of his problems were her fault after all. He tried for a lighter outlook:

"OK. I'll meet you at the beach about 8 Sunday morning. And I'll even buy you an icecream if you behave yourself." he said.

"What if I don't behave myself?"

"I'll buy you two icecreams."

At least she got a rise out of him, and they shared a little laugh.

Aiden tried to shake off his gloom and despair as he sat by the beach waiting for Isla that Sunday. He felt his mood rise as he heard her gaily call his name. She ran to his side and beamed a sunny smile that instantly lifted his heavy heart.

"Sorry I'm a bit late, had to get fuel and there was a line up." she said.

"Surf's up," Aiden smiled back, "but the water might be fairly cold this morning."

"It will be bracing. Last one in is a rotten egg."

Isla squealed as she hit the cold water. Aiden would never have swum in such cold water except for Isla being there. He couldn't ignore her playfulness. Gingerly he tiptoed in trying to become accustomed to the chill slowly. Like a mermaid, Isla already floated beyond the breakers, her beckoning dare to come in seemed as tempting as any siren call. Aiden dove under the next wave and struck out towards her. Isla disappeared from view. Aiden looked around wondering where she had gone before she rose up in a whoosh of water behind him.

"Boo." she laughed.

"You don't scare me." he lied.

His heart thumped not out of fear but for being so near to her. As she tread water her foot fleetingly stroked his leg. It took all his will power not to grab for her.

"I owe you an ice-cream." he said to break the moment.

"Yep, that's the deal and I'm holding you to it. A double cone."

"I didn't say double cone."

"You didn't say single cone either. Open contract."

Isla laughed before swimming strongly overarm to catch a wave to shore.

Sunday at the beach attracted plenty of visitors, people strolling the esplanade, sunbathing, swimming and the ever-present surfboard riders.

Aiden and Isla rinsed off under the open-air freshwater shower in front of the surf club building. Sunshine and a warm ocean breeze would soon have them dry as they ambled along the path leading to the ice-cream parlour.

Isla's happy smile froze as she spotted her old boyfriend, Troy Van Baas, walking towards them. Troy was the last person on earth she wished to meet. In the next instant she decided to let her ex-heartbreaker see she was well over him and was with someone much nicer now.

"Kiss me Aiden. Quick."

Aiden was taken by surprise but didn't object as Isla stopped him in his tracks and flung her arms about his neck. He readily bent to her command circling his arms about her waist. Isla extended the kiss parting her lips suggestively and leaning into Aiden's body as Troy neared. Ethan was on life saving duty back at the surf club that Sunday. One of his mates said it looked like his big brother was having a win. If Ethan was surprised at seeing Aiden and Isla in a clinch, what happened next amazed him because he had never known Aiden to be violent. Troy had walked right up to the kissing couple and uttered some malicious words:

"She's not bad for a bit of rough on the side hey mate?" Troy sneered.

Startled, Aiden drew back from Isla. He recognised the face from the porn show brothel. It was the good looking dude with the hank of fair hair boyishly flopped over one eye.

"What did you say?"

"You heard me. She's good for a root if nothing else. I'll give her that."

"Ignore him Aiden. He's just a stupid moron."

Isla lay a calming hand on Aiden's arm. Aiden didn't take Isla's advice. He stepped towards Troy and pushed him hard in the chest with both hands. Isla's old boyfriend stumbled backwards into a palm tree that saved him from falling over flat on his backside. Troy recovered in an instant and poised himself into some sort of karate stance, albeit appearing rather ludicrous. Watching in alarm from the surf club building, Ethan could see this would not end well for his brother. He ran over as back up, calling on some other mates as well. Several other lifeguards stood up prepared to help. The lifesavers including Ethan were all strong well-built young men who competed in Iron Man Competitions and surfing marathons. Outnumbered, Troy nimbly vaulted a fence into the car park with a final barb smirked at Aiden:

"Seems we have a lot in common, if you don't mind sharing that is."

Only Aiden knew he might refer to his attendance at the brothel as well as to Isla. A screech of tyres and taunting blast on the horn of his sports car, was Troy's parting shot.

"Alright?" Ethan patted his brother's back.

"Yeah. Thanks kid. Catch you later. OK?"

Ethan returned to the club house and thanked his mates for their show of support.

"I'm so sorry Aiden. That was Troy my ex-idiot mistake." Isla said.

"I got that Isla." Aiden replied quietly.

Aiden felt stupid and let down for loving the kiss before finding it was only Isla's ploy to annoy her old boyfriend. Isla realised how he felt and was kicking herself. Aiden's eager response had not been lost on her. She had to smooth it over.

"Suppose I don't get that ice-cream now." She said.

"Maybe later." Aiden said shortly. He just wanted to go home.

"You have every reason to be miffed Aiden. Thanks for helping me out."

"I'm all heart." he replied bitterly.

"Also really very lovely to kiss." Isla whispered, shyly touching a finger to his lips.

"You must desperately want that ice-cream." Aiden said as he melted to her touch.

"Come on Sweet Cheeks." Isla said, less shyly.

"OK. I can buy ice-cream. I'm not just a kissable face you know." Aiden softened.

"I know. I've seen you in wet board shorts." Isla gave him a cheeky wink.

Isla held out her hand to Aiden. He accepted knowing he remained a pushover. Isla had him hook, line and sinker.

Ethan had gone back to the surf club but watched them walk away hand in hand. He guessed his brother might have some luck for a change. He liked Isla and hoped his brother would not think her too unsophisticated after that glamorous tart Jenni he married.

Sitting in the ice-cream parlour garden, enjoying double cones of vanilla and chocolate, Aiden tried to work out how the encounter with Troy came about to degenerate in the way it had.

"Your old boyfriend was seething. Didn't you say he dumped you?"

"Yes. Troy dumped me for his public image. But he still wanted me as a shag on the side. I wasn't good enough for anything else." Isla said plainly.

"So you actually dumped him after he dumped you."

"I guess. Anyway I bruised his ego. Having a common supermarket chick refuse him insulted his high opinion of himself. That's what he can't stomach, and it angers him. It's more about him than me. There'd be a lot of other women begging for his favours. Not like he actually needs me."

Aiden tossed up whether to tell Isla that Troy had been at the brothel. He had an idea Troy might bring it up in some later confrontation with Isla so perhaps he should preempt that by telling her now. He wouldn't mention the peep show or being present during the murders.

"Isla. There's something I should tell you in case you found out later and wondered why I didn't say upfront. You probably don't want to know, so sorry in advance."

"What is it?"

Isla couldn't imagine what it could be. Aiden ventured a short version:

"I recognised Troy's face. I saw him at the same brothel where I'd followed Fergus Rudin."

"No kidding? Troy Van Baas at a brothel? I'm sure he'd have so many women at his beck and call he wouldn't need to pay for it."

Isla was truly astounded.

"Maybe the brothel provided something he couldn't get elsewhere?"

"Like what?"

"I don't know. Maybe group orgies. Bondage. Or just no strings sex." Aiden deliberately didn't say porn shows.

"I just can't imagine Troy paying for sex. I reckon he'd more likely be one of the pimps in a brothel. He always had plenty of ready cash. I never did find out exactly what his business entailed but I know he conducted interviews and hired and fired people."

Troy being part of the brothel management hadn't occurred to Aiden. If true, it explained his presence at the porn show. He'd be checking how it went down with clients and how well the actors performed their roles. It hit him that Troy might have been one of the talent scouts who'd interviewed Jenni and conned her into thinking she was set for movie stardom.

Suddenly Troy's parting comment about sharing took on a more complex meaning. Troy Van Baas could know Jenni was once married to him although she went by her maiden name McKinstock. Jenni always said Birdwhistle was too ridiculous a name. As it turned out, Aiden and indeed Ethan as well, became thankful that Jenni had never taken their surname.

Jenni's apparent return to live in their marital home brought the criminal connections right to Aiden's own doorstep. He feared her presence involved him. He might be forgiven for leaving the bloody murder scene but he was culpable for not immediately going to police with what he knew. The longer he left it the worse it looked. At least he had the thin excuse of being on a case of his own. All this Aiden mulled over in the ice-cream parlour garden with Isla.

"Penny for your thoughts Aiden." Isla smiled to reassure him. He looked so worried.

Aiden forced his thoughts to the present; aware he must be acting oddly.

"Not worth a penny...um...it just occurred to me that your old boyfriend is the most likely one to have thrown that brick with the note."

"You're right. I hadn't thought of Troy because he'd backed off bothering me lately. Until today, I had Fergus Rudin down for it. Now I'm not so sure." Isla said.

Aiden didn't mind putting that doubt in Isla's mind in case she still had any hidden feelings for that handsome bastard. After the recent confrontation, Troy van Baas definitely seemed the person most likely to have smashed his window, given the slur on Isla in the note.

"It would be very difficult to prove who did it. Probably impossible."

"I know. I'm sorry I brought this down on you." Isla said.

"As you said Isla. It's about him not about you. You've done nothing wrong."

"Thanks. Anyway the glaziers are due this week at last. Maybe as soon as tomorrow."

"Good. I mightn't be available myself. I have business to attend to tomorrow morning. You and Ethan can man the ship and talk about me." Aiden added.

"OK. We will." Isla smiled. And they would.

Isla liked Ethan and they got along well together, sharing jokes and work at the agency. She really appreciated how he'd sprung to help Aiden against Troy that Sunday morning. Also Ethan was the only one with whom she could discuss his older brother.

Ethan and Isla were both aware something was really troubling Aiden and hoped he would snap out of his blue funk soon.

9

AIDEN & POLICE

Monday. Aiden eventually found the detective in charge of the brothel mansion murders. After having his own name and I.D. details laboriously checked by a desk sergeant, Aiden was eventually ushered into an interview room, bare apart from a table and four chairs. A window into the room did not fool Aiden that it would be two-way for outsiders to watch his reactions. The stern steely eyed senior detective, Dougall Grimslade, wore a permanent expression of dubiousness. Aiden guessed he often had his time wasted with nut cases.

"So...Mr...er...Birdwhistle you're a private investigator yourself."

Grimslade said it like the profession stank. Aiden wearily met his smirk.

"Yes. Birdwhistle Solutions. I know it's BS. Thanks."

"You want to make a statement?"

"That's why I'm here. I know that double murder house is a porn show brothel. I was there checking out an errant husband for a client. She is the man's wife of course."

"Hard work." The older man rolled his eyes. "But someone has got to do it. Right?"

"There is a ready market for this type of surveillance. The industry might stink but so do the cheaters and criminals we get hired to expose. I'm sure you realise those we catch are just the tip of the iceberg."

The detective sighed and leaned back in his chair. The comment coming from a lay man irked Grimslade and he couldn't wait to give him the bums rush and go get his morning tea. His wife had packed his favourite salami and pickle sandwiches.

"What can you tell us that we don't already know."

He sighed with a glance to the window where a colleague observed proceedings.

"In a nutshell: The black woman found dead in bushland was in the sex show the night the murders took place. Everyone in the audience witnessed her abduction done by a group of three tall negroid men. One had a knife. The knife dripped with blood. Before those men barged into the bedroom, a fight was heard happening outside in the hallway. Everyone saw the two slain men. They couldn't miss them. One man's huge body lay across the doorway and had to be jumped over to get out."

Dougall Grimslade sat forward, suddenly all ears. His colleague, Dulcy Vestige, entered and sat in. She'd obviously been watching and listening. Probably as bored as the other detective until the unexpected tip off. Aiden agreed to have his statement recorded. He told them as much detail of the altercation, the woman being taken, the male brothel clients running away as he remembered.

"Did anyone touch the bodies?"

"One did. He robbed a wad of cash from the dead doorman."

"Did that thief move the body?"

"He just slipped his hand in the guy's coat pocket. That's all I saw him do and he was quick about it. The big wad of notes was pretty obvious."

Asked how he gained access to the place, he told how he found out about the password ads for dirt bikes. Aiden paused over the next question. He did not want any link to Isla, but he did very much want Troy Van Baas investigated.

"Did you know any of the other men in the room?"

"I recognised the younger one from somewhere, but I don't know him. Only that his name is Troy Van Baas."

"You didn't know any of the others?"

"No. They were all older. Van Baas is about my age. He sports a hip hairstyle that covers one eye. That's why I remembered him. He has a habit of flicking it back. Like a girl would."

"Sounds like you don't like him."

"No reason to like him." Aiden replied.

"Did you know anyone else you saw on the premises? Or that you knew to be on the premises? Either then or any other time?"

Oh God. Aiden dropped his head down into his hands. He couldn't lie to the police. The tension caught up with him and it had to all come out. Involuntarily, Aiden broke down and began to sob. It felt like a proper nervous breakdown as he couldn't stop it. He felt so ashamed. The interviewers exchanged glances. They didn't expect this sudden reaction. Water and a box of tissues was offered to Aiden. After a while he composed himself.

"I'm sorry. This has been a nightmare. Is still a nightmare. I do know one of the porn show prostitutes. My ex-wife Jenni. Divorced six months ago."

"Was she the real reason you were there?"

"NO. I gave you the real reason. That was the first I knew of her being there. It was a terrible shock seeing Jenni playing the sexpot for a roomful of strange men. Her mask and wig fell off during the invasion."

"You're saying she was also present during the murders. And her name is Jenni Birdwhistle?"

"No. She goes by McKinstock. Jenni McKinstock. Her maiden name."

"Where is your ex-wife now?"

"I don't know for sure, but she might have gone back to our marital home. I moved out months ago before the divorce but she kept on staying there. Then, she recently auditioned for some talent scouts and supposedly landed a plum movie part, and moved out."

The police twigged how Jenni's habitation in the marital home effected Aiden.

"Does your ex-wife contribute to the mortgage?"

"No. She didn't work while we were married. I have always paid for everything."

"So you have every reason to want her out of your life."

"That is correct."

"Did it anger you seeing her in that pornographic role?"

"Not at all. I'm glad she finally found a paying occupation and I'm sure she enjoys the part to be honest. It suits her. She's finally found her forte." Bitterness tainted his reply.

"It sounds like you've lost respect for your ex-wife."

"Of course I have. Do you find that unreasonable?"

Questioned further, Aiden explained he had engaged contract cleaners to prepare the house ready for inspections. He hoped to sell it as soon as possible to finalise terms of the divorce. He told them how the cleaners made a last check and found someone had used the bath towels. So he believed Jenni may have gone back there, possibly having nowhere else to run after what happened at the brothel mansion.

"Have you been back to your house yourself since?"

"No. I didn't want to see Jenni."

"So Mr. Birdwhistle. Aiden. You've wanted to finalise your divorce. Your ex has stood in your way causing you financial difficulty. Then you discover her in a compromising situation in a sex show. Yet you tell us you tried to get her out of the brothel house."

"I did try. But the house seemed empty. I was sure she had already fled the place. Of course she didn't know I was there or she would have appealed for my help."

"You believe your ex wife would appeal for you help?"

"Oh yes. I am absolutely sure of it." Aiden replied.

The interviewers appeared sceptical.

"Did you search the entire brothel house?"

"No. I called out and knocked on the wall in the hallway. The two dead men were on the floor. Blood oozing. I could smell it. It really freaked me out. So I left."

"Why didn't you immediately contact us?"

"I know I should have. I don't know. I was in shock."

Aiden realised he was being questioned as if he were at fault.

"Is there more to this you're not saying?"

"Like what? I don't know what you want from me. I came in to help with what I know."

"Let s go back to the men who invaded. You said earlier they looked African. Couldn't they have been, for example, Indigenous Australians?"

"I think that highly unlikely. The invaders looked to be the same ethnicity as the woman they abducted, and I heard on the news she was described as Sudanese."

"But you didn't know that until you heard the news did you?"

Aiden didn't see why that would matter. He got that they aimed to trick him into changing aspects of his story. He soldiered on sticking to the facts:

"The first impression I got was that the woman must have been from some very tall African race. The men who took her all had the same appearance. Why is this an issue?"

"Just clarifying the facts. Aiden." Grimslade smiled like a crocodile.

"I need to get back to work."

Aiden felt nauseated having his attempt to help turned on him.

"Before you go. Has your ex-wife any distinguishing marks?"

"There are plenty of photos of her if you need identification." Aiden said.

"Has she any distinguishing marks?" Grimslade doggedly repeated.

Aiden paused, puzzled. It seemed an odd question to ask. It seemed more like information needed for identification of a body.

"Has something happened to Jenni?" he asked suddenly going cold.

"What distinguishing marks has she? Scars, tattoos, birthmarks?"

Aiden's own question was ignored.

"Jenni has a vaccination scar on her upper left arm. And a mole on the back of her neck and another mole down below covered by her pubic hair. Her opinion of tattoos is they are a sign of lower class and even lower I.Q. There's irony for you hey? Anyway, I doubt if she'd have gotten a tattoo at any time, and I didn't notice one when I saw her naked."

"Thanks for you co-operation Aiden. We will talk to you again."

Aiden felt they fell just short of telling him not to leave the country. He got up to leave.

"One more thing Aiden. We'd like to inspect your house. Today."

Wordlessly Aiden handed them his house keys. He had already removed the hidden cameras from the master bedroom and couldn't think of anything else he need worry about.

"Please return the keys to my office when you're done." he said.

The original video evidence Aiden retained of Jenni's adultery was stored on a flash drive in his sock drawer. Destroying that would be the first thing he did on returning to the flat. He had every right to keep that footage but sensed the turn of tide shifting against himself.

Aiden returned to the agency office that Monday, barely noticing the front window had been renewed in his rush to destroy the flash drive. He soaked the flash drive in boiling water then pocketed it, soon to be thrown into the sea.

"Are you ok?" Isla asked.

"Sure. Just ducking out again for fifteen minutes. Where's Ethan?"

"He ducked out as well. But he said he'd see you here tonight."

Isla felt fobbed off. She'd been alone and bored for much of the day. She rationalised that Aiden was very busy and counted her blessings that her situation was still miles better than at the supermarket job. Having cleaned the office and kitchen, Isla looked for something more to do. She decided to invent a database of client names in alphabetical order to streamline finding anything in the hard copy filing system. It wasn't absolutely necessary but helped fill the hours.

While Isla beavered away at the office, Aiden drove along the shore to an old jetty and took a stroll to the end. He had palmed the hot flash drive while still in his car in case the police watched what he did next. It was what he would do in their position.

The small storage device was surreptitiously dropped between a wide gap in the old jetty timbers as Aiden sat for a while, cooling off in the sea breeze.

Aiden's subversive sex thrill material was gone with an inaudible plink into deep water beneath the jetty. He felt half regretful and half relieved to be rid of it.

10

ETHAN SPRUNG

That Monday night, Ethan planned to visit Aiden at the flat above the office, curious to know what actually went on with his brother's show of temper at the beach. Aggressive behaviour was so out of character for Aiden. Isla hadn't been very forthcoming when questioned and Ethan felt she was holding back.

When Aiden returned from the jetty, he thanked Isla for overseeing the new window installation and for minding the office. Saying he was tired out, he encouraged her to go home early, and he locked up for the day. Just on dusk, Ethan returned to visit his brother, bringing fish and chips and a six pack of stubbies.

"You there big brother?" Ethan called out from the bottom of the stairs.

"Yeah. Just out of the shower. Come on up. Do I smell fish and chips? You're a lifesaver."

"That is a known fact. Speaking of which, I might have saved your life yesterday from that karate goose."

"Knew you had an ulterior motive to visit. Guess you didn't extract the whole rundown out of Isla."

"I tried but she was tight lipped." Ethan laughed.

They didn't bother with plates. Just spread the fish and chips out on the paper it came wrapped in. Aiden got the vinegar out of his pantry as his small contribution, and they drank the cold beer straight from the brown bottle stubbies.

"You and Isla got a thing going?" Ethan asked with a casual burp.

"No. Yes. Not really. Not yet. I'd like to." Aiden admitted.

"That's clear then."

The situation was actually absolutely clear to Ethan. His big brother was totally hooked on Isla.

"She's alright don't you reckon?" Aiden also tried for a casual remark.

"Isla's great. Really down to earth. Probably too good for you." Ethan laughed.

"I know. I've been thinking that too." Aiden said it, suddenly seriously downcast.

"I was only joking Bro. I think you suit each other. Looked to be going well at the beach."

"No. That was just Isla play acting, trying to irk an old boyfriend."

"Bloody good acting. It looked really authentic. You could both be in Hollywood."

Aiden smiled remembering Isla's comments. Saying he was lovely to kiss. Calling him Sweet Cheeks. Hinting it was his tight buns that earned the nickname. He'd checked his bum out with the aid of two mirrors after that and vainly thought she'd made a fair assessment. His little brother might be the taller muscular athlete in the family, but he could possibly earn a pass in the right light himself, especially with those sweet cheeks of his.

That made Aiden think of Isla's well-rounded attributes and his throat went dry. He drained his beer. Ethan pressed his interrogation:

"So that was her old boyfriend? Good looking dude. Hard act to follow. What did he say to make you so mad?"

"Insulted Isla. Cast aspersions."

"Had to be something bad to rile you up."

"More or less said she's just a bit of rough. Said she's only good for a root"

"What a bastard. No wonder he lost her."

"Thing is, he dumped her. She doesn't fit his highfalutin public image. He more or less told her he was happy to bestow his favours in private. Like he expected her gratitude. She gave him a polite suggestion. Actually, 'polite' might be an exaggeration."

"Good for Isla. Bet she told him in no uncertain terms too."

"She would hey. Since then, we both reckon that sook was behind the brick throwing."

"Seems the prime suspect." Ethan agreed. "What's his name?"

"Troy Van Baas. There's more to his story too. If I drink enough beer I might tell you."

Ethan got another two stubbies from the fridge.

"What have you been up to yourself?" Aiden asked.

"Today? Apart from failing to get any info out of Isla, I checked new enquiries. Sylvia Rudin got back to us. Seems her wonderful hubby is still tom catting about."

"Truly? So she didn't dob him in to police for going to the murder mansion. Pity."

"No. She hasn't even told him she knows either. She's still thinking about the best way to use it. So she wants him followed some more. I see you didn't charge her very much the first time."

"That's true. I really wanted that account after what Fergus Rudin did to Isla."

"I figured we won't want to spend much legwork on him. So I attached one of the locator bugs to his car. I can follow him remotely."

"Jesus Ethan. I reckon he'd be a mean mongrel if he caught you doing that."

"I was careful. He always parks in the space reserved for manager behind the supermarket. I couldn't see any CCTV but there could be some. Anyway, I parked nearby and undid my shoelace before I got out of my car. I pretended to be engrossed in my phone until a couple of people came along. Then I walked away in front of them pretending to trip. They pointed out my shoelace. Thanks I said. I was just behind Rudin s vehicle so while I tied my laces, I nimbly stuck the 4G magnetic thing under his fender."

"Nimbly hey. Nimbly is always good." Aiden smiled.

Ethan had been demonstrating his movements in a pantomime.

"Yep. Pretty slick hey."

"Yep. The old shoelace trick. So what have you found out. Anything? By the way that device will have to be retrieved eventually. Too expensive for a once only use."

"Oh ye of little faith. I know. And I tracked him to that big hacienda on the cliff."

"So what does that mean I wonder?"

"Maybe it's another brothel?"

"Have you driven past since then?"

"Yes. But not up to the house. The driveway is long and steep with a few switchbacks. It doesn't seem the sort of place where customers would park on the street and walk up. There could be parking spaces up near the house of course." Ethan said.

"Not good for speedy getaways." Aiden replied.

"No. The place is really private and there is only one way in. There could be a helipad of course and I've seen choppers out that way before. A sleaze bag like Rudin must have a reason to go there. I doubt if he's delivering groceries."

"Ha ha. I doubt that as well. Maybe time will tell. So have you given out the info to Sylvia Rudin yet?"

"Not yet. I didn't know how much you'd want to bill her this time."

"I suppose she is a returning client and I'd really like to land Rudin in trouble. Just charge her a token fee like last time."

"OK. I said I'd meet her at a playground where she takes her kids so she didn't have to get a babysitter again. She says she's there most afternoons at three thirty."

"Good thinking."

"I'm not just a pretty face." Ethan grinned.

Although Ethan knew Aiden followed Fergus Rudin to what became the murder site brothel, he didn't know the extent of what went on inside. Aiden thought his younger brother was lucky to have gotten away with bugging Rudin's car but had to agree it was far safer to track a target remotely if at all possible. They talked about brothels traditionally being linked to a shadier side of life involving pimps and drugs.

"You were lucky to get away with that first brothel thing yourself Aiden." Ethan said.

"The thing is, I haven't gotten away with it. I spent all morning talking to police in charge of the mansion murder case. I had further information that might have helped with their enquiries. Except I seem to have wound up landing on their suspect list myself."

"What! Why? How could that happen?"

"I actually went into the brothel to check it out. Long story. Had to get a password. The main attraction is a live porn show with a roomful of viewers watching anonymously from a dark room. There's a two-way mirror."

"So you watched it yourself. Was it any good?"

"Erotic. Full on action. Music. Coloured light show."

Aiden began bringing his younger brother up to speed although only with an edited version of events. He shied off revealing what Jenni had been doing.

"You get all the good jobs." Ethan said enviously.

"Good until the murders Ethan. I was there when it happened. So was Troy Van Baas and a bunch of other men. In the dark viewing room."

"Shit Aiden. Why didn't you tell me sooner? No wonder you've been out of sorts lately."

"During the porn show, three frigging enormous black dudes burst into the bedroom scene and abducted one of the women. A Sudanese woman. After they left all the men including myself, scarpered. I waited a few days before going to police. And that apparently doesn't look good for me."

Ethan put it together. "The mutilated body! Was that the same Sudanese woman?"

"Had to be. That's why I went to the police. In case they didn't get the connection to the brothel. Also I wanted to let them know Troy Van Baas had been there. Isla says he would more than likely be a brothel pimp than a brothel client."

Aiden got the remaining beers from the fridge. He didn't know if he could make sense to Ethan without disclosing Jenni's part in it all. Ethan had been mulling it over.

"So. I don't see how the police find you to be suspicious. I mean you went to them voluntarily."

"Jesus. This is where it gets dirtier and more involved Ethan."

Aiden took a deep breath. Ethan felt a twinge of foreboding.

"What?"

"Jenni was working at the brothel. She was in the sex scene with the Sudanese woman. I waited until the others all left and tried to get her out of there. But she had gone by then. I told the police all of that."

Ethan was astounded at what he was hearing and that his brother had been keeping it bottled up. On reflection, he wasn't amazed that Jenni would participate in a porn show. Aiden had already told him she aspired to star in adult movies. They had both agreed it was good that she finally moved out of the house for whatever reason.

"I still don't get it. Why would you be under any suspicion Aiden?"

"They focused on making me seem vengeful. They brought up that I paid the mortgage even though I didn't live in the house anymore. And that Jenni staying on in the house put me under financial stress. They suggested I had every reason to want to be rid of her. I agreed. I said I was glad she had finally moved out so the house could be sold."

Ethan digested the implications and worried about possibilities.

"It sounds like they want to blame you for something. Or for anything."

"I know. Then they asked if her part in the porn show angered me. I said it didn't. But I also said Jenni would enjoy it and I thought the career suited her. I was being truthful but they jumped on it. They asked if I'd lost respect for Jenni. I said of course I had."

"Shit. What a bitch she is. Jenni's got you into this."

Ethan was angry but he stopped short of telling Aiden that Jenni had tried to seduce him years ago. No need to worsen it. Aiden went on to describe the interrogation he was given, asking if Jenni had any distinguishing marks. Then the demand to search his house.

"Those questions are like seeking info to identify a body." Ethan said.

"My thoughts exactly Ethan. I asked if something had happened to Jenni but they wouldn't say. Just ignored my question. They were searching the house today. I asked them to return my house keys to the office."

Ethan paled. They both swigged more beer.

"Do you think something has happened to Jenni?" Ethan asked at last.

"I don't know. I was sure she went back to the house because the cleaners said someone had been there after they'd thoroughly detailed it for real estate inspections. Just minor things like a bathroom and towels had been used. I didn't go to see Jenni because I didn't want to. I just couldn't believe she was back in the house after I'd finally gotten her out. She'd left the place looking and smelling like a pigsty before I'd got the cleaners back in. I thought I could finally get the house on the market and sold and that would be closure on the divorce at last. And I would never have to see her again. But after the porn show episode she was apparently back again and I could see the whole cycle repeating."

Ethan reddened. He had a confession to make:

"Oh no Aiden. I'm so sorry. It was me."

"What? What was you?"

"I used your house. I'm really really sorry. I took a girl there for...you know. We had nowhere else to go at the time. There's no privacy at the beach house. I shouldn't have done it. But just so you know. It wasn't Jenni who used the shower. It was me and the girl."

Ethan had his own key to Aiden's house in case he ever needed to get in. His older brother had not even thought of Ethan going there as he'd never done so before, to his knowledge.

"Jesus. What does this mean then. If Jenni didn't go back to the house...where is she?"

"Do you think we should tell the police?"

Ethan asked the question, suddenly fearful of the consequences.

"Let's think about it. I don't see how it affects anything they're doing. And they've pissed me off big time already. I don't feel inclined to offer them any more info. Everything I told them this morning just seemed to make them suspect me of wrongdoing." Aiden said.

Ethan became more ill at ease and confessed a significant reason for his discomfort:

"To be honest. I'd rather not get involved either. Not the least because the girl I took there is still at school. High school. She's almost sixteen. Going on twenty though."

"Almost sixteen! Bloody hell Ethan. That's fifteen!"

"Tiffany looks older. And I didn't know she was underage. The subject didn't come up before....well before it was too late."

"Jesus Ethan. I hope you practised safe sex with what did come up."

"Sure did. I wore a hard hat and hob nailed boots." Ethan joked half heartedly.

Aiden thought of another aspect of Ethan's sexy romps in his house.

"So Ethan. Have you ever used my house before or was that a one time only?"

"Only that once. I promise. And I won't ever do that again. At your house I mean. Without your permission. Tiffany will be sixteen in two weeks time by the way."

Aiden knew the chances of talking Ethan out of the young girl were zilch. He imagined Tiffany would be a silly little strumpet with an entitled attitude and no respect for authority. In other words, like half the kids at high school seemed to be. He thought the romance wasn't likely to be a long-term commitment on either side. However, as the older brother, he decided to give Ethan a lesson on the morals of some females:

"I guess you're old enough and ugly enough to know everything now little brother."

"Like what?"

"Remember that stake out I did last year where the husband was clear on video but not the woman? Well, I recognised the woman he was playing up with as my own darling wife. I added up several odd things I'd noticed at the time. I put up some hidden cameras set up in our bedroom. Sure enough, Jenni was bringing men home and using our own bed. That's why I divorced her.

Therefore, you and *The Child Tiffany* might have starred in your own porn show if the timing was right."

The brothers eyed each other realising the embarrassing implications and what ifs.

"Might have starred if we used your bed but I'm not that bad Bro. We used the spare room."

"Thank heaven for small mercies. If there's a next time, make sure you fold the towels lengthwise and polish everything afterwards. And put the chain on the door. I don't want to walk in on you."

"OK Aiden. I would. But I hope to find somewhere else anyway."

"And wherever you go, remember...."

"I know. Practice safe sex."

Aiden envied Ethan's popularity. His younger brother could take his pick of the beach bunnies who eyed him off. And frequently did. It was a worry he'd nailed one under the age of consent though Aiden understood how girls could look a lot older in a bikini. He could hardly presume to lecture Ethan knowing he'd probably do the same given the chance. Aiden had to concede his little brother had far greater experience with conquests.

"Suppose you don't need that much practice anymore. You're getting more than I ever did."

"You'll have to work a bit more on Isla. If she can stand you that is." Ethan laughed.

"She can stand me. You know she calls me Sweet Cheeks." Aiden preened.

"Behind your back?"

"That's where it started. After she saw me in wet board shorts."

"That's promising then. She must be easily pleased." Ethan laughed.

Aiden might not have disclosed the Sweet Cheeks nickname if he hadn't just drunk three stubbies in quick succession.

11

IT'S A DATE

A young duty police officer had returned Aiden's house keys to the office after closing time that Monday. He dropped them through the letter flap on the front door while Ethan and Aiden were upstairs eating fish and chips, drinking beer and sharing secrets. Ethan stayed overnight on a sofa since he'd drunk so much.

Isla arrived early the following Tuesday morning and felt surprised to see both brothers already at their desks, thinking there was a first for everything. She greeted them cheerfully:

"Anyone want coffee? With fresh cinnamon scrolls from the bakery?"

"Aiden if you don't marry this woman I will." Ethan exclaimed tactlessly.

Isla and Aiden both blushed and hurried to get on with their separate tasks. Ethan smiled to himself. He could see the attraction in matchmaking.

The pleasant Tuesday morning was marred when the young policeman arrived asking Aiden if he would accompany him to the station for further questions.

"Why? Am I under arrest?"

"No. Just a courtesy request. If you've no objection that is."

Aiden deemed the baby faced officer to be only a junior gofer who wouldn't know the reason he was being recalled anyway. Aiden went out of curiosity. To refuse would be uncooperative and worsen attitudes against him. The same two detectives from the day before, interviewed Aiden again. He thanked them for promptly returning his keys, adding that he hoped they hadn't made a mess of the place as real estate agents were booked to inspect and take photos.

"I think you'll find it is in order." He was told. "Can you remind us why you believe your ex-wife had gone back to that house?"

"The cleaners said the bathroom had been used. The towels were damp. You can check with the lady manager. She told me this in case I thought they'd been neglectful."

"We will check. She must be a very exacting cleaning lady."

"The firm specialises in preparing homes for real estate inspections. They detail everything down to the last wrinkle and speck of dust. They will even come in and replace fresh flowers in vases and fresh fruit in bowls if necessary. For a price."

Aiden recalled already going over all of this with the detectives. The difference now was he knew Ethan had used his house. He didn't want to involve his brother or the schoolgirl and was not about to mention them. But the police cast doubt on whether Jenni had gone back to the house as if it had some significance to them. Aiden tried to glean information for his own peace of mind:

"Has something happened to my ex-wife? Otherwise, I can't see why her whereabouts is so important."

"You seemed sure your ex Jenni McKinstock went back to your house after the incident at her place of work."

"No. I was not sure. I only thought she might have. I don't know where else she has to go to. We've been divorced for six months. I don't keep tabs on her."

"Except you were present at her peep show." The inspector reminded.

"That was coincidental. I was on a case of my own."

Neither detective replied to that. They both stared at Aiden waiting for some reaction. He hoped his guilt didn't show. He had already resolved the Rudin case and had really only gone back to the brothel again lusting to see another sex show. His thin excuse to himself was confirming Jenni was a player. But the real reason was he craved the thrilling stimulation of the live porn show. The experience was addictive.

He realised it counted against him if detectives thought he'd been obsessed with what Jenni got up to. Visibly annoyed at the stalemate, Aiden's only option was to be upfront with his real feelings at that moment:

"Is that all? I have a business to run. And since you won't or can't tell me anything about Jenni, we are just wasting each other's time."

He stood up to leave.

"Just one more item we would like you to clarify for us concerning Troy Van Baas."

"I will if I can."

Aiden sighed. Would this never end?

"Your previous claim not to know him is at odds with the fact you engaged in an altercation with him two days ago."

Aiden surmised that information had to come from Van Baas himself.

"What has he been saying?"

"We want your version."

The detective spoke sternly, in a comment that may or may not confirm Troy Van Baas had already given the police his own account. Aiden replied:

"I pushed him. That's all. He backed down and took off in his car."

"What was your reason to push him."

"He made crude and disparaging comments."

Aiden realised this was about to bring Isla into the frame.

"You allege to not know the man. So why do you think he did that?"

"I was accompanying a young woman who works at my agency. Isla Tickle. Van Baas used to be her boyfriend. The slurs were directed at Isla."

Aiden had to give Isla's name; they'd find out soon enough anyway. Hedging would only alert the detectives to suspect some ulterior motive in withholding information.

"So Van Baas backed down after you pushed him?"

Grimslade asked it with a hint of disbelief and a wry look. Aiden knew it seemed unlikely he scared the man off with one push.

"At first, he did some martial art posturing, shaping up to fight. But I have friends at the surf club who were watching. When a bunch of them stood up ready to help me Van Baas jumped the fence into the car park."

Aiden edited what actually happened. He did not want to bring Ethan into it as well as Isla. The detectives referred to some notes and summed up.

"So Aiden. You named Troy Van Baas as being at the brothel saying you only knew him by name. Then you become embroiled in an altercation over his ex- girlfriend, an Isla Tickle who works for you. You, Troy Van Baas and your ex-wife Jenni McKinstock were all present when the abduction and murders took place at the brothel. A lot of coincidences here."

"Nevertheless, that's how it is." Aiden replied.

Despite his innocence, Aiden began to sweat.

"Have you reason to believe your ex-wife and Van Baas are known to each other?"

"I have no idea." Aiden told them truthfully.

"You made sure to tell us Van Baas was at the brothel."

"You asked me if I knew any of the other men. I told you I knew Van Baas by name. Why do you keep going over this? I volunteered to tell you what I knew." Aiden said.

"You wanted to implicate Van Baas, didn't you?"

"I had no reason not to tell his name. And since he seems a complete and utter arsehole, yes, I hope you do investigate him."

The interrogators met Aiden's riled expression blandly. He could not tell what they thought or whether they were only fishing for clues.

Aiden returned to the agency feeling like he'd been dragged over hot coals. He knew he must warn Isla that her name had come into it. Taking her aside, he explained how it had gone down with the detectives probing the case. He told her she might also be questioned, if they left no stone unturned.

Next problem, it bothered Aiden that police might demand access to his files, to check when and where he had followed Rudin. Being under suspicion made him paranoid.

At least he had not recorded anything about Isla's matchmaking case. It had been so trivial and at the time, he hoped she would join them at the agency. Since Isla had renovated the filing system, she must know there was no record of Fergus Rudin hiring Birdwhistle Solutions to catch her out at the supermarket.

"No need to tell police about your previous employment Isla. I mean the matchmaking and all that. But they know I was following Fergus Rudin for his wife."

"I don't care if they question me." Isla said defiantly. "I haven't committed any crimes and I'll take the opportunity to let them know exactly what I think of Troy bloody Van Baas. Don't worry about that."

Aiden admired her spunk. Her plucky attitude encouraged him. He wanted more of her company and he needed his day to improve so he asked Isla to dine with him that night:

"Have dinner with me tonight? I'll cook."

He added the last part to let her know he was asking her up to his flat again.

"That would be lovely. Thank you Aiden. What time suits you?"

"As soon as you like."

"What can I bring?"

"Just yourself. I don't need anything else."

Isla took that more than one way. Aiden warmed as she returned his shy smile.

"It's a date then."

12

ISLA & AIDEN

Isla went home to shower and change. Hoping dinner at Aiden's flat might lead to something more intimate, she packed an overnight bag with a change of clothes and stowed it in her car.

She knew Aiden was attracted to her and felt excited over what delights the night might hold in store. It had been so long since she'd been with a guy and Aiden was a delectable possibility. Isla chose what to wear carefully with one thing in mind. Lastly she spritzed a little perfume behind her ears.

Aiden could cook a few dishes well. He chose to do a ginger flavoured vegetable stir fry with sea scallops and prawns. He didn't take himself too seriously as a chef and wore a pink frilly apron that Ethan had given him as a joke one Christmas. Ethan knew Jenni never cooked which was behind his pointed choice of gift. The significance had gone well over Jenni's head but Aiden got the drift and the brothers shared a moment at her expense.

Isla was greeted with a peck on the cheek. Aiden still wore his girly apron to keep the moment lighthearted. Isla admired a table set nicely for two, with candles, wine glasses, shining cutlery and good china.

Aiden tossed the prepared stir fry ingredients together in a wok and soon delicious aromas filled the room. He'd opened a chilled bottle of Sauvignon Blanc earlier and poured for them both as an aperitif. He bid

Isla pick music from his selection and was pleased when orchestral strains of a Beatles medley drifted in as background. They had similar tastes in music and the volume Isla set was perfect for romance. He had wanted her to choose that ambience herself, so he wouldn't appear too forward or hopeful.

A bowl of steamed white rice warming in the oven accompanied the stir fry. Aiden presented the meal and removed his apron. Isla felt like a princess as he pulled out a chair for her and lit the candles.

They spoke little during the meal. Neither wanted to bring up work or any of the recent troubles. They smiled together when they'd finished eating. Aiden asked if she'd like coffee after he'd stacked the dishwasher saying he also had a box of after dinner mints to go with it.

"Maybe later. That was a fabulous meal. Thank you Aiden."

"I'm glad you liked it. Why don't we have more wine and sit on the sofa."

"That sounds like a nice idea." she replied. "The wine is really delicious too."

Aiden carried the ice bucket with the wine to the living room area.

Isla thought kissing Aiden would be even more delicious than the wine. She felt he was holding back and guessed he didn't want to come on too strongly. They sat together in the darkening room facing the view, admiring a full moon reflected on the seascape. The bi-fold doors were opened fully and the night was quiet enough to allow sounds of waves crashing on the distant shore.

Isla kicked off her shoes and relaxed curling her legs up on the sofa. She wore a short cotton dress with flared skirt and stretchy shirred bodice. Aiden felt his blood pressure rise seeing the expanse of tanned thigh exposed in the twilight. Isla knew. She bent forward to pick up her wine glass, leaning closer to him as she did so. Aiden breathed in the spritz of perfume she had applied. His breath exhaled onto the nape of her neck giving her goosebumps.

Aiden casually placed his arm along the back of the sofa without touching her. He felt like a gawky teenager again. Isla liked how this was going but wished Aiden would make a bigger move. He was wasting time and needed a nudge. Isla stifled a pretend yawn.

"It's been a long day." she said.

"Are you tired?" Aiden whole heartedly hoped she wasn't going to leave.

"No I'm not at all tired. But I'd like to go to bed. Wouldn't you?"

Her nudge was more of a shove. Her voice was low and husky. His was even huskier replying to her suggestion.

"Do you mean? Together? With me? Now?"

"I thought you'd never ask."

Isla smiled and softly touched a finger to his chin. Aiden grasped her hand, turning it to kiss the palm, adding a small lick from the tip of his tongue, then pulled her closer to face him on the sofa.

Isla straddled his lap, knees apart either side of his body and arms about his neck. He circled her waist feeling her warmth through the thin dress fabric. They kissed hungrily as ripe buds of desire bloomed.

"Mmmm. That feels so right."

Isla murmured with pleasure feeling his hardened response poke her in the best place.

"Sweet Jesus. Isla. I've got a hair trigger. Slow down." Aiden moaned.

"Bring it on Aiden. We have all night at our leisure."

Aiden knew he'd met his ideal woman. The pearly glow of moonlight dimly lit the dark room. Isla stood up and slipped her panties off then knelt on the floor and helped peel down his shorts and underdaks. He lifted his bottom eager to speed the undressing.

Isla fixated on his burgeoning erection that gleamed moistly and pulsed in readiness. She took a mouthful of icy cold wine, knelt between his parted legs and dribbled a little best Sauvignon Blanc over his intense throbbing. The chill slowed his arousal a little before she took him into her mouth, stroking with her tongue and lips then sucking deeply.

"Oh my God."

Aiden gasped as he built to the point of no return. In a paradox of fevered wishes, he wanted her foreplay to last forever but craved his climax that would end it. At the final second Isla mounted him again, joyous to have him fill her completely. Aiden cried out in ecstasy and held her hips hard down as his shuddering after tremors eased.

"I've wanted to feel that for so long Aiden." Isla whispered, kissing his forehead.

"Sorry I was so quick..." He began.

"Don't be sorry. I wanted you like that. It's not over yet. This is just the beginning."

Still astride Aiden's lap, Isla easily pulled her dress over her head. Ever since seeing her in that wet swimsuit Aiden fantasised over seeing her naked. He unclipped the lacy bra with trembling hands and freed her ample breasts. Isla softly growled her approval as he began kneading her fullness and kissing her nipples. She clutched his shoulders almost desperately and began to gyrate her hips.

"More. Suck me. Harder. Mmmm. That's right. Oh Aiden. Don't stop. I'm in heaven."

Enthralled, Aiden watched her moonlit face, seeing how much she was loving it. He felt her juices mingle with his own although he was only at half-mast inside her. Aiden amazed himself when he brought her to a soft orgasm. She sighed her satisfaction, and they parted to lay together on the sofa.

"Nice?" He asked.

"Bliss." She replied.

They entwined together, each in love or in lust without any way of separating the twin sensations. The night began to cool.

"Let's take this to the bedroom." he whispered eventually.

"Can I have a shower first? I'm all sweaty and fucky."

"Sure. I'm holding you to the promise of all night. I'll bring the coffee tray into the bedroom."

Aiden anticipated this to be the first of many wonderful sweaty fucky Isla nights.

Isla looked forward to refreshing herself in Aiden's modern bathroom. It was the one room he had remodelled in the flat. A walk-in shower took up most of the space and the mirrored vanity had a low beam overhead downlight. She used his spicy scented soap and rinsed her mouth with his peppermint mouth wash. She saw that her nipples had darkened from Aiden's expert manipulations. She loved that he had worked her just right and relished having more. Aiden was even more of a prize than she imagined he would be. He handled her breasts exactly as she liked, far better than Troy ever did. Isla had little experience of different lovers but knew what she liked.

Isla admired her own reflection in Aiden's bathroom mirror and felt assured she looked ok. Or at least pretty enough not to need a paper bag over her head.

The coffee tray was already on the bedside table when Isla entered Aiden's bedroom. She could hear him closing the bi-folds across the verandah and locking up for the night. Eagerly waiting for her lover to return from his shower, Isla sipped coffee and ate an after-dinner mint. The hour was past her usual bedtime, so a caffeine and sugar hit seemed a good idea for the bout ahead.

Aiden returned and stood at the end of his king-sized bed, taking in the sight of Isla waiting for him there, softly lit in the warm glow of a dimmed bedside lamp. He made a softly spoken confession:

"You look so beautiful Isla. I can hardly believe this is really happening. I've been dreaming of you like this, here in my bed, ever since the first time we met."

"Then come to me, my dream man."

Isla opened her arms. Aiden moved up from the end of the bed and Isla drew him closer inviting him to settle between her legs. Aiden supported his weight on his arms as they kissed between murmurs of love. Isla ran her cool hands down his back, dropping them to his buttocks with gentle squeezes.

"Hello Sweet Cheeks"

She crooned and goaded him to press in, sighing in pleasure as he accepted her welcome with gusto. Aiden needed no persuasion. They began to rock in harmony losing themselves in the timeless rhythm they craved.

Aiden revelled in meeting Isla's keen response. He increased the tempo at her urging and drove with enthusiasm, confident he could last longer this second time around. When he felt her give, tighten and blow in a shattering release, he reaped his reward, coming into her pulsing aftermath. They cried out their mutual rapture and collapsed, sweating and elated.

Aiden had never felt so empowered with a woman as he did with Isla, who embraced everything he wanted.   As for Isla, she had found her Nirvana with Aiden.

"That was amazing." Isla whispered as they lay cooling.

"You're amazing." Aiden spoke in soft reply.

They kissed, gently now and slept, sated until the early hours of the new day. Sleepy and a little sore, in a nice way, they reached for each other again, greedily hungry for more.

The following morning, Ethan arrived at the office around nine, puzzled to find no one about. The cars were there so he wondered where his brother and Isla could be. He called out. No answer. He went upstairs to the flat and in one quick glance, took in the two wine glasses and the clothing strewn around the sofa. He crept back downstairs and quietly left, deciding it must be his turn to get the bakery treats.

When Ethan re-entered the building, he slammed the door, whistled a tune and made a lot of noise clattering about in the kitchenette. Aiden came downstairs, dressed for the day and with his hair still glistening wet and dripping down the back of his shirt from a hasty shower.

Ethan observed Aiden's face, relaxed with no furrowed brow or signs of anxiety his brother had worn for such a long time. He hadn't seen Aiden looking as serene since long before his divorce.

"You're looking mellow. Nothing like a good nights sleep hey." Ethan remarked.

"Nothing at all like a good nights sleep little brother." Aiden smiled dreamily.

Isla crept downstairs, wearing one of Aiden's big t-shirts that fell to her knees. Both brothers seemed studiously absorbed in their computer screens, with their backs to her. Very quietly she went outside to retrieve spare clothes from her car and just as silently crept back upstairs to the flat. *Phew.* I think I got away with that, she wrongly supposed.

Eventually Isla entered the office, neatly dressed for work, in jeans and prim pin striped business shirt.   She spoke casually as if she wasn't two hours late:

"Anyone want morning tea? Coffee? I didn't get to the shops this morning, but there might still be some raisin loaf in the 'fridge for toast."

Ethan replied:

"That's okay. I brought in fresh cheese rolls and cinnamon scrolls this morning."

"Both? Wow. I'm sure we'll make short work of that."

Aiden rubbed his hands together in anticipation. He was starving. Ethan added:

"Yes I am sure it will go down well. And I recommend that combination. It's my personal go to choice of calories after a marathon."

Ethan grinned broadly. Aiden kicked his younger brother under the table. Hard.

Isla blushed and dropped her gaze demurely.

Both brothers noted her Mona Lisa smile.

13

ISLA IN QUESTION

Birdwhistle Solutions had won a lucrative contract with local government. Hidden cameras were to be installed in the public library. The job meant Aiden and Ethan would be out of the office most of that Wednesday. Restored by all the calories at morning tea, the brothers went to work with a will. Aiden had a particular spring to his step.

This was another unusual case for Birdwhistles: Library staff were routinely finding chewing gum stuck between pages of hardcover books on the shelves. CCTV in the library did not cover enough area to catch the vandal. Damaged books came from all sections and genres, hence the need for the extra coverage Birdwhistle Solutions specialised in.

School kids were suspected but chewing gum was banned for anyone entering the library. A bin placed outside the entrance had a notice ordering that any chewn gum be binned and any packs of unused gum to be handed in at the desk. The packets could be collected on exit.

Ethan left for the library just ahead of Aiden, who took the opportunity to embrace Isla in the kitchenette, telling her it was ok to lock up early and go for a snooze upstairs. He acted thoughtfully for her comfort but also didn't want her to be overtired for the coming night ahead. He took her hand in his, and kissed it as he gazed into her eyes.

"I hope you'll stay with me again tonight. If you're willing."

"I'm willing." Isla smiled.

Even with the constriction of lace and fabric, she gasped and closed her eyes as he touched her intimately. Her reaction exhilarated him. Aiden groaned his longing:

"Wow. I'm on a promise. This will be a long day."

"For me too. I can't wait to be with you again. I'll go home to get a change of clothes after closing time and see you this evening." she said.

Isla locked the office and went upstairs, stripped the bed, found where he kept the fresh linen and remade it with smiling anticipation of rumpling it up again during the night ahead. Next, she tidied the living room and put a load of washing on.

A few loose ends remained to be tied up in the office, but Isla decided to take that snooze once that was done. She returned downstairs in time to answer a knock on the closed front door. It was the same baby-faced junior police officer who'd called to take Aiden in for further questioning.

"Hello. I'm afraid the manager is out at the moment." she said.

"I've been sent to accompany a Miss Isla Tickle downtown."

"That's me. But I can't leave now. I'm here alone and in charge of the office..."

Isla realised she was to be questioned over the incident with Troy. Although she could lock up and go with the officer, she was tired and didn't want to. The young policeman looked uncertain. He hadn't expected a refusal. Isla felt sorry for him, and suggested a compromise:

"...but if the interview can be done here, I am happy to assist."

She said it to placate the young office but really hoped they would make it another day. Unfortunately, they did not.

Shortly, two detectives arrived to interview Isla. One was a plain-clothes female officer who held a briefcase. She introduced herself as Dulcy Vestige. She said to call her Dulcy. The other was Dougall Grimslade. He did not say to call him Dougall.

Having been about to close up and go for a sleep upstairs, Isla felt inconvenienced. The night before had been strenuous, and she wanted to boost her energy reserves for another pleasurable marathon with Aiden.

Grimslade's intense stare seemed rude. His eagle eyed inspection seemed to cut right through Isla. It made her want to give him some back-chat but she managed to hold her tongue. She just wanted them to get the interview done and leave her in peace.

The questions began:

"Miss Tickle. Can you confirm you were in a relationship with Troy Van Baas?"

"Yes. I was. He broke it off with me because he needed someone more suitable."

"More suitable for what?"

"To further his career or image. He is a high flyer. I don't even know why he picked me as a girlfriend to begin with."

Isla answered with the plain truth as she knew it, hoping they would wind it up quickly so she could crash for an hour or so on a sofa, with the bi-folds open to let in the sea breeze.

"How did you meet Troy Van Baas?"

"To put it bluntly, he picked me up on the beach. I was charmed by his handsome face and his smooth talking. Pretty soon I began dating him seriously. I didn't know his true nature at the time. If I had known what he was really like, I wouldn't have touched him with a barge pole."

"Had you seen him on the beach before?"

"Sure. I noticed him. Hard not to. He was always the centre of attention, hanging out with a bunch of bikini girls. That's why I was flattered when he asked me out because I'm the opposite to a glamorous bikini girl. I don't even wear bikinis. I only go to the beach for swimming or surfing and not to parade about. I always wear plain ordinary one piece bathers with baggy board shorts as well. I haven't tried to impress anyone that's for sure."

"Were you with other people when Troy Van Baas first spoke to you?"

"No. Not really. But there are always others I know around on the beach whenever I go. Usually there would be some people I recognise who shop at the supermarket and a few of the regular lifeguards and other locals."

"Did you ever go out on the yacht with Troy Van Baas?"

"Yes. A few times. But usually he took me to his big house. I have to admit his wealth impressed me at the time. Now I know he isn't worth it."

Dulcy the policewoman watched Isla's face as she voiced an observation:

"So you say he broke off with you. But the altercation with your employer Aiden Birdwhistle suggests jealousy."

"Troy neither wants nor needs me. If he did, he wouldn't have dumped me. Right? He just can't hack that I wasn't thrilled to accept his terms."

"What terms?"

"He wanted a loose arrangement where he did whatever he liked with his fancy women but still had me as a sideline. And he thought I would go for that! Well, sorry for the language but to put it crudely I told him to go fuck himself. So he's been really peeved because he thought it was a reasonable arrangement. I guess he couldn't stand seeing me with Aiden. And while I'm on that subject, someone threw a brick through the plate glass window here. It's just been fixed. But there was a nasty note tied to the brick. I believe it was probably Troy who did it. We kept the note. I'll show it to you."

Isla found the note where she knew Aiden had locked it in a desk drawer: WHAT A SLUT. BONKING THE BOSS IN THE LUNCH BREAK. The insult still needled.

"Can we keep this?" The detective asked.

"Sure. We only kept it in case any clue ever came up over who did it. No luck for us. But it's the type of thing Troy said about me and why Aiden pushed him that day."

"Apart from work, are you in a close relationship with Aiden Birdwhistle?"

"Yes. I am now. Just beginning. But I wasn't at the time the brick was thrown. In fact, that happened on my first day of working at Birdwhistles. And I only met Aiden one day before."

The questions took a different path:

"Did you know Jenni McKinstock before meeting Aiden?"

"Who? Oh, is that his former wife Jenni? We sort of met once."

"When was this?"

"She accosted Aiden at a hotel restaurant when I was with him in a work related meeting over dinner. I had only just met Aiden that same day and agreed to try the job on trial. I hadn't started work at Birdwhistles yet. Anyway, she must have imagined we were on a proper date, and I guess she was jealous. The woman was really offensive and quite drunk at the time. I only saw her that once. The place wasn't well lit and she was ranting and wild looking. Hotel security escorted her out. Aiden apologised and said that was his crazy ex who loved to make a scene."

"Did you or Aiden say anything to her at the time?"

"No. Nothing. We just sat there stunned. It was so unexpected and embarrassing."

Hotel CCTV of that incident had already been checked, but the detectives wanted to hear what Isla had to say in case her version differed with what they saw. It didn't.

Next, two professional studio photographs of Jenni McKinstock looking like a star pin up girl were produced from the policewoman's briefcase and shown to Isla.

"Is this the same woman you know as Aiden Birdwhistle's former wife? And are you sure you hadn't seen her on other occasions?"

"Yes and no. I think it's the same person but she looks a helluva lot better in these photos than when she made that drunken scene. I don't remember ever seeing her before but she might have been amongst the models who partied on Troy's yacht. They were all like clones of glittering film stars. Flash jewellery. Heavy make-up. False eyelashes. Probably wigs as well. I can't be certain now if she was one of them, after all this time. Obviously, I was really outclassed amongst the glitterati."

"There's more to class than paint and bling." Dulcy said, somewhat primly.

"So. Is that all?" Isla asked.

"Not quite."

The interviewers paused. Isla noticed a pointed look pass between them. Grimslade nodded a go ahead to Dulcy Vestige who asked:

"Isla, were you aware of being video taped while you were privately with Troy Van Baas?"

Isla looked aghast. She visibly paled then reddened. Her hands flew to her open mouth and her eyes widened as she gasped. Dulcy and Grimslade paid close attention to her reaction and predicted she wasn't faking.

"What? No! I hope you don't mean...Is that what you mean?"

Isla received no reply to her anguished question. In fact, the investigators did not know whether Troy had filmed Isla having sex with him but inadvertently hit on a truth. They fished that line of enquiry after receiving an anonymous complaint from another woman, who said Troy had videoed a personal activity without her consent, on his yacht. They had been unable to locate that complainant and whoever she was, she did not contact them again.

That case thickened when partial female remains were discovered under an old timber jetty. It happened to be where Aiden had disposed of the flash drive with footage proving Jenni's deceit.

Efforts to identify the body parts pointed to it being someone from Troy Van Baas' yacht. DNA had been taken but no match found. Jenni McKinstock was the possible victim since her whereabouts were unknown, and she featured in the mansion murder fiasco. No viable DNA material could be extracted from the marital home she recently inhabited, since her former husband, Aiden Birdwhistle, had the house thoroughly cleaned by professionals.

The lone fisherman who netted the grisly catch from the jetty, had been sworn to keep it secret for the time being. Investigators did not want to forewarn Van Baas his yacht was under scrutiny while they pursued the case. The old fellow felt important for being trusted by the police and looked forward to five minutes of fame when his name might be in the newspaper for his part in it.

Isla's fears of being videoed inappropriately had not been confirmed by the detectives but she had no doubts Troy must have done so.

"Thanks Miss Tickle. We might want to talk another time but that is all for now."

Dougall Grimslade and Dulcy Vestige left Isla in a state of shock and anger.   Before their split, Isla had loved indulging in fabulous sex romps with Troy. He must have recorded their steamy sessions. Otherwise, Isla reasoned, why would the police even ask? There was no way she could now relax for an afternoon nap.

"That bloody rotten bastard mongrel." Isla ranted while pacing the floor.

Oh hell. What would Aiden make of it. She didn't know if she should tell him. He might think less of her. Ethan had hinted about losing respect for that Jenni creature. He'd said they were relieved Jenni hadn't taken their surname, giving Isla the distinct impression Ethan loathed Aiden's wife and been glad when his brother divorced her.

Isla ran upstairs. She'd earlier noticed an opened bottle of vodka in the back of the fridge. She poured a good swig into a glass of orange juice and sculled it to settle her nerves.

After the alcohol buzz kicked in, Isla decided it would be best to level with Aiden about the police interview. After all, his ex had come into it quite a lot. With the knowledge of how beautiful Jenni appeared in the studio photos, Isla revisited her own deficiencies.

She had hoped something more might develop between herself and Aiden but now saw she was only kidding herself. They were not equals. At least they were compatible for great sex and she'd have to be happy for just that. Isla had to mock her own thoughts of *only just great sex* because they were both eager to continue enjoying each other carnally and hungered for a second night together.

Isla rehearsed how she might begin the awkward conversation with Aiden and went for a second hit of vodka and orange.

In other business, Ethan planned to meet up with Mrs. Sylvia Rudin at the playground that afternoon to give her the cliff side address where he'd tracked her errant husband. He would omit saying he employed a bug attached to Fergus's vehicle.   As with most private eye businesses, Birdwhistles preferred not to divulge their methods. Ethan also didn't want Sylvia looking for the bug out of curiosity and risk having Fergus see her doing that.

At the playground, Sylvia sat on a bench beside her baby in its pram and watched her other two children climb over a jungle frame. Ethan greeted the mother and sat beside her. He looked at the baby and the baby looked back. Ethan thought *crikey*. The kid looked so much like a Troll Doll that he pitied Sylvia, who seemed to be waiting for his comment.

"What a...um...remarkable child." Ethan managed.

"Thank you. Yes. I am blessed with my beautiful children." Sylvia smiled, flattered.

The little troll pointed at Ethan and said "Dada".

Not guilty Ethan backwheeled in horror.

"Don't worry, he calls all men Dada. The kids hardly know their father, we see so little of Fergus."

"Speaking of Fergus: I can tell you he has been going to that big house with white arches up on the cliff. Do you know it?"

"That one with the steep zigzag road up to it? Is it another brothel?"

"Yes that's the place. Sorry I haven't found out what goes on up there. It could be a brothel of course or perhaps something to do with gambling, like a private casino. But we doubt if your husband goes there to deliver groceries, Mrs. Rudin."

"I doubt that as well." Sylvia said sadly.

Ethan felt terribly sorry for the careworn young mother. She had probably been quite pretty at one time and seemed to have wasted herself on Fergus.

"Tell me, Ethan, in your experience of similar cases, do husbands stray more often than wives do?" Sylvia asked.

"There's a question. I'd say percentage wise; men seem less faithful. Or at least, we get more enquiries from women wanting their men checked on." Ethan replied carefully.

"Maybe women have more of an instinct when something is not right, and they act sooner." Sylvia mused.

"That is very likely. Someone close to me found out his wife was unfaithful but only after heaps of obvious clues. Then he only checked on her hoping to find out he was wrong."

Sylvia gave the little troll a rusk and offered Ethan a milk arrowroot biscuit. He accepted it to be polite.

"I'm not sure what to do about Fergus. I was going to give him a second chance if only for the children. But I can't keep turning the other cheek. You understand?"

"I think you have been very patient. And strong."

Ethan felt out of his depth trying to offer an opinion or give counselling advice.

"Yes. I have been patient. Maybe not strong. I have been weak by not facing up to Fergus."

"Well Mrs. Rudin. It doesn't always pay to act rashly. For what it's worth, I think you will come out of this better off. I really do."

Ethan thought about how Aiden had unexpectedly met Isla. His brother was so much happier now. This sad woman would have to be better off rid of her bad husband. With so many people in the world, there would have to be someone else for Sylvia in the future.

"It can be difficult to let go when you have loved someone," Sylvia said, "have you been in love yet Ethan?"

"There is a girl I like a lot. I'm not sure how to tell if it is proper love. She has to go away soon to further her career ambitions and I know I'm going to miss her. Though she drives me crazy a lot of the time."

"Crazy can be a clue. Maybe she will come back to you." Sylvia smiled kindly.

"Once we're apart I think we will both play the field." Ethan admitted.

"Better to play the field before you commit seriously than after."

"True. But if one partner really wants out, they should let the other know so they can get on with their own lives. The worst is keeping them sidelined in the dark. It seems selfish and even cowardly." Ethan said.

"Vows should be sacred but also, I think you are right. It is very unfair and hurtful on the unwanted one. Have you made promises to your girl Ethan?"

"No. Neither of us make promises that we probably can't keep."

"Even knowing your girl will play the field, as you say, would you take her back if she came back to you?"

"In a heartbeat, Mrs. Rudin. Yes. I would."

"Sounds a lot like love." Sylvia said.

Ethan knew he would be over the moon if Tiffany returned after Uni and wanted to be with him again. On the other hand, Sylvia Rudin knew her own dilemma was a far different kettle of fish than Ethan's.

14

ABDUCTION

Isla went out to the car park after the normal office closing time, with the plan to go home for more clean clothes which shouldn't take long. She now regretted having the double hit of vodka but would drink a black coffee when she got back to her own flat and maybe take a cold shower. She reckoned to be back within the hour when she planned to discuss her police interview with Aiden first thing, up front, to get it out of the way.

The existence of personal videos with Troy really threw a spanner into the works and it worried Isla greatly. She had done nothing wrong and hoped Aiden would be forgiving.

Slinging her shoulder bag and clothes from the night before into her car boot, Isla palmed her car keys. She was about to get into the driver's seat when a racy sports convertible with the roof down, drove in and blocked her exit. It was Troy.

"What do you want arsehole?" Isla fumed, hating him.

"Don't be like that Isla." Troy smarmed.

"The police have been asking questions about you. They asked if I knew you videoed us together. You despicable bloody pervert."

"Relax Isla. It's no big deal. It isn't a crime between consenting adults you know."

"I didn't even know you filmed me. So how is that consenting?"

Isla's rant gave Troy inspiration to carry out a certain plan in a different way. He improvised a mock apology.

"It was very wrong of me. And I sincerely apologise for all the wrongs I've done to you, my darling Isla."

"Huh. Too little too late Troy."

"But Isla my sweet, I have all our charming little home movies right here to give to you. That's why I'm here. You might like to watch them and remember what you're missing. We were so good together. The films are proof of that. Anyway, you decide if you'd rather destroy it all. But you do look fabulous on screen. It isn't sleazy. It's just a beautiful record of our time together. After you view it all, hope you might consider being mine again."

Troy put on a sorry face and indicated a small bubble wrapped box on the back seat of his sports car. Isla wasn't fooled by his sorry act but rashly dropped her guard with the effects of vodka in her system. She strode to his car to grab the package.

As Isla bent over to reach for the package, Troy plunged a loaded hypodermic needle into her behind. Isla knew something was terribly wrong the second before she blacked out. Troy heaved her bodily over onto the floor behind the front seats and covered her with a car rug. He then casually put the overhead hood up, hiding her from view.

Troy drove slowly out towards his destination, observing all traffic signs and speed limits. It could be disastrous if he were to be pulled over by a traffic cop. But he made it to his cliff top home without incident.

Troy chuckled at how dumb Isla had been. He would never have put any private videos in his car. He kept his extensive library of fun viewing locked away on the yacht, including all the times he had been with Isla. The box on his back seat only held music CDs.

Troy delivered Isla, now temporarily disabled, to his secluded Spanish style house situated high on a headland overlooking the ocean. It was where he and Jenni McKinstock carried out many sordid escapades.

Nonetheless, he had to be careful what Jenni had access to. She'd go nuts if she knew he watched video of himself with Isla, whose beautiful body was far more luscious and voluptuous than her own. Jenni didn't like playing second fiddle.

Jenni and Troy were kindred spirits and soul mates in many of their warped and sadistic adventures. But not all. Troy knew Jenni to be insanely jealous of his past romps with Isla, so had taken elaborate steps to ensure his latest housemate would not be home for this exciting session of thrills and retribution.

Troy had given Jenni tickets to concerts in the city and prepaid a few nights accommodation at a plush hotel. He made sure room service would deliver a large bottle of best single malt whisky, with his compliments. That should keep her sweet and too inebriated to bother contacting him. Jenni had her uses and was up for anything Troy suggested but he didn't want to hear from her for at least a few days. Not while he had Isla Tickle at his disposal.

The golden opportunity to get revenge on Isla came about when the local supermarket manager, Fergus Rudin approached Troy to procure that particular woman for his own devious pleasures. Rudin didn't care how it was done or what became of her afterwards, but he wanted a full night with the former check out chick. He knew Van Baas had run the mansion brothel and might achieve what he wished.

Troy assured Fergus it could be done in fine style with feasting, drinking and access to the woman awake but rendered helpless to resist. For a price.

Subsequently, Rudin agreed to pay a five-figure sum to have his way with Isla Tickle in an all night festival of excess. He'd embezzled funds from the supermarket to finance his pathological obsession.

Troy had at first planned to obtain Isla by stealth and strength. He knew she would never be bought or cajoled and she did not trust or respect him. He'd overpowered other difficult ones in the past, using a drug filled syringe. This time, his ploy worked far better than he hoped when Isla gave him the clue about their sex movies. When she actually bent over the side of the convertible reaching for the so-called box of films, jabbing her bum was ridiculously easy. She had played right into his scheme. Troy swelled with pride over yet another successful procurement, plus fat old Fergus Rudin's cash was a bonus already in hand.

Isla was kept hidden in Troy's car until after the caterers had been and gone. The banquet was delivered and set out attractively on a long table. Nothing in the room gave rise to suspicions or any clue to its wicked purpose. The single bed that later became a sacrificial altar was pushed against a wall and covered with rugs and cushions.

Between them, the two men, Rudin and Van Baas, carried Isla's drugged and limp body up into the house to a dedicated suite set up to receive participants. It had been the scene of many other events usually enjoyed by Troy and Jenni and some other customer who paid an extravagant fee for a similar privilege.

The men made sure to tie this one down well before she came around. Troy knew Isla would be a wildcat. All the better. He couldn't wait to humiliate her himself and watch her being raped by dirty old Rudin as well. He would toast her with champagne and laugh in her face.

The specially appointed sound proofed games room had the bed set up for the purpose of sex with bondage. An ensuite bathroom with clean white towels was available for paying clients to shower and wash away traces of their activities afterwards.

Troy was particularly pleased with a hog tying invention that Jenni McKinstock perfected. Manacles and anklets joined by strong ties crossed underneath the hostage. Wrists were secured to ankles on opposite sides. Raising a right wrist bent the left leg and vice versa. Attempts to fight against the hog ties pulled the legs apart exposing genitals. The perverted couple were most entertained when struggles caused abdomens to hump suggestively.

Some paying participants requested the novelty of being in the contraption themselves, at first enjoying the perverse thrill of bondage. But when their pleas for release were repeatedly ignored, they knew they'd been duped. Ensuing blackmail demands then came as no surprise. Troy Van Baas credited himself as a master puppeteer pulling the strings, toying with his live marionettes.

Jenni loved to be put into the hog ties herself, but Troy refused to be enslaved. Wisely, he did not trust Jenni's masochistic traits. Her appetites departed even further from normal than his own.

Hidden cameras filmed the entire scene from various angles. Most buyers wanted victims to be fully aware and a surprising number preferred them struggling frantically. Paid sex workers acted the part but unwilling victims sometimes needed greater incentives. Threats of torture usually had a desired effect but Jenni McKinstock had a blood lust for inflicting real pain to make the hog tied subject fight harder.

Human life meant nothing to people like Troy and Jenni other than as playthings for their own gratification and financial rewards.

Games room events were orchestrated according to clients' requests and how much they were willing to pay. Initial payment of cash upfront was comparatively small against huge blackmail demands that followed.

Fergus Rudin paid handsomely for his chance to demean Isla and hoped his criminal embezzlement would go undiscovered until he escaped the country. A one way ticket to Malaysia and a suitcase packed ready were in the boot of his car. His plan was to hop from country to country ending in an ultimate getaway to South America where he could effectively disappear.

Rudin reasoned his sow of a wife would be happy enough having the kids to herself. She had wanted children. He hadn't. Fergus thought his snotty brats all took after Sylvia, a definite fault in his opinion and he had never taken to his offspring.

As always with similar events, the entire scene with Isla being secretly filmed to blackmail Rudin later. Troy Van Baas had no idea this client planned to flee Australia as soon as he had finished with Isla.

Troy had Fergus pegged as a family man who occupied a respectable managerial position, a man of some standing in the community, with a valued reputation to protect. Rudin seemed an ideal blackmail subject.

Extortion boosted Troy Van Baas' lifestyle. The brothel mansion porno theatre had gleaned future suckers from the most gullible in the audience, but that source of income dried up after the murders.

Van Baas acknowledged his mistake in taking on that Sudanese woman without any clue she would be hunted and punished by her strict countrymen in their traditional subversion of females. He only saw the tall ebony skinned amazon as something exotic to be enjoyed as a variation. Troy tried all his actors first, male or female. It was part of his personal audition process.

Loss of two able bouncers with the Sudanese invasion could be easily shrugged off. Dim witted thugs happy to work for peanuts and a free go on the women after others finished, were a dime a dozen. Troy had been quick to make his escape, sprinting to where his fast car was parked. He left Jenni to her own devices as she had her own car nearby.

Even before Aiden had stepped around the bodies and called out to Jenni in a rescue attempt, she sped on her way to the hacienda shared with Troy. The pair had been careful to distance themselves from the mansion brothel in case shit like what just happened, ever hit the fan. The mansion practice had been set up within a maze of false business names.

In a brief wistful aside Jenni said she'd rather liked that doorman. He was stupid but keen and grateful. Troy assured her there would be others. In his experience, people were expendable. There were always others in an overpopulated world.

Closure of the mansion brothel now worked in Troy's favour. He congratulated himself for being a superior entrepreneur. His innovation of filmed sexual perversions with blackmail, proved to be his best money spinner yet.

Troy never had any shortage of women to be used. Some regulars actually liked the work and the easy money. The majority of silly bikini girls and street workers who vied to party on his yacht had no idea they were hunted for his projects. The pick of them were auditioned by Troy himself and secretly filmed. In recent history, one risky dissenter became crab bait. In the distant past, a few others also disappeared efficiently without trace, in the convenient garbage disposal of shark infested waters.

Since the mansion brothel and porn show closed down, Fergus Rudin's request came at an opportune time and couldn't be better with Isla as the target. Troy Van Baas rubbed his hands together, gloating. It was all working out well and he felt lucky.

Atop the clifftop at the hacienda games room, a smorgasbord awaited the latest guest. The table was lavishly set with linen napkins and elegant crystal flutes, and laden with bowls of lush fruits, joints of roast meats on silver platters and magnums of champagne in ice buckets sparkling with frost. Ornate carving knives and corkscrews matched the silver hardware. The reproduction antiques were all part of the fine experience promoted to paying guests. And pay they did. On and on. Nothing happened without Troy who always personally hosted the games room parties.

Isla had her wrists and ankles secured in the shackles without delay in case she woke, so Troy cut her clothing away with scissors, keeping Fergus away until he gave the okay. Fergus Rudin with his coarse manners and obese flabbiness disgusted Troy but his money was as good as anyone's, and Isla would be thoroughly abased by the disgusting man. As Rudin bit into a ripe peach, the juice ran down his chins to mingle with drool from his bulbous lips. He slavered like a rabid animal to get started on Isla.

"Why can't I start on her now while she's out to it." Fergus whined.

"No. I want her to know what's happening. It's payback time. Isn't that what you want?"

"Sure. I want to get back at the bitch. I've got all night right? She can see me later and know I've already done her and haven't finished yet."

"Come on Fergus. Give the girl a fighting chance. Otherwise, it'd be like bumping a corpse."

Troy smiled knowing Isla might yet get her final bump after death. She was never going to survive but he would not tell a fool like Rudin who might get cold feet.

With a mental shrug, Troy admitted to himself it was a shame Isla didn't like to play his way, she had been one of his favourites. That was why he'd kept her all to himself for so long. But what the hell. He'd make her final days a lesson in regret for crossing him. So, she wasn't a complete loss.

Isla might last a few days if Jenni stayed in the city longer. Troy gave ample credit on a plastic card for Jenni to have a grand shopping spree, yet told her to phone if she needed more funds. Troy was confident Jenni would always want more money and would phone for extra, keeping her away longer.

Running hands over Isla's slumbering body, Troy roughly pushed her legs apart and invaded with savage fingers. Pain registered in Isla's benumbed brain prompting her to first fuzzy awareness.

"Hey!" Rudin shouted in anger. He didn't like his prize purchase being handled.

Troy ignored his complaint. He smelt his fingers and waved them towards Fergus.

"Get a whiff of that Fergy. I love that female cunty scent. Don't you? She smells ripe and ready. At least she'll enjoy the first one with me. Then it's all downhill with you."

Troy couldn't resist rubbing in his superior status over lesser mortals at anytime. But he identified an oops moment as the disgruntled client riled up. Maybe he should have exercised more tact. Nevermind, it was not as if Fergus Rudin was ever going to be a lifetime buddy. Champagne and food sprayed from Rudin's mouth as he spluttered in rebellion:

"She's mine. Not yours. I go first and you stay out of it until I'm done. That's what I paid for. You can't take that away from me now."

Troy used his most persuasive tone:

"Ha ha. I go first. You can watch as a bonus. I'll loosen her up for you. Have some more of that delicious pork crackling or the lamb roast. We've got hours yet Fergy old boy."

Fergus slammed a fat hammy fist on the table. He had a volatile temper and was accustomed to being in charge. He considered Troy his employee since he hired him for this job. The younger man's assumption enraged Rudin. He demanded his rights:

"Bullshit! NO! I go first. I paid enough. You do what you like after me. Tomorrow."

"That was never the deal Rudin. I call the shots around here." Troy asserted.

"Have I paid so much just to help you get her here like this for yourself?" Rudin shouted.

"Fergus old boy. It doesn't make any difference who goes first. But it will be me. It is always me. My prerogative as host. You'll have hours with her after me."

Troy did not relish going second after the pig of a man and had no intention of doing so. He would thoroughly wash Isla out after Rudin, before he continued the next day. Troy thought of cleansing Isla as quality time. It would give him a chance for a nice chat to lecture her on the error of her ways.

At this stage, Rudin's air of entitlement aggravated Troy, who saw the man as a guest who abused his hospitality.

"Do you think I am stupid?" Rudin spat.

"No. I don't *think* you are stupid. I *know* you are. But if you want anything you'll obey my rules," Troy told him sternly, "otherwise you can piss off now and get nothing."

Frothing at the mouth, Rudin's eyes bugged out at the ultimatum. Troy was disrespecting his authority, just as Isla Tickle had always done. And look where that got her. His seniority was again being overridden by an upstart.

Fergus Rudin seethed with anger.

15

PANIC

In the meantime, Aiden returned home from the day spent installing surveillance equipment at the library. He arrived with a bunch of flowers for Isla and a tasty take-away dinner.

Aiden was overjoyed to see Isla's car there, thinking she'd been home already and returned waiting for him. He went inside happily calling her name, but the place was empty. At a loss, he went back outside to her car. Then he noticed Isla's car keys on the ground.

In haste to grab the package from Troy's car, Isla had dropped her keys. Troy hadn't noticed as he'd been engaged in carefully extracting the syringe from his pocket and jabbing her with the needle.

Aiden picked up the keys. He found the car to be unlocked but no clue to explain Isla's whereabouts. He called Isla's number and heard her mobile ringing faintly from inside the car boot. Soon her shoulder bag with cards, money and phone were discovered where she had put it. Her togs bag was there as well, with swimming gear. Not that he expected Isla would have gone to the beach. She was as keen to get together again as he was. Something seemed very wrong, and Aiden had every reason to be alarmed. Half panicked, Aiden took Dougall Grimslade's card from his wallet and called the private number scrawled on the back.

"Slow down. Say it again."

The detective had just sat down to his own evening meal. Aiden explained it all again. He felt time was wasting and was beside himself with worry so he called Ethan immediately after.

"I'll be right there." Ethan said and arrived within minutes.

"Van Baas has to be behind this," Aiden said, "who else could it be?"

"What about Jenni?"

"Not impossible. But if it came to a fight my money would be on Isla."

"Didn't Isla have problems with her old supermarket boss?" Ethan said.

"Fergus Rudin. But he was caught out. I don't know what his wife did about it."

"I do. Remember she got back saying he was up to his old tricks and she wanted him followed again?"

"Did you find something more?"

"More of the same. I've tracked him remotely going up to that big Spanish style place on the cliff a few times. You know the one? Up a steep drive. White arches. I didn't drive up to the house of course. Just drove past for a gander. Seems he could be going to a different brothel now. Or the original might have moved to that place."

"That's our best bet then. Van Baas might hang out there as well. Come on. Let's go there now."

"Call that cop first." Ethan said.

"I already called him. He was eating dinner by the sounds of it. Here you call him again on the way."

Aiden handed his phone to Ethan, and they sped out onto the highway together, taking Aiden's faster car, making haste for the clifftop house. A traffic squad car with flashing blue lights gave chase but Aiden did not slow down.

"Holy shit Aiden." Ethan yelled clutching his car seat in alarm.

"Let him follow. It might be the quickest way to get police back up. Tell Grimslade what's happening."

"We're going to feel bloody stupid if no one's there." Ethan said.

"I'll cross that bridge when I come to it." Aiden said through gritted teeth.

He had to do something and the hacienda was his best lead. Aiden was certain Isla must have been abducted and Troy Van Baas was prime suspect. He suddenly remembered the yacht and prayed Troy hadn't put out to sea with her.

"Ethan. Tell Grimslade to alert the Coast Guard. She might be on Troy's yacht."

Ethan did as told but Grimslade had already got his act together in a hurry and had called Dulcy Vestige telling her to meet him at the marina. Dulcy reluctantly abandoned her soldier husband who only had a short leave before being deployed overseas. But this was an emergency, another link tying a missing woman to that damn Van Baas yacht.

Grimslade's wife, Bella, frowned as he stuffed half a slice of bread in his mouth and shoved his shoes back on. Another meal put on hold. Maybe it could be nuked later. Or not. It all depended on how long he'd be away this time. Dougall couldn't say, because he didn't know.

Back at the hacienda, Isla came to consciousness slowly. She was groggily aware but smart enough to play possum. Feeling cool air on her skin, Isla knew she lay naked. She recognised both the voices of Troy Van Baas and Fergus Rudin. They were arguing over who went first with her. Aware of her bondage, Isla prayed Aiden would miss her and try to find her in time. If she hadn't planned the night with Aiden and been abducted from the beach or her own flat, no one would have missed her for another day or more.

Isla's mind raced. Troy didn't know she planned to meet up with Aiden that evening. But he must expect she'd be missed eventually. Her car would be noticeably still parked at the agency but that could be for a number of reasons. The most obvious would be she'd walked down to the beach for a swim. Isla couldn't remember if she'd locked the car boot where she'd stowed her bag and other belongings. She often put the keys in her pocket and if she had done so, Troy probably had them now.

Isla felt sure Aiden would try calling her mobile, but its ring might be inaudible from inside her shoulder bag. She might have also covered it with some clothes to take home for the wash but couldn't recall if that is what she did. Even if Aiden realised she'd been taken, he would not know where she was. Isla had no idea where she was either and worried she might be sailing away on Troy's yacht.

Aiden's best break had been finding Isla's car keys on the ground. Isla didn't know she had dropped them, but then, neither did Troy.

Jenni McKinstock had been mistrustful of Troy's motives from the beginning. He was not usually as generously inclined and had no reason to arrange her extended absence with all the treats and so much tempting spending money. It reeked of something fishy going on behind her back. Halfway to the concert, Jenni changed her mind and screeched a U-turn suddenly terribly afraid for Pitbull her adored toy poodle. She had an idea Troy didn't like her dog.

In fact, Troy despised the dog and went out of his way to torment little Pitbull whenever Jenni wasn't looking. Earlier, as soon as Jenni left for the city, Troy booted the small poodle into the deep end of the swimming pool, hoping the useless mutt would drown. To his disgust, Pitbull proved to be an excellent swimmer and smart enough swim to the shallow end, ably getting himself out of the water by the concrete pool steps.

The little dog vigorously shook his curly coat dry and aimed a baleful eye at Troy. Pitbull then scampered off to lift a leg on his enemy's car tyre. He might have peed on something else if he could get inside. But Jenni's poodle had been locked out of the house, adding insult to injury and fuelling the small dog's hatred of Troy. Thwarted by the dog's talent for self-preservation, Troy decided he would take the damn mongrel out on the yacht with Isla later and see how long they'd both last in the open sea amongst the predators.

He locked the poodle into a small enclosure that housed the pool pump and equipment. Left without drinking water or bedding, Pitbull glared at Troy from between wooden slats. Troy knew the dog would have little fight in him after a few days thirst and starvation. He might even cark it before he got thrown to the sharks but the voracious sea creatures would eat him anyway.

Troy rehearsed how he might explain Pitbull's absence to Jenni:

"He was such a cute little guy; someone must have stolen him."

Oops. Revise that:

"He IS such a cute little guy; someone must have stolen him."

Maybe he'd even run some sham ads to report a lost or stolen dog. Troy had it all worked out. If Jenni wanted another dog, he'd beg off, saying he couldn't go through the awful tragedy of losing another one. He could say it would dishonour Pitbull's memory. Or, he'd say, what if he came home and found himself replaced. Blah blah. No end to ideas. Troy saw himself as a gifted ideas man. Another award to his ego.

While Jenni made haste homewards to check on Pitbull and whatever Troy was up to, another highly motivated woman also sped towards the hacienda.

After their chat, when Ethan informed Sylvia of Fergus's regular visits to the clifftop house, she began to plot a showdown for the next time he went out at night. The next time soon arrived. Fergus had not come home to eat the good meal Sylvia cooked for him. He hadn't even bothered to call. Sylvia finally reached the end of her tether. Her neighbours agreed to babysit the kids for a few hours.

Sylvia told herself: This is it. No more pussy footing around.

Initially Sylvia blamed losing Fergus on Isla the check out girl. But after Isla mentioned the order for condoms, Sylvia was not so sure. Thinking a lot more about it, that comment seemed guileless. Nevertheless, Sylvia explored possible motives Isla could have for mentioning the condoms. If Fergus used them with Isla, was she likely to mention the order to his wife? Unless Isla deliberately dug for information wondering if Fergus still shared the marital bed. As the wronged spouse, Sylvia analysed every nuance in paranoid anguish. Fergus certainly had no use for condoms with his wife. Even before the youngest baby arrived, he withheld any form of affection or physical contact from Sylvia.

During the preceding weeks, before Sylvia became certain her husband was up to something, she began to keep tabs on him whenever possible. Curiosity grew after seeing him go into Birdwhistle Solutions across the road from the kindergarten where she took her children. Sylvia was at a loss, having no idea why her husband would go there but she would never ask him outright. She did not know Fergus had hired the firm to embarrass that check out girl or anything about the matchmaking incidents he'd caught Isla doing. Fergus Rudin did not discuss anything with his wife and never sought her opinion.

So Sylvia watched Birdwhistle's agency while on volunteer playground duty at the pre-school or lingering in her car in the kindergarten car park. One morning, she happened to spy Isla through Birdwhistle's shopfront window. The former check out girl was obviously working there in the office. This surprised Sylvia greatly as she didn't know Isla had left the supermarket. In fact, Isla had only just begun at the agency and was on her first day.

Around midday the pre-school children were herded indoors for lunch, story time and naps. Sylvia placed her one year old baby in the pram, about to walk down to the esplanade for her own lunch, when she glimpsed Isla and Aiden through the open verandah doors above the Birdwhistle office. She saw a cushion fly across the room and Isla seemed to recline on a sofa. Sylvia misread what was going on. And in the middle of the day! What a harlot! Not enough to steal my husband but now she's latched onto another boss. How many men does she need?

Overcome with anger and the injustice of her lot, Sylvia searched the kids' activity bag kept in the storage rack under the pram. She tore a blank page from the back of a colouring book and used a thick black crayon to write an angry note: WHAT A SLUT. BONKING THE BOSS IN THE LUNCH BREAK. String holding a mobile toy across the pram was adequate to tie the note to a loose brick found nearby beside an old construction site. Bent on revenge, Sylvia hid it all in the pram.

The street was deserted during that lunch hour. She pushed the pram right up to Birdwhistle's door and hurled the brick through the plate glass window with all the weight of her discontent. Hearing some big dogs start barking savagely, she hurried away as the baby woke and began to howl. Turning the corner, Sylvia was soon out of sight of the agency. Afterwards, Sylvia couldn't believe her own audacity or that she'd gotten away with it.

Sylvia Rudin had already thought about engaging Birdwhistle's agency to have her husband followed. It would be poetic justice if they caught their own promiscuous employee with Fergus and that outcome became Sylvia's fondest wish. Maybe they would sack the slut.

Therefore, it came as quite a revelation to learn Fergus had not been meeting up with Isla at all. Instead, he had frequented a brothel. Sylvia's shock multiplied tenfold when that mansion of ill repute was all over the news for the murder deaths of two men.

Sylvia bided her time saying nothing to Fergus. She bleached his towels and washed his clothes separately because God knows what diseases he might pick up. Not that he had physical relations with her anymore, but he crawled into their shared bed after he imagined she was asleep. Fergus's total disregard combined with his interest in Isla and his nefarious nighttime outings alerted Sylvia to his betrayal in the first place. Over the years, Fergus went from giving his wife a quick servicing once a week, to once a month, to once a year, then nothing. Sylvia accepted that she had aged but then, so had Fergus and he was ten years her senior.

If Sylvia thought the mansion murders would cure her husband's habit, she was wrong. Learning he now frequented a different place, she felt defeated. When the lad from Birdwhistle's told her the next place could be another brothel, or perhaps an illegal casino, or both, Sylvia knew her marriage was kaput. However, there was no way she was letting Fergus get off scot-free because he had caused her so much misery for too long.

Sylvia knew the posh Spanish style house on the clifftop, it was a well-known local landmark. White knuckled, she gripped the steering wheel as her escalating heartbeats pounded in her ears. Fergus Rudin's wife was hell bent for a showdown at the hacienda.

16

THE HACIENDA EVENT

Isla lay frozen in terror, knowing she was at the mercy of two sadistic men who both hated her and wanted revenge. She heard the argument intensify over who should go first with her. It took every skerrick of her willpower to remain still and keep breathing steadily, as if unconscious.

"Do you think I am stupid?" Rudin had shouted.

His exclamation was met with insults and the ultimatum from Van Baas. Troy was in control and enjoyed needling the chump. Fergus Rudin's loud angry words echoed in what seemed a large room, making Isla hopeful that she wasn't on the yacht sailing out to sea.

"Settle down. There's no need to argue. You'll get your turn."

Troy repeated mildly, though it was a little late to placate the older man.

"Enjoy the buffet Fergus. I said you can watch. That's a bonus. You can have that at no extra charge."

Van Baas wasn't afraid of the heavy panting supermarket manager. Let him suffer. Troy knew Fergus would never demand his money back. Not that it was ever an option.

Rudin's anger and frustration boosted Troy's ego and his perception of power over others. The situation only added to his anticipation of demeaning Isla. He felt his lust rising to the occasion since the time drew near.

The idea of having Fergus watch him added to Troy's arousal. His erection expanded with the unique and titillating opportunity at hand. He dropped his pants to let Rudin admire his superb engorged appendage in its full naked glory. Fergus Rudin turned scarlet with rage. He knew himself to be not particularly well endowed but the younger man's boner outdid his best by double.

Fergus Rudin had long fantasised over having Isla submit to his own macho mastery. The cherished dream had been his driving ambition and obsession. Now Troy Van Baas' unexpected intervention with his superior tool was spoiling everything. The supermarket manager thought the uppity bitch wouldn't even feel his own puny efforts if Troy Van Baas went first with such an enormous cock.

"You should see your face!" Troy laughed mocking Rudin.

Troy enjoyed belittling Fergus, seeing him wriggle on the hook. Rudin knew full well he was beaten and would never get his money back. The only option was to bow to Van Baas' terms because he still hungered to rape Isla.

Hands on his hips, Troy leaned back, proudly waggling his amply distended pride and joy from side to side to further taunt Fergus, revelling in the envy and resentment he saw cross the older man's face.

"Eat your heart out old man." Troy chuckled.

It was too much for Fergus Rudin to accept. His steaming fury rose to fever pitch. Grabbing the razor-sharp carving knife from the roast meat tray, he lunged at Troy. In one swift rage driven downward swipe he lopped Troy's rigid penis off in a clean cut.

Troy Van Baa's impressive manhood fell with a gentle plop onto the floor.

Both men froze in shock.

Troy couldn't understand it at first. His brain wouldn't process what just happened. This was impossible. He began to scream as realisation dawned. Falling to his knees he grappled to grasp the shrivelling piece of himself, but it slid away out of his reach. The room spun before his eyes, and he blacked out. Fergus Rudin, immediately horrified at what he had done, dropped the knife onto the floor. He cried out a stuttering sentence:

"It..it can be reattached. I..I will put it on ice."

Passing by the swimming pool on her way in, Jenni heard her darling Pitbull whimpering from the pump enclosure, which fully justified her suspicions and added to her anger. She'd picked her dog up for a kiss and cuddle and let him follow her into the house.

Fergus didn't want to touch the quivering remnant of Van Baas' sinewy flesh but reached for a clean linen napkin to pick up the awful thing.

At the same moment, Jenni used her key to gain entry to the locked games room. Without any surprise at the sight of Troy kneeling half naked on the floor, since their adventures had them adopt various attitudes, Jenni's focus went straight to Isla lying on the bondage bed with her legs pulled up and her genitalia pinkly exposed.

"You sneaky frigging bastard Troy!" She shouted. "I knew you had to be up to something."

Fergus Rudin, in the act of reaching for a napkin, jumped in alarm at Jenni's abrupt appearance. He almost upset the entire smorgasbord table. Some fruit rolled to the floor. Pitbull the poodle followed his mistress into the room and began sniffing around. Troy came around to consciousness on hearing Jenni yell his name. He saw the dog sniffing at his severed penis and began screaming again.

"The fucking dog! Get the fucking dog!" Troy screamed in panic.

Jenni looked askance still not realising what had happened. Then she saw little Pitbull pick up a morsel of something from the floor. She scolded an aside to her poodle:

"Don't eat that my darling. You don't know where it's been."

Jenni bent to pick up the little dog and clear his mouth of whatever he had but the pooch evaded her grasp. Pitbull cast one last disdainful glare back at Troy before racing away with his tormentor's severed dick clasped between his sharp little teeth.

Fergus's irate wife had driven in and parked behind Jenni's Audi. She easily gained entry into the house as Jenni had left all the doors open. Sylvia marched in primed for battle. She noticed a small growling dog on her way through the house. It worried at something meaty, shaking its head. Maybe it was trying to kill a rat or something. So intent was the dog, it ignored Sylvia and she strode right on by. Sylvia didn't know and didn't care what the dog was up to. She had only one mission and that was to confront her rotten husband and hopefully catch him in the actual act of adultery.

Troy Van Baas knew the dog had taken his most loved and valued part of himself, never to be recovered. His system went into overdrive, unable to cope with that horrible realisation. He began to tremble and shake uncontrollably in a ruinous seizure that twisted him onto his back. His whole body stiffened, and his heels drummed a tattoo on the hard floor while his flippant lock of hair flopped about, dancing to the beat. Troy's eyes rolled back in his head, showing only the ghastly whites, matched in colour to his pearly teeth, clamped together in a rictus grin.

Jenni got the clue. Something was dreadfully wrong with Troy. She knelt beside her favourite lover who had his genital area covered with one hand. Jenni took his hand in hers but dropped it in horror on seeing what was... or wasn't, underneath. A red raw stub dribbled blood-stained urine where his magnificent penis should have been. Jenni noticed the carving knife on the floor near Fergus Rudin's feet.

Revolted, shocked and outraged Jenni turned on Rudin:

"You did this. You've hacked him off. You've destroyed him." She rasped.

"I tried to save it. I-I was p-putting it on ice...but but but...the dog..." Fergus stuttered.

Jenni picked up the carving knife. All the force she could muster went into plunging it into Fergus Rudin's lower gut, aiming for his genitals but his fatty overhang protected his small shrunken handful. Fergus clutched at his stomach in astonishment, feeling no pain at first.

Jenni got over her initial sickened reaction in exacting that quick reprisal. She'd avenged Troy and felt virtuous for doing so. Ever optimistic, Jenni immediately identified a bright side: At least Troy wouldn't be diddling other women anymore. Too bad. Too sad. Alas poor Troy, I knew him well. Somehow those words came to Jenni. She prided herself in owning a poetic side. Oh well he'd been good while he lasted but the bastard shouldn't have locked Pitbull in the pool shed. That was unforgivable.

Jenni withdrew the wide blade from Fergus's guts and calmly wiped it on the shoulder of his black shirt.

"I dub thee Sir Lancelot. Or lance a little as the case may be."

Jenni tittered at her own wit.

Having wiped off the heavy silver carving knife, Jenni placed it back beside the tasty leg of roast lamb that Fergus had been enjoying. The mint garnish had fallen off the joint of meat, so she arranged it artistically back into place. All neat. All fixed. Now there was just that slag Isla to deal with. Jenni chose the silver handled antique corkscrew. The long sharp spiral spike would do just nicely.

There was very little bleeding from Fergus's wound. He stood upright staring straight ahead for stunned moments. Sylvia entered the room just as Jenni rearranged the mint garnish and did not realise her husband had been mortally wounded. Sylvia yelled at Fergus in her loudest voice:

"Aha! So this is what you do."

Fergus did not reply but a trickle of acrid smelling urine wet the front of his pants. Sylvia felt triumphant that she'd put the wind up him enough to make him piss himself. Jenni stared in surprise and demanded to know who was this mad looking stranger who burst in.

"Who the hell are you?"

"Whose asking bitch?"

Sylvia remained buoyed and brave after catching Fergus out at last. Incensed, Jenni shrieked:

"Get out! Get out now! Or I'll use this on you instead of that trollop."

Jenni threatened Sylvia while brandishing the corkscrew towards Isla. Sylvia had hardly looked at the woman on the bed but now recognised Isla and saw she was restrained somehow in a crude and vulnerable position. Sylvia had never imagined seeing such an appalling debauched scenario.

"What is wrong with you people!?" Sylvia cried, aghast.

"I told you to get out." Jenni screeched again.

The instant Jenni lunged at Sylvia with the corkscrew, Fergus crashed to the floor between them. Jenni tripped and fell face down to lay over the top of his fat form. Sylvia grabbed a heavy champagne magnum by the neck and tapped Jenni on the back of her head. Not so hard as to smash the bottle. But she hoped to knock her out. That seemed to do the trick for the time being and Sylvia felt pleased with her accomplishment.

"Don't mess with the big girls honey." Sylvia advised.

In light of what she now saw, Sylvia felt contrite for blaming the former check out employee for Fergus's betrayal. Isla was clearly not a willing participant and Fergus was obviously completely at fault. Sylvia told herself she should have known an attractive young woman like Isla wouldn't be interested in someone like Fergus. He was well past his prime.

Sylvia wistfully admired Isla's body, recalling with nostalgia she had once looked that good herself. Maybe that was why Fergus felt so drawn to this poor girl. Huh. Small comfort. The way Isla was trussed up was beyond what Sylvia imagined her husband to be capable of. It must have been that mad woman with the corkscrew who'd done it, and she probably killed that guy on the floor as well. Sylvia couldn't wait to get out of there. But first she had to help Isla.

Sylvia fetched a couple of big white towels from the bathroom to place over Isla's nakedness. The manacles and anklets had some kind of locks Sylvia couldn't release. In haste to depart, she had to leave Isla bound up, telling herself at least the young woman was modestly covered now.

Isla hid in the only place she could, behind the walls of her own mind. If she opened her eyes the fear would manifest. Isla remained catatonic in her self- induced stupor. She heard Sylvia quietly apologise for throwing the brick with the nasty note. Although the woman thought Isla to be drugged asleep, she had spoken her thoughts aloud, feeling it atoned somewhat for her vengeful act.

Jenni lay across Fergus who had begun a mournful groaning. Sylvia showed no sympathy:

"What? You tired of this slut already Fergus? She not doing it for you any more?"

Sylvia kicked Jenni over onto her back and saw that the corkscrew had pierced her smooth rouged cheek and gone right through her mouth. The sharp tip protruded with a trickle of blood from the other side of her face. Jenni gained awareness and tried to prise the corkscrew from her face but it caught on her molars. Pulling on it was unbearably painful. She began keening and trying to dislodge it with her bloodied tongue, to no avail.

"Glah glah glah"

Jenni made the guttural noises as her mouth hung ajar frothing with blood-stained spittle. Her long, beautifully manicured fingernails clawed and scratched her once flawless skin, carving deep red welts.

Sylvia thought it quite the ugliest exhibition she ever had the misfortune to witness. So, she averted her eyes.

Fergus groaned more pitifully and reached a hand up to his wife beseeching her help. His guts had begun to ooze with a corrupt foul odour, but Sylvia still didn't know he had been stabbed and was fatally wounded.

"Oh, now you want my help. I pity you Fergus. I really do. But you can just lay there under that dirty slattern and enjoy what you paid for. And smells like you've pooped your pants as well. You filthy stinking old bastard. Have fun."

Troy Van Baas remained a silent witness. His lips stretched agape over his perfect brilliant white teeth. Even in death, he appeared inappropriately amused.

Sylvia spared him a disgusted glance believing he probably got what he deserved. The unloved wife did not change anything else in the room apart from placing the towels over Isla. She supposed Fergus might phone someone for help eventually but he could clean up after himself and deal with his own problems from now on. She fired a parting shot:

"I wash my hands of you, once and for all Fergus Rudin."

It was late and Sylvia had to get back to her children without delay. Barely out of the steep driveway and on her way home, Sylvia passed a speeding car with a traffic cop hot on its tail, blue light flashing.

"Idiots." she said to herself. "What is the world coming to."

Turning onto the highway home, Sylvia did not see both vehicles roar around the zigzag hairpin bends up towards the picturesque Spanish house, its gardens subtly lit with night lights that gleamed on the elegant white arches. The alert little grey poodle came out and barked at the newcomers.

17

FREEING ISLA

The three men, Aiden, Ethan and the traffic cop burst into the house. Pitbull scampered about yapping at their heels.

The poodle ran ahead leading them to the games room where he sniffed over Troy's dead body. After anointing the peekaboo fringe with a drizzle of his doggy scent, Pitbull turned tail to scrub his feet backwards in a burying motion, *implying that's that.*

Fergus Rudin had died in a reeking mess of his own bowel contents. The poodle regarded the smelly body with disdain apparently finding it beneath his dignity to bother pissing on it.

Jenni had fainted with pain but was alive, breathing shallowly. Pitbull licked some blood from her face and sat on her, growling at the new visitors but wagging his tail in apology at the same time. The concerned little dog wasn't sure who could be trusted.

"Holy Mother of God. What happened here?"

The traffic cop exclaimed in dismay. It was as bad as any traffic accident he'd seen. He immediately ran back outside to call for back up and ambulances.

Aiden and Ethan rushed to Isla's side. She was groggily aware enough to register immense relief at being saved, mixed with distress from her cramping limbs. Between them the brothers freed Isla from the cruel bonds. Aiden wrapped the towels more securely about her naked body. Isla instinctively knew Aiden's touch, heard his voice and was encouraged to re-enter the world.

"Just try to relax. You're safe now."

Aiden kissed Isla's brow and eased her legs down into a more comfortable position. He straightened and rubbed her limbs to increase circulation, speaking softly to calm her discomfort as pins and needles prickled.

"At least you were covered up."

"Sylvia Rudin covered me."

Isla croaked the words. Her throat was so dry she could hardly utter anything at all. Aiden fetched a glass of water for Isla to sip. He had at least one immediate question:

"Fergus's wife was here?"

"Only just before you got here." Isla whispered hoarsely.

Aiden could not imagine how Sylvia Rudin breached Troy's security but he would never underestimate the capabilities of a scorned woman.

Isla fell into an exhausted sleep as the brothers discussed the situation very quietly between themselves. Ethan had detected hidden cameras in several places including light fittings, ends of curtain rods, within artworks and above a false ceiling. He told Aiden, who felt an urgent priority to get rid of them so Isla's prior exposure would not be viewed by a bunch of police detectives and others associated with the case.

"I know how you feel. I get it. But we mustn't do that." Ethan said. "It would be tampering with evidence."

"God. I hate this." Aiden replied.

"Just be thankful we've found her this soon. They couldn't have had time..."

"There was time." Aiden said quietly.

"She'll be ok. You'll both be ok." Ethan hoped he was right about that.

The brothers knew Isla must have suffered depravities but couldn't be sure to what extent, or that she would be able to talk about it. Video footage was the truest record otherwise it might only ever be speculation.

Within the hour, Dougall Grimslade and Dulcy Vestige arrived with a host of forensic people, photographers, ambulance bearers and uniformed police so it was too late to dismantle the spy cameras anyway.

It was unanimously decided that Isla would be the first casualty taken to hospital. Ambos ascertained the victim was traumatised, aching, had a thumping headache and felt nauseated but otherwise had no severe physical injuries. Mental torment would be Isla's cross to bear.

Jenni was taken next. The corkscrew remained in her face, to be removed surgically under anaesthetic. Medicos gave Jenni pain relief and taped the silver handle securely to prevent it wobbling about and enlarging the holes.

The deceased, Troy Van Baas and Fergus Rudin were left until last. They would go to the morgue for autopsies. Ambulance bearers cringed over the gory wound where Troy's long thick penis had recently reigned supreme.

Aiden insisted on accompanying Isla in the ambulance. Ethan was to drive Aiden's car back and at the last minute, decided to take the poodle home as no one else was there to look after him. He put the little dog down beside Fergus Rudin's vehicle and removed the magnetic tracking device from under the fender, slipping it under his belt and pulling his shirt down over it. A policeman placed on guard duty asked what Ethan was doing.

"Just trying to get the little dog. He's frightened by all the activity."

"Is it your dog?"

"He's a family dog. My brother Aiden bought him, but he went in the ambulance with one of the victims."

"What's the dog's name?"

Ethan mumbled Pitbull. He'd always thought it an absurd name for a toy poodle. The officer misheard thinking Ethan said Pebbles. The poodle scampered under the car.

"Pebbles, Pebbles, come here boy."

The policeman got down on his knees and coaxed in a girly voice. Pitbull ran to him. Apparently Pebbles sounded a lot like Pitbull to the dog. The officer grabbed the poodle and was nipped on the thumb for his trouble.

"Ow. He's a real little carnivore isn't he."

"Dogs will be dogs." Ethan replied.

He thanked the policeman and placed Pitbull/Pebbles in the back seat of Aiden's car. Jenni's poodle jumped into the front seat as Ethan drove away back to the agency. Ethan swapped Aiden's car for his own and went back to his shared beach house.

By that time, the sun was up on a new day. Ethan's surfing housemates had already been out at daybreak on their surfboards and were now back cooking breakfasts. They all exclaimed over the cute little silver-grey doggy.

"Who's this?"

"Collateral damage from an event. There was no one to take care of him."

"What's his name?"

"He's been Frou Frou, Pitbull and Pebbles so far in his short life. Take your pick."

The name Frou Frou wasn't given the time of day. The lads argued over Pitbull or Pebbles. It didn't matter as the poodle answered to either. He was given a dish of water and offered some scrambled eggs, but he didn't seem at all hungry.

The poodle was more interested in running outside to explore. The back door to the beach house stayed open as someone would always be home at any given time. The little dog enjoyed the luxury of a choice of trees in the large back yard. He soon met three small next-door terriers through the chain wire. After strutting their stuff for a bit, the dogs decided to be friends and enjoyed a game of running up and down the dividing fence line.

With freedom of a big yard, all the surfer boys and other dogs for company it was the best Jenni's poodle had known it could be, in his tormented life so far.

18

AIDEN & GRIMSLADE

For the remainder of the eventful night after leaving the hacienda, Aiden sat beside Isla's hospital bed. A nurse came in and told him he might as well go home and get some sleep. The patient needed to rest and was not likely to wake anytime soon as she had been sedated.

Aiden dragged his feet to the hospital canteen to grab a coffee, remembering he had no car as he'd come in the ambulance with Isla. About to call Ethan to pick him up, he was joined by a bleary eyed Dougall Grimslade.

"How do they make this coffee taste so bad?" Grimslade said as a friendly opener.

"Morning Grimslade. How did it end up?"

"Troy Van Baas dead. Fergus Rudin dead. Jenni McKinstock scheduled for surgery today sometime. Probably early this morning."

"So now you know I didn't do away with my ex." Aiden said.

"Why would I think you did?"

"Your line of questioning about her distinguishing marks. Also your comments about me wanting to be rid of her."

"Those were mainly run of the mill prodding. But the distinguishing marks question was to eliminate your ex from another case."

"Give me a lift home and I'll let you tell me about that." Aiden said.

"OK. This hasn't been released to the media yet but you might as well know. Human remains were found tangled around footings under the old jetty. Not much to go by except white female with a tattoo. We've since had help with the I.D. Apparently the tattoo design is common to a particular group of hookers who worked for Van Baas."

Aiden had gone to that old jetty not so long ago which he didn't care to mention.

"You might have told me. I worried something really bad had happened to Jenni."

"Something bad really has happened to her now. But she should survive whatever went on in that room. It's looking like one of them went berserk and chopped Van Baas' penis off. My money would be on the woman doing that. Your ex that is."

"Jenni?"

"Only hypothetical. I could be wrong. But I think that at some point she's stabbed Rudin and maybe copped the corkscrew in the face when he tried to defend himself."

"That's a theory."

Aiden replied. Personally he couldn't imagine Jenni mutilating Troy's equipment.

"But surely you've got the footage from the hidden cameras?" Aiden said.

Grimslade paused in confusion and worded his next question carefully:

"What do you know about hidden cameras?"

"My associate detected them almost immediately. They are well hidden but we know what to look for. Surveillance is our business."

Aiden felt proud of Ethan's expertise and realised perhaps police investigations had not yet discovered the cameras. Admittedly it was still early morning and only hours since the crimes were reported. Aiden made a remark with raised eyebrows:

"Don't tell me your crew haven't found those spy recorders yet?"

The senior detective made no reply but excused himself and went outside to make a phone call. Aiden watched him pace up and down, hands gesticulating wildly. He guessed a search for cameras would be the imperative pursuit now.

Grimslade returned and with a nod of his head, beckoned Aiden out to his car for a lift back. On the drive, Grimslade remarked it would be too easy if the entire event was recorded. And he hoped it had been. Aiden replied:

"I'm certain Van Baas would video it all. Unfortunately it will include my girl Isla exposed naked and I hate to think of her being ogled by everyone on the case."

"It's normal to blur victims' faces after they are identified. But she was covered with towels wasn't she?"

"Not at first. Fergus's wife covered her up when she got there."

"Mrs. Rudin was in on it?"

"No. Not as such. She hired us to follow her husband. We told her the address and she must have gone there to catch him out."

"How do you know so much Aiden?"

"Isla told me Fergus's wife covered her up. That was before you got there. Anyway, it should all be recorded on the spy equipment."

Grimslade gave Aiden a lift back to the Birdwhistle Solutions premises. Before Aiden left the car there was one more question:

"Just one more question Aiden. What were you doing down on the old jetty after you were brought in for your second interview?"

As Aiden suspected. He had been followed that Tuesday to see what he'd do next. Probably his phone calls were intercepted as well. It was all grist for the mill and police had to do their jobs. So Aiden told Grimslade exactly why he'd gone to the jetty:

"I was getting rid of sensitive material involving my ex. Records of her infidelity to be exact. If your enquiries led to my flat being searched, I didn't want all and sundry seeing what my wife did behind my back, while I was away."

"What form was that evidence?"

"One USB flash drive containing films of Jenni with several partners at different times. In our own bed I might add. I felt more ashamed of it than she ever did. She laughed in my face when I confronted her."

Grimslade probed further and Aiden expounded woefully on Jenni's many deceptions that caused his alienation and marriage breakdown. He didn't know if the detective could fully understand how much Jenni's behaviour devastated and diminished him. Grimslade's bland expression belied a growing compassion he felt for the younger man. He liked Aiden and despised women like Jenni McKinstock.

"Are you married Grimslade?"

"Happily. Twenty-one years. And call me Dougall."

"Thanks. OK Dougall. A good woman must be worth her weight in gold."

"Bella is a rough diamond. She'll will tell me I look like shit when I get home. And say I'm getting too old for this job."

Dougall Grimslade returned to his own home and gave his wife a rare hug appreciating that he had a good one. Bella told him to put his smelly clothes in the laundry hamper and get in the shower while she made him something to eat, adding:

"And don't even think about going back to work for the next few hours . You'd be no use to them dead of a heart attack. Did I say you look like shit? Because you do. You're getting too old for this job Doogie. Bacon and beans on toast alright?"

When Sylvia Rudin was duly informed of her husband's death, she was beside herself with sorrow and guilt remembering how Fergus had reached out to her and all she'd given him was the brunt of her acid advice. Yes, she told herself, he had done wrong but he didn't deserve to be cruelly ignored when he suffered so terribly. If only she'd known her poor Fergus had been stabbed in the guts and was dying even as she thrashed him with her scorn.

Once his car was returned, Sylvia decided she would clean it thoroughly, sell it and use the money to buy a top notch funeral for him. Maybe a big headstone as well. With nice engraving and a stone angel to look over him. She doodled what that epitaph might say on notepaper that soon became spotted with her heavy teardrops.

The widow's grief lasted only until she found the good leather suitcase full of newly bought clothes and her husband's one way plane ticket, stowed in the boot. That bastard was leaving her in the lurch! Anger was a great salve to her grief. Sylvia looked into the cheapest budget funeral possible and washed her hands of Fergus for ever. Again.

Sylvia Rudin used the proceeds from selling Fergus's car to buy herself new clothes, go to a hairdressing salon and take the kids on a holiday, luxuries she hadn't enjoyed for years.

The supermarket chain discovered Fergus Ruden's embezzlement and was able to recoup most of the money from a bank account he'd loaded with his getaway stash. They decided not to go after his car and house out of sympathy and respect for his widow and children. Sylvia counted her blessings. She had her home and children and was free of her uncaring depraved husband for good.

Jenni McKinstock underwent surgery to remove the corkscrew and repair internal and external lacerations. Dulcy Vestige interviewed Jenni who was being fed intravenously and could not speak properly due to tongue damage. Jenni's statement, painstakingly written with Dulcy's assistance claimed accurately that Jenni had not known Troy Van Baas would have Isla Tickle as his guest in the home they shared. After the first paragraph, Jenni McKinstock's statement slewed from the truth:

Jenni stated that Isla Tickle would definitely have been agreeable to the bondage event, saying Isla would do anything to please Troy trying to win him back after he dumped her. Jenni excused her own vicious attacks on the Rudens claiming self-defence, with the lie that she had been terrified of the couple, who she believed were in cahoots. Jenni continued with a request for legal representation with the aim of suing Sylvia Rudin and Isla Tickle for what led to the maiming of her face.

To date, no legal eagle jumped on that challenge.

19

BUSINESS AS USUAL

Isla Tickle gratefully came out of hospital within ten days time and returned home to occupy her own small single flat.

During hospital visits, Dulcy Vestige had engaged in kindly conversation that answered her questions without interrogating Isla too harshly. Hazy over exactly what happened, Isla also had some of her own questions met:

"You're telling me Troy and Fergus died? In that room. While I was there as well?"

"Yes. Both of them. And Jenni McKinstock was injured. She is hospitalised in custody."

"I shouldn't be glad about them dying. But I am." Isla admitted.

"Can't blame you. They were evil men. Strange that they came from very different backgrounds, yet both goaded you to stick up for yourself, then wanted to punish you for it."

"I remember them arguing. Fergus was yelling. I was frozen with fright."

"Just as well you were able to contain yourself and not panic."

"I do remember Sylvia covering me up. I am so grateful to her for doing that."

Dulcy thought about Fergus's wife taking the time to cover Isla and was reminded of something her mother told her which she shared with Isla:

"It's often the extra things women do. My mother once said that women peck at the small details necessary to keep everything together. Maybe Mum arrived at that notion from her quilting bee craft group, thinking of the thousands of tiny stitches and scraps sewn together to make something good and whole."

"Your mother sounds very wise. Must be wonderful having a Mum. I never knew mine."

"I'm sorry for that Isla."

Dulcy did feel compassion, she liked and admired Isla.

Aiden visited to sit by Isla's hospital bed every evening. He couldn't stay away. Happy to see him, Isla always smiled her greeting as he arrived, carrying flowers or some little treat.

Isla was falling ever more deeply in love with Aiden. She was certain he had loved sex with her, at least before the interference of other men and her shameful naked exposure. Isla's natural defence of pessimism had her wonder if his attention was now pity based, or in an associated guilt response because his ex-wife played such a part in her abuse. She would not declare her love in case he didn't feel as she did, and attempted to keep his visits lighthearted:

"Hello Aiden. Thanks for coming again. I feel lucky to have you tuck me in every night. Do I get a bedtime story this time?"

The man pecked a kiss onto Isla's pale brow. No longer the robust beach girl, Isla appeared wan and delicate propped up against the white pillows and dressed in a plain tent-like hospital night gown. A purple tinge around her eyes underlined her depletion.

Aiden was careful not to overstep the mark by indicating his physical needs. Though he longed to take Isla into his arms and feel her body pressed against his, he realised her dreadful experience must curbed any desires she might have.

"You want a bedtime story? Sure. I can do that...let's see...here's one: Once upon a time, there lived a noble knight, who was known throughout the land as a pathetic pushover..."

"Ha ha. Noble was he? Do go on."

"...so, this sad but noble soul fell under the curse of a wicked witch who dragged him down to a very dark place, where he floundered in misery. Until one day, a beautiful enchantress magically emerged from the gloom of the knight's despair...and she cast a charmed spell on him that lifted the curse."

"Did she look like an angel?"

"Not in the least."

"What was she wearing?"

"A cheeky grin that brightened her eyes and made her nose wrinkle a little bit."

"You were blessed. Did the good witch have a name?" Isla fished.

"He called her his IT girl."

Isla smiled. She had always liked initialling things as IT. The orphanage had kept the note found on her as a newborn, simply calling her 'it'. That pitiful scrawled scrap of a paper was the closest blood link Isla had to family.

The problem child who grew into lovely young woman longed to find her true beginnings and loved Aiden's fairy tale of how she evolved. Aiden sat with Isla for each and every night she spent in hospital, until she fell asleep, then he gently kissed her forehead and crept out. Alone at home in his bed, Aiden no longer craved any form of sexual release. He only yearned to have Isla back in his everyday life.

Much of Isla's hospital stay was far from a fairy tale: Kept in under observation, Isla reluctantly underwent free counselling given by a youthful professional, who could not have been long out of university.

Isla resented being analysed by someone her junior who referred to his laptop most of the time. It made Isla feel like a guinea pig, just an interesting case used as a learning curve for a person with little personal worldly experience of their own. Isla felt the young consultant's questions dug for gory or sexy details of her abduction for his own entertainment. She told him as such and would not be going back for his recommended return appointments.

In a way, the counselling sessions helped, since Isla fell back on her own stubborn resilient nature that she had always relied on. Yet the ordeal weighed heavily, and she did not bounce back immediately after being discharged.

Although Isla greatly appreciated having Aiden and Dulcy Vestige visit her in hospital, on release, she craved time alone, needing to put some normality back into her disrupted life.

Aiden respected Isla's need to resettle into a routine. He could only assume she might, in time, welcome his sexual overtures and he must be patient. Yet he began to long for their unfulfilled second night together.

Business continued as usual at Birdwhistle Solutions. The library chewing gum vandal had not been found and no new incidences had occurred since the extra spy equipment had been installed. Aiden included Isla in discussions to let her know she was relevant and necessary. She'd been quieter and somewhat withdrawn ever since coming home from hospital.

"This reeks of an inside job." Ethan said.

Aiden agreed and looked to Isla who was back at her desk. She only nodded.

"OK. So we know there are three permanent librarians and a few temps. The permanents would definitely know more surveillance has been put into play."

"What about the cleaning staff?"

"The council only used cleaners for administration offices. Not in the library. Vacuuming and dusting is shared amongst the normal staff, mainly relegated to the temps."

"Let's suggest they give the story to the local paper. It might flush something out."

"Can't hurt."

An article was published within a week with photographs of the library building and some of damaged books with gummed up pages. Birdwhistle Solutions received a mention in the text as providing additional security measures.

Nothing came to light until one afternoon, two students in high school uniforms walked into the office. A tall thin boy and a short chubby girl nervously fronted up to Isla's desk and introduced themselves as senior class captains chosen for a certain task. Ethan and Aiden were out on another case at the time. Isla smiled at the school kids.

"Hello there. What can I do for you?"

"It's about the library story in the paper. The chewing gum thing."

"Oh yes?"

"We used it as a class project. Brain storming ideas onto a whiteboard. Anyway we thought our findings might be useful. We printed it out."

"Would you like an appointment to see the manager?"

"Can we just leave our report with you? Our email addresses are on it so please let us know if anything comes of it. You see, our study group will be marked on this exercise."

"Of course. Thank you for bringing it in."

Isla opened the folder of neatly printed pages after the kids left. They had numbered several ideas but left conclusions up to the reader. Plainly, the kids implicated a former teacher who had resigned her post after she completed a librarian course and gained a position with the local council. The students' findings were itemised:

Number one stressed the teacher's abhorrence of chewing gum in school. Two: The teacher made kids spit their chewed gum into sealed plastic bags which they believe she kept. An aside was added that the school kids remembered this well as they used to joke she must chew it herself later. Three: The teacher clearly disliked all the kids and particularly the gum chewers. Four: The group unanimously decided the former teacher would want school kids blamed for the library vandalism. Five: At the library, this former teacher always overlooked school kids in any queue and made them wait longer. Six: Everyone thought that librarian would want school children permanently banned from the library. Seven: They all agreed they might be banned from the library if the chewing gum damage was attributed to students. Eight: No one wanted to be banned from the library.

Isla read the submission and thought the class captains were on the ball. The effort the youngsters had put in, renewed her interest in the private eye business and helped her climb out of the doldrums.

Aiden and Ethan also admired the work done by the school kids. Despite using caution in not actually naming the former teacher, it was not difficult to pinpoint who was believed responsible.

Council put employee records at their disposal and only one had been a former high school teacher: A Miss Millicent Wendall who was also the most recent new librarian recruit.

All the library staff were questioned. Of course none admitted to ruining the books with gum. Millicent Wendall protested more than anyone and was adamant the gum had to come from high school students.

General opinion gleaned from private conversations, hinted that Millicent Wendall seemed bitterly inclined. A failed marriage and inadequate results in her role as an educator added to her poor attitude. Aiden made pertinent enquiries to the school board and found that even straight 'A' students had done poorly under that teacher although she blamed it on the children themselves.

Students counselled over failed subjects or low marks, claimed Millicent Wendall only ever instructed them to read from their text books during lesson periods. She never actually tutored them or offered helpful input. They accused the teacher of spending the lesson times on her iPhone or reading magazines.

The teacher had been unpopular, and students had high motives for revenge, but everything pointed to Millicent Wendall as the chewing gum perpetrator. Without proof it was only hearsay, and nothing could be done.

In other developments, a handful of hookers and desperate would-be star-lets, who had been employed by Troy Van Baas, attempted to lay claims on his estate by forming a class action. However, the man had only appeared to be worth millions. His wealth had been all smoke and mirrors main-tained by a network of hefty loans.

Once news of Troy Van Baas' demise was made public, the extortion payments dried up and his empire collapsed. The swank residences and fancy car were repossessed.

The luxury yacht mysteriously exploded and sank one dark night. Records of sexual exploits involving high profile players, politicians, busi-nessmen and various celebrities were destroyed in that blast. Troy's home movies with Isla and others also disintegrated in the massive fireball.

For all intents and purposes, Troy Van Baas and his misdeeds disap-peared from the face of the earth.

Jenni McKinstock slowly recovered from surgery to remove the corkscrew. Aiden had forgotten she was still on his private health insurance but let it slide out of pity when she claimed her medical expenses against it. Her face and tongue were extensively damaged, largely worsened by her own frantic efforts to remove the metal spiral.

Ongoing reconstruction surgery could possibly improve scarring if it were considered essential surgery by prison officials. Aiden realised his ex-wife might face years in prison, if she were sentenced. Time would tell. Remanded in custody, Jenni had yet to face court.

Jenni McKinstock stuck to her story of being so terrified of Fergus Rudin and his wife, that she acted in self-defence. Jenni had threatened to use the corkscrew on Isla, but it could be argued she'd only said it to scare Sylvia, as she so claimed.

Aiden's marital home finally sold at auction including all the furniture and contents. He wanted to keep nothing to remind him of that place. He appointed a solicitor to invest Jenni's half of the proceeds for her eventual release. Aiden decided he might use some of his money to further improve the little flat above the office. There were definite advantages to living there. It was not only convenient but meant Isla was in close proximity. And having Isla near was paramount for Aiden.

Initially Jenni McKinstock was hospitalised in a mental institution where Aiden reluctantly visited, at her request. He found Jenni to be greatly diminished both in spirit and appearance.

Having always traded on her great beauty, Jenni could no longer bear to look at herself in a mirror. Barbed retorts were also a thing of the past for Jenni, as the damage thickened her tongue, affecting her speech, making her sound moronic. People with intellectual disabilities had always been a source of ridicule and improper jokes for Jenni, so her speech impairment felt as dreadful to her as the facial scarring.

Jenni quietly thanked Aiden for organising a solicitor to manage her finances. However, her one concern was for Pitbull her poodle.

"He's fine and being well cared for. Ethan took him in. There's a lot of company and a good big yard. Plus he has the run of the house as always." Aiden told her gently.

Jenni began to cry then. Aiden realised it was the first time he had ever seen her shed a tear in genuine emotion. She asked that a stipend be organised out of her funds to cover keep, medical bills and beauty parlour visits for her poodle. Aiden promised to get onto her solicitor and have it done. The poodle could live for another twelve years or so but Aiden knew the dog might not be around by the time Jenni was released.

Aiden wondered if it could be possible to take Pitbull on prison visits in the future but he did not mention this unless it was disallowed. He privately vowed to look into it, realising his connection to Jenni would now be ongoing, possibly for years and years. The thought greatly depressed him.

With a heavy heart, Aiden drove home in a blur of his own tears. He really needed to be with Isla, if only just for her company. But she had closed the office for the day and gone home by the time he returned, after sunset.

20

THE BOOK CASE & ISLA

The following morning, Dougall Grimslade dropped by to ask for Aiden's take on another case. It was a friendly visit. The detective also used his case research as an excuse to check on how Isla and Aiden were handling the recent upsets.

Entering the office, Dougall greeted Isla and Aiden. Isla blushed and lowered her eyes. The men were aware of her embarrassment. Isla knew Grimslade would certainly have viewed her naked bondage in the hacienda case evidence tapes. She could not shake off the feeling of being publicly demeaned with no idea how many others had access to the humiliating evidence.

Aiden took Grimslade upstairs to the flat, so Isla needn't be discomforted by the detective's presence. Being near lunch time, Aiden made sandwiches and coffee to share with Dougall. They were now firmly on first name basis.

"Aiden, I believe you made extensive inroads into a Millicent Wendall who works at the public library. Can you share your findings?"

Aiden was curious why he was asked but had no reason not to share findings. He told Dougall the gist.

"I've no proof of anything." Aiden admitted. "Circumstantial hints only. May I ask what is your interest in that librarian?"

Dougall said the librarian had since run her car up onto a footpath narrowly missing a large group of school kids at a bus stop. Fortunately the children all managed to jump aside suffering only minor bumps and bruises from falling over. It had been a near thing with one child's school bag ripped from his grasp by a side mirror. The vehicle rammed into the bus shelter causing considerable damage to the structure. Millicent Wendall was unhurt and her small 4x4 vehicle escaped relatively unscathed as she'd recently had a roo bar fitted.

The librarian claimed to have blacked out momentarily, causing her to lose control. She couldn't recall any of what happened and could not explain why she took that particular route past the crowded bus stop. It was not part of her usual way home and did not lead to the shopping centre or other places she frequented.

Several school students disputed Millicent Wendall's story, coming forward to say the former schoolteacher had always had it in for them. Evidently, an ongoing feud existed between the school students and Wendall. Police realised the kids would surely like to see her in trouble so they could be exaggerating.

Nonetheless, the driver's actions were deemed serious as the accident may have been deliberately staged. Officers first on the scene, who quizzed the driver, thought it likely she had acted on purpose. Again, nothing could be proven against Millicent Wendall.

"Millicent said she planned a road trip to the outback in the future. That's why she got the roo bar fitted. I had to take that with a grain of salt." Dougall said with a wry quirk of his mouth.

"I can tell you she has a history."

Aiden elaborated on what he knew so far and called down to Isla asking if she could find the numbered list the school class captains had provided. She found it quickly and brought it up to the flat.

"Would you like a sandwich Isla?" Aiden asked her.

"No thanks. I have my lunch in the fridge downstairs."

She fibbed about having a lunch in the fridge and retreated back downstairs, avoiding having to meet Grimslade's eye.

Isla had planned to ask Aiden to join her at the hot dog stand for lunch that day. She was going to order her hot dog *without* onions, hoping he'd get the kissing clue. Instead, she made some tea and Vegemite toast in the kitchenette and ate a spartan lunch at her desk.

Grimslade read over the student notes:

"This ties in with what Millicent Wendall brought up in questioning. Our interview only concerned the car accident but the woman obsessed over the chewing gum vandalism, saying DNA would prove the students did it."

"Would the department go so far as to DNA the chewing gum found in the books?"

"I seriously doubt it." The detective said. "Not rocket science why she'd want it done though. She must know for sure whose DNA would be found if she planted it herself."

"I get it. The kids say she made them spit their gum into plastic bags that she kept. They joked amongst themselves reckoning she'd be chewing it herself later. It's sounds crazy but it is feasible Millicent kept the gum to use against the kids somehow. The library job gave her the perfect opportunity. But our surveillance got nothing useful. Unfortunately."

Dougall said he was taking it further and not stopping at a possible nutcase being on the loose:

"I'm pushing for Millicent Wendall to be assessed by government psychiatrists. Depending on the outcome, she could be detained under the Mental Health Act. At the very least she might be tripped into confessing."

"I'm glad there is a thorough investigation. I just wish we'd caught her at it."

Grimslade changed the subject:

"I know Isla doesn't want to speak to me and I fully understand why. But perhaps you can let her know the evidence footage now has her identity blurred out. She might feel better knowing that."

Aiden had been walking on eggshells around Isla and had not pushed her for details on what happened during her abduction and bondage.

"She might feel better. If she believes it. But she doesn't want to talk about it. I'll try to tell her if an opportunity comes up and the time seems right. I just don't know how to handle this situation now. Any ideas Dougall?"

Dougall gave it some serious thought.

"Well. I wouldn't be avoiding her. On the other hand, I wouldn't be coming on too strong either."

"That's how I'm trying to play it Dougall, but I don't think it's working out too well."

"Why not start over like you just met. You know. Flowers. Gifts. Hugs. All that crap. Women like that sort of thing."

"You're a romantic at heart Dougall." Aiden laughed.

"Been there. Done that." Dougall looked pleased with himself. "And a nice bottle of wine never goes astray, if she likes it."

Aiden thought of the last bottle of wine he shared with Isla. Then his mind went to how she'd used it on him in foreplay.

"Yes. Good idea Dougall. I believe she is partial to a good Sauvignon Blanc."

Aiden would be out the door to stock up on more of that very soon.

"Well don't rush it. She's been through a terrible ordeal and it could take some time. You have to deal with the thought of the other men as well of course. I don't mind admitting I'd want to kill them, in your shoes. Fortunately, that option has been taken care of. How are you feeling about it now Aiden?"

"For my part, this is killing me. I still want her regardless but she might be repulsed by my interest now after going through all that. Or she might think I'm repulsed because of whatever Rudin and Van Baas did to her. It's torture thinking about it. I don't even know if she was raped."

"I can tell you she wasn't."

Aiden felt enormously relieved to hear that.

Dougall omitted mentioning the invasive fingering Troy did before Isla awoke.

"You've got it all on film? The whole thing from beginning to end?"

"Yes thank God. It would have been hard to piece together how it all went otherwise."

"Can you please enlighten me?" Aiden asked.

Grimslade knew he must try to be delicate with his wording yet delicacy was not one of his strengths.

"Sure lad. I'll try to get it straight: Both the men brought Isla in and put her on that bed where you found her. She was limp. Unconscious. That could have only been within about ninety minutes or so after her abduction from your car park. Troy put her in the shackles and cut her clothes away with scissors, meaning Isla would not be leaving the place dressed again. Or not in her own clothes."

"He never intended to let her go." Aiden said grimly.

"My thoughts exactly, Aiden. I believe he would have taken her out on his yacht afterwards."

They both thought of the dire implications and came to the same conclusion: Troy planned to murder Isla. Dougall picked up the story again:

"Fergus watched and pigged out on this bloody great feast that was laid on. Apparently the elaborate food and champagne was all part of the package he paid for."

"That sounds highly organised. I bet it wasn't the first time Van Baas staged something like it." Aiden said.

He knew Jenni would have loved all that pageantry and debauchery.

"For sure. It was a huge source of income for Van Baas. We ascertained Rudin probably paid twenty-five thousand in cash up front, going by how much he embezzled from his workplace against his far greater getaway stash. He planned to scarper overseas once he'd done the deed."

Aiden swallowed hard and dared to ask what he dreaded knowing.

"Did they touch her?"

"Only Van Baas did. While he was undressing her. And he, ah, you know, ran his hands over her."

Grimslade had to tell him something but left out the crude fingering. If he'd alleged Van Baas had not touched her at all, Aiden would never believe it.

"Was Jenni watching all this?"

"No, she wasn't there then. She arrived shortly after."

"When did Isla start to wake up?"

"The video shows she flickered her eyes briefly when Troy and Fergus began disagreeing. Fortunately they didn't notice. She either feigned unconsciousness or actually was really out to it after that. If she pretended to be senseless it was a smart strategy, being all she could do to delay them. Our experts who examined the footage think she could have been aware after the men began arguing."

"What did they argue about?" Aiden had to ask.

Dougall paused knowing the facts would upset Aiden. Nevertheless, he decided to tell him straight. If Isla had heard the argument, Aiden needed to know what she'd suffered through, if he was ever able to help her get over it.

"Fergus Rudin wanted to start on her right away but Troy Van Baas wanted her awake. His main agenda was her humiliation."

"That bastard." Aiden seethed.

"He gives bastards a bad name. Anyway, then Troy said he always went first, as the host."

"It had to be a regular thing." Aiden said.

"Apparently so. But Fergus wanted to be first saying he'd paid enough for it. He erupted in anger, shouted and thumped the table but Troy seemed unmoved by that."

"Oh Christ. It must have been terrifying for Isla." Aiden felt her horror. "No wonder she doesn't want to talk about it"

"That is understandable." Grimslade agreed. "She was given free trauma counselling by a newly qualified young man. But she sacked him and said she wasn't going back."

"Maybe she would have been better with a female counsellor."

"Yes maybe. Dulcy got along well with her at any rate."

They both privately wondered if Isla was done with men.

Dougall continued:

"This is where the plot fell apart. Troy drops his pants and wags his bloody enormous prick about. He's taunting Fergus with his super-sized boner, smirking and laughing. Fergus goes ballistic..."

"Wait... You're saying Troy Van Baas was really well hung?" Aiden hated that.

"Like a bloody horse. I kid you not my friend. Unbelievable..."

Grimslade held his hands apart describing Troy's outsized member as he recalled the collective awe in the room when his cohorts witnessed that part of the evidence tape.

Aiden was well enough blessed with his own parts but began to feel the old inadequacy that Jenni instilled in him. He reminded himself that Isla seemed pleased with his efforts. If only he got another chance to test that theory.

Dougall belatedly twigged that Troy Van Baas' mighty dick might not be welcomed news to Aiden since the lad entertained being with one of Troy's conquests, namely Isla.

So Dougall rushed ahead with the story:

"...anyway, Fergus grabs the carving knife and in one fell swoop that impressive article is twitching and shrivelling on the floor. It would fair make your eyes water."

"Ouch! I'm glad Jenni didn't do it. I doubted she would have done, to be honest."

"Nope. Fergus did it. Then he's sorry and wants to put the severed bit on ice."

"Could a penis ever be sewn back on?"

"Maybe. Of course it might not work like it used to. But I think the operation has been done before."

Aiden and Dougall both crossed their legs, deep in thought.

"But that's when Jenni bursts in. She's focused on ogling Isla and doesn't notice anything amiss, as you might say, even though Troy is on his knees."

"You would be on your knees, hey, having that happen."

Aiden flinched at the very idea.

"Yeah. I'd be praying that's for sure." Dougall agreed.

"So then what happened?"

"Then, the dog comes in and sniffs about at some fruit and food that rolled off the table. Troy starts screaming to get the effing dog. But the dog grabs the piece of dick and runs outside with it. I suppose he ate it or buried it. Whatever. It would be of no use anymore."

Aiden assessed the poodle in a different light and was guilty of thinking:

"*Good boy.*"

"Holy cow. I bought that poodle as a puppy for Jenni. My brother keeps him now."

"Hopefully the pooch hasn't developed a taste for the exotic salami."

Dougall grimaced. It made him think of his salami and pickles snacks.

"Pitbull...that's what Jenni named him, was always rather a fussy eater. Jenni thought it was because he came from a celebrated pedigree line. I think maybe because she fed him best fillet steak most of the time. He would turn his nose up at ordinary dog food. I don't know what Ethan feeds him. I should ask."

"He better keep him well fed. That's all I'm saying."

Aiden wasn't sure if he should tell Ethan about the poodle's little lapse of table manners. As Grimslade's story continued, Aiden realised Pitbull had been the catalyst for both Troy and Fergus dying.

"Did Troy die from blood loss or a heart attack?"

"Not sure but there wasn't much blood. Looked like he had some kind of fit. I guess from knowing he was unmanned when the dog took off. He might have survived if there had been any chance of saving his pecker."

"The shock of it, I suppose." Aiden said.

Unsaid was Aiden's conviction that justice had been properly served. He wasn't a spiteful man but couldn't have dreamt up a better punishment.

"What happened after that?"

"Jenni sees how he's been maimed and realises Fergus must have done it. She goes nuts and knifes him in the belly."

"So, there is proof. Jenni is up for murder."

"That seems likely. It's all on the video. A good lawyer might get her off with an insanity plea. But I can't see her walking free. She handled it well too. Cool as a cucumber afterwards. She wipes the knife on Fergus's shoulder and makes some smart jokey remark. Then puts the knife back on the meat tray and neatens the food table."

"Even I find that hard to process. But then, Jenni has always been rather cold blooded."

"Cold as ice, if you ask me." Dougall said.

Aiden felt a shiver go down his spine, having lived with and lusted over a woman who was probably a psychopath, his instincts not to rile her too much had been spot on.

"Then what?"

"That's when Sylvia Rudin came in to join the party." Dougall said.

"We had to be on our way there by then or not far behind." Aiden added.

"True. It all happened quickly. Apparently, Fergus's wife didn't know he'd been stabbed because he's still standing up looking like a stunned mullet. Jenni and Sylvia argue. Jenni goes for Sylvia with the corkscrew, but Fergus falls down like a ton of bricks and trips her."

"Not on purpose?"

"No. His injury kicked in at the right moment. Fortunately for his wife. All the same, Mrs. Rudin hits Jenni on the head with a bottle while she's down. Can't blame the woman after being attacked like that. I'd call it self defence regardless, but it's not my call."

"She has got a few little kids to think about." Aiden said.

"True. Then Mrs. Rudin covers Isla with the towels then rolls Jenni over and sees she's been impaled through the face. That happened when Fergus fell and tripped her."

"Shit. It was accidental? So Jenni ruined her own face. The poor silly bitch."

"Don't waste your pity mate. She meant to use that corkscrew on Isla."

"Thank God that didn't happen."

Aiden was horrified at what Jenni might have been capable of doing to Isla. He wouldn't put anything past that devil woman any more.

"So your ex wife panicked trying to claw the thing out of her face. It seemed stuck somehow. It must have been really painful with all the nerves in the tongue and face. Probably just as well she passed out again."

"She's always been so vain. I do pity her. I can't help it." Aiden said sadly.

Dougall couldn't help thinking Aiden was a bit soft.

"Well then, you have a kind heart." he said.

"Isla managed to tell me Sylvia covered her up. I was grateful for that."

"Mrs. Rudin was definitely a very lucky break for Isla. She'd spoken quietly while covering her with the towels but we couldn't catch exactly what she said. Sounded like an apology. Suppose she felt responsible somehow for her husband's part in it. Anyway Isla didn't seem aware of it at the time. Then the locks on the fetters proved too hard for Mrs. Rudin to get them undone."

Aiden recalled the desperation in trying to free Isla:

"They were tricky to get open. Poor Isla was really cramping. But I suppose Sylvia didn't want to waste any more time there."

"No. Couldn't blame her really. Fergus was given a few choice words saying he can just stay there and enjoy what he paid for. Then she left him for dead, though she didn't know it at the time. She seemed genuinely sorry and grief stricken when told of his death because she had no idea he'd been stabbed."

Aiden understood the woman feeling sorrow for her spouse despite everything, they had shared a marriage and must have loved each other once. Dougall seemed less forgiving, being accustomed to taking a hard line in his work.

"Will Sylvia Rudin be charged for hitting Jenni with the bottle?"

"Doubt it. Not in the circumstances. Jenni didn't seem to know about it anyway."

"I'm pretty sure she'd press charges if she did know." Aiden said.

"I don't think anyone will be telling her." Dougall said.

Sylvia dodged another bullet:

In deep gratitude for the kindness given in covering her up with the towels, Isla never told anyone who threw the brick. She adopted the motto 'let sleeping dogs lie' and with Grimslade's presence upstairs, the slogan came to mind. It seemed apt when Ethan came into the office with the silver-grey poodle on a leash. He'd begun taking Pebbles aka Pitbull on his rounds whenever possible.

Isla told him Aiden was upstairs with the detective Grimslade, discussing the library chewing gum case. Isla had no doubts they discussed much more regarding herself, but she didn't want to go there, wishing the whole debacle would just blow over.

Ethan could have added more to the librarian saga as his schoolgirl lover, Tiffany Dellapinto, was full of anecdotes about Grumpy Old Millicent as she was known to classmates.

However, Ethan deemed it tactful not to draw attention to his youthful girlfriend. Although Tiffany had by now reached the age of consent, that stern detective would surely take a very dim view of a twenty-two-year-old man sporting a sixteen-year-old schoolgirl as his partner.

Out of school uniform, Ethan knew Tiffany could easily pass for eighteen, but six years age difference was a lot at this stage of her life. He felt chastened by his older brother's disapproval as well.

21

TIFFANY CUTS TO THE CHASE

ater, after Dougall Grimslade had gone home, Ethan learnt of the librarian's recent car accident that almost mowed down a group of high school students. After school was let out, Ethan brought young Tiffany in to meet Aiden and Isla for the first time. He thought Tiffany might fill in more about the Millicent Wendall saga, but as it turned out, they never got around to that subject.

Tiffany Dellapinto looked nothing like the cheap smart-arsed little dolly bird Aiden had imagined she would be. The tall, slim sixteen-year-old wore heavy rimmed spectacles making her appear seriously studious. Her dark auburn hair, worn drawn up smoothly into a neat ponytail, shone naturally with burgundy highlights. Although in school uniform and by far junior to the others, Tiffany's manner was forthright and outgoing. The girl greeted Isla and Aiden as any self assured adult might and her presence pervaded the room with an energetic vibe.

Aiden saw a chance to engage Isla socially by inviting Ethan and Tiffany up to the flat for refreshments so the four of them could relax, chat and get to know each other.

Isla helped lay out carrot sticks and dip, salted nuts and sparkling apple juice. Aiden pointed at some beers in the fridge with raised eyebrows, but Isla shook her head, mouthing NO with a frown. Aiden blushed. He acknowledged it would be wrong to serve alcohol to a sixteen-year-old, but the circumstances of Ethan's intimacy confused him.

Ethan's attraction to Tiffany was easily understood. Although she was not overtly beautiful, her full rosy lips, bright green eyes and creamy complexion needed no enhancement. Tiffany carried her stature with grace as she walked up the stairs and entered the living room.

Aiden knew Tiffany would not look like a schoolgirl, on the beach in a bikini. He shared a glance with his younger brother communicating that thought. Ethan smiled self consciously and shrugged imperceptibly. Aiden rolled his eyes.

Tiffany's refined manner and elegant deportment had a time limit. She sat sprawl legged on a sofa, feet pigeon toed in the gangly attitude of girls her age. Which was ok and quite endearing. Isla liked the younger girl and asked what she aspired to do after finishing her education. Tiffany had a few ideas and was not shy about speaking up, which soon exposed a glaring fault: The girl had a tendency to run off at the mouth:

"Mostly I'd love to be one of those reporters who does in-depth interviews. Or a sports physiotherapist. Or an actress. I wouldn't mind being a bikini model on the side as well. Pity my boobs weren't bigger but Ethan likes me in a swimsuit. You do don't you Ethan? That's how we met. On the beach."

Isla smiled with a reply:

"Sounds like you're open minded. The world is your oyster at your age."

"I know. Hey Isla it was awful what you went through getting kidnapped and all."

"It was no fun." Isla admitted.

"Were you gang raped?" Tiffany asked with avid interest.

Aiden and Ethan almost fell through the floor but Isla handled it mildly:

"No Tiffany. At least I escaped that horror. But thanks for your concern."

"Gee that's good. I suppose it would really stuff up your sex life if your partner thought you were tainted. Would you think that of her if she got gang raped Aiden?"

"No. Of course not." Aiden went beetroot red.

The sixteen year old had cut straight to the chase and named Aiden as Isla's lover in one go. Ethan intervened:

"Hey babe. Not so much of the in-depth interviewing. Ok?"

Tiffany laughed out loud.

"He's just afraid I'll say something out of place."

At that, Isla burst out laughing as well. The guys joined in with nervous attempts at laughs. Tiffany was unstoppable:

"So anyway. That's how I met Ethan. He liked me in a bikini. Personally, I hope my boobs do get bigger. I'd love to have your boobs Isla. Well not your actual boobs of course. That would be weird. My best friend at school, Chantel, says as long as you have a handful. Otherwise best go looking for a guy with small hands. Ha ha. But then there is supposed to be a correlation between hand size and penis size isn't there? Even though size is not supposed to matter. I might take a survey sometime. Hey Ethan would the surf guards be in that do you think?"

Ethan covered his face with his own hands.

"Ooh. I made Ethan blush. Isn't he cute? Aiden's cute too. Don't worry Isla I'm not going after your man. He's much too old for me anyway."

"Phew." Isla said. "You had me worried for a moment."

Aiden liked that. Isla accepted him being called her man. Maybe she would stay with him again soon. It couldn't be soon enough for Aiden.

"My friend Chantel has the hots for Ethan too. But I swam outside the flags so he had to save me. What a hero. Now he's my first proper boyfriend. I'm not his first lover of course. But Ethan says I am his first virgin. So that's something isn't it?"

"Babe..." Ethan squirmed in embarrassment, wishing she'd shut up. "What?"

Tiffany's innocence was not convincing. Isla had an idea the girl got a kick out of being precocious and embarrassing Ethan. Aiden's ideal change of subject was to tell them the gory details of how little Pitbull featured in the horror story at the hacienda. Tiffany was fascinated and scandalised in equal measure.

"You mean he actually ate it?"

"Or buried it. Probably ate it though. And please keep that under your hat."

The image that comment conjured up had Tiffany and Isla chorus together:

"Yuck!"

"Metaphorically speaking." Aiden added.

Ethan imagined how that news would go over with his surfer house-mates.

"So I've taken in the pecker eating dog? That's great. Wait till I tell the other guys."

"Takes *feeling peckish* to a whole new level." Tiffany declared. "That's what we'll call it from now on, hey Ethan? I'll just say *feeling peckish* whenever ...... "

Ethan clamped his hand over her mouth just in time. Tiffany nipped him lightly but shut up with a smug smile. Isla recognised that the brash schoolgirl liked putting Ethan on the spot to make him blush. Ethan said:

"I better get you home. Six o'clock curfew and I'm sure you've got homework."

"Yeah. It's a bugger." Tiffany agreed. "Hey guys. This has been great. Loved meeting you both at last. Hope we can do this again sometime. Adios amigos."

Tiffany exited with a salute and a wink that confirmed Isla's opinion of the girl's scallywag nature. That left Aiden and Isla alone together in the flat for the first evening since her abduction.

"Well now, isn't Tiffany a breath of fresh air." Isla said with a fond smile.

"Yes. If you mean being tactlessly juvenile equates to fresh air." Aiden said.

"Oh come on. I like her. Says what she thinks."

"I noticed that."

"I hope they practice safe sex."

"Ethan says they do and I can't see them abstaining at this point. Can you?"

"No. But I do think they suit each other. Talking them out of it would be like trying to turn back the tide."

Aiden was trying to cope with his own tidal wave. Tiffany's naïve comments brought his desperate need for intimacy with Isla to the fore. An impasse was reached as Isla didn't want to be the one to make the first move and Aiden was unsure how to conduct himself without seeming like a sex starved brute.

They cleared the living room table, rinsed the few glasses and dishes, then both seemed at a loose end. Isla didn't want to go home to her lonely flat again but couldn't bring herself to say it. Aiden yearned for her to stay with him but felt unable to broach the question. He thought of a compromise enabling more time together:

"Do you want to go for a stroll along the esplanade. Maybe get fast food?"

"Sure. I feel like fried chicken and mashed potato with gravy and peas."

"Sounds good. You've talked me into that." Aiden smiled.

Isla could have suggested dog turds on toast and Aiden would have agreed.

"We could get some of those nice after dinner mints to go with coffee for later."

"That would keep me awake all night." Aiden replied cluelessly.

Isla wondered what it would take for him to get the hint. Aiden tried to read her. He thought about suggesting another bottle of that nice white wine they'd enjoyed together. Then he chickened out in case Isla saw it as the broad proposition he intended and felt like he pressured her. As the sun sunk below the hills to the west, they strolled down towards the sea, enjoying relief from the heat. Twilight of evening remained warm and muggy.

After their chicken dinner in the fast-food restaurant, Aiden and Isla avoided the pavement of the esplanade that held inherent heat from the days hot sunshine. They strolled back along the deserted beach, barefoot, carrying their sandals, digging their toes into the damp sand.

A sliver of moon, peeping from clouds, illuminated white frilled crests sparkling over dark water. The heaving ocean seemed to breathe deeply in accord with the couple, while a fresh salty breeze flirted with their hair. Wavelets from a calm surf dissolved soothingly on the shoreline where they paddled, the seawater warm to their bare feet.

Aiden felt at a crossroads, he didn't want to overwhelm Isla after her abduction ordeal but there might never be a better time to act. The setting was ideally romantic, and they were on neutral ground. If the opportunity passed him by, he'd be kicking himself later. Spurred by that thought, Aiden stopped walking and gently pulled Isla closer.

Isla was glad she'd waited for him to make that first move. Though he had taken his sweet time about it.

"I've missed you." Aiden whispered.

"What have you missed most?"

"Just you. Everything." He said stroking her back.

"I've missed you too." Her eyes sparkled in the soft moon glow.

"I'd like to kiss you." He said, looking at her mouth.

"Now might be a good time to do that." she smiled.

They kissed softly at first. Then more urgently. Then frantically.

"Mmmm. You taste of salt."

Isla sighed between kisses as his hands roved her warm body. Her hands delved under his waistband, seeking and finding. Aiden moaned with mounting desire. At that moment, he had never wanted anything more. He choked out a plea:

"Isla. Sweetheart. If you're willing...I want you here and now."

"I'm willing."

Isla assured him as she sank to the firm sand at waters edge. The wash of seawater swirled about their legs and feet serving to temper Aiden's spontaneous combustion.   Finding their rhythm, the lovers rocked in harmony with the ebb and flow of the sea, climbing slowly to peak in a long overdue shared rapture. Theirs was a joyous, wet, briny and sandy coupling.

They descended at last from euphoria to face reality. Aiden just managed to salvage their discarded shorts from an incoming tide while Isla rescued their sandals. They laughed trying to get dressed. It had been much easier getting the pants off than working them back on gritty and sodden with sea water. Isla made a practical suggestion:

"We could just run home naked. There's no one about and it's not far."

"No way." Aiden replied. "You know what would happen if I did that? I'd be suddenly stopped in the middle of the road and surrounded by squad cars and armed police with megaphones. And a helicopter with a big spotlight and a news camera would hover overhead."

"I almost want to test that theory. But guess we'll have to get sandpapered in the interests of decorum." Isla laughed.

An uncomfortable gritty walk got them back to the flat, where they showered together soaping sand out of places it should never be, before going to bed. They had forgotten the after-dinner mints and didn't want coffee, content to cuddle together all night.

Before sunrise, they made love again, slowly savouring each other.

"Last night was magic. On the beach like that." Isla whispered.

"I want you to stay with me." Aiden said. "Every night. If you're willing."

"I'm as willing and able as you are."

Isla smiled loving the way he always checked for her consent and acceptance. She loved everything about Aiden. Aiden blessed the day he met Isla Tickle. She made him feel like a man. Her man.

The next morning Ethan arrived with his apologies for Tiffany's tactless comments. Isla laughed and told him honestly she though his young girlfriend was delightful.

"She has a great talent for elephant hunting." Isla said.

"Eh? Elephant hunting? I don't get it."

"Outing elephants in the room." Isla laughed.

"Oh that. Well thanks for understanding her. I know Tiff is too young but I just can't resist her now. And I don't want to hurt her either. I guess this thing we have at the moment will run its course. But not yet. For a while." Ethan was candid about that.

Isla hit on an idea she thought might appeal to Ethan:

"Say Ethan. Wonder if you'd do me a favour?"

"Anything."

"Well since you're upfront with me, I have to tell you I'll be sleeping upstairs with your brother for the foreseeable future...so if you're in the neighbourhood of my flat, can you look in and check everything is ok occasionally? You can park in my space there."

Isla handed Ethan the spare keys to her flat. He was quick on the uptake.

"Oh my god. You are an absolute angel Isla." He exclaimed.

Ethan clasped his brother's girl in a great bear hug, lifted her off her feet and spun her around.

"Hey! Unhand my lady!" Aiden walked in at that very moment.

Cradling Isla's precious flat keys like gold, Ethan ran outside to message Tiffany, telling her he had a place where they could get it together, starting that very afternoon. His lover replied with hearts and hand clap emojis.

"May I ask what that was all about?"

Aiden made the demand with a crooked smile, hands on hips.

"I'm guilty." Isla said.

"Of what?"

"Ask your brother. You'll probably find him in my flat later"

"What!?"

"With Tiffany."

"Oh."

"You didn't think..?"

"No. Of course not. Never. I was just taken by surprise." Aiden flustered.

Isla saw that Aiden had always been somewhat in his younger brother's shadow when it came to the opposite sex. She imagined that witch Jenni must also have undermined his self confidence. Now he was embarrassed at his own jealous reaction.

Isla stood up and faced Aiden. He offered his lips expecting a kiss and a hug. Instead, he received a smacked face and a tweaked nose. The smack was light, the tweak not so much.

"Ow. You feral woman!" Aiden cried, rubbing his reddened nose.

"I'm yours while ever you want me and no one else will ever do." Isla scolded.

"Anyway, that didn't hurt." Aiden retorted lamely.

"Just so you know. And remember it." She said calmly turning back to her work.

"I might get you for that later." He threatened.

"Promises promises." Isla muttered.

They went about their tasks with secret smiles. Isla decided to buy a good bottle of white wine and show him just how feral she could be later. Aiden also decided to buy another bottle of Sauvignon Blanc hoping to encourage Isla's wild side later that night.

They ran into each other in the bottle shop just on dusk and couldn't wait to get back to Aiden's flat.

22

RESULTS

Aiden enquired about bringing Pitbull to see Jenni but prison administration disallowed pet visits. He was told selected inmates might be given rescue dogs to train and socialise at some stage but with no guarantee Jenni would be chosen.

The corrective services personnel Aiden spoke to were sympathetic but said surely if the pet had been happily re-homed, it might be just as well not to upset it. Aiden grasped this logic as good reason never to visit Jenni again and that burden lifted from his shoulders.

In due course, Jenni McKinstock was diagnosed with Psychopathy and Antisocial Personality Disorder. Aiden researched ASPD and had to agree his ex-wife fitted the profile. Jenni did manipulate others for her own selfish needs by using charm and intimidation.

Video footage from Isla's abduction proved Jenni was also capable of violence with no remorse, another classic trait. The diagnosis deemed her to have a personality disorder rather than a mental illness. So Jenni was housed in prison alongside other inmates.

Millicent Wendall's classification also came under Psychopathy and Antisocial Personality Disorder. Under scrutiny, the librarian lapsed out of a prim and righteous persona to engage in a rant that totally disregarded social conventions, showing her true colours. Authorities subsequently reasoned she had schemed to perpetrate the chewing gum damage and tried to lay blame on students. Failing that, she then plotted to run down children at a bus stop. Driving the different route and having the roo bar installed on her vehicle preceding the collision, suggested prior intent. The risk of re-offending to harm children was considered high. Since the former schoolteacher's assessment of ASPD did not excuse her behaviour on grounds of mental illness, she was also incarcerated with other inmates while on remand.

Jenni McKinstock and Millicent Wendall shared the same gated community. In a quirk of fate, the sexual deviant and the holier-than-thou librarian with a schizo personality, became best friends and an odd couple.

Other best friends, Ethan and Tiffany, had somewhere safe and private to indulge their passion, thanks to Isla. However, more opportunity for sex did not hasten their torrid affair to run its course. Instead, the young couple fell ever more deeply smitten.

Only as the school year came to a close, Tiffany's career ambitions forced sorrowful farewells. Ethan and Tiffany shared heartfelt vows to always cherish their time together. However, their vows still did not extend to promises of fidelity. They both knew that might not be possible and each strove to keep their relationship honest.

Tiffany Dellapinto finished high school and moved to the city to attend university. Her excitement over acceptance to university, confirmed Ethan's belief of how that would go. He knew Tiffany's keen curiosity to broaden her horizons, would lead to other guys.

Tiffany's aim to acquire an eventual Bachelor of Communication aspiring to Journalism, meant the young couple would be separated most of the time over the next few years. Tiffany's parents had plans of driving into the city to see their daughter most weekends and study commitments limited other free time.

Occasional visits home when Ethan and Tiffany could be together, dwindled.   Inevitably, the young couple drifted apart. Ethan pined for Tiffany but took comfort from casual encounters readily available from a bevy of beach girls.

Pebbles the poodle made it even easier to meet girls. The cute little dog attracted attention as unofficial mascot to the surf club. A big playpen with a portable kennel placed under the shade of a large Pandanus palm kept Pebbles safe whenever Ethan was on lifeguard duty at the club, or just out to catch a wave on a surfboard.

Ethan took his casual lovers indifferently, merely as means to an end, unable to connect with any other like he had with Tiffany. Cautious with hindsight, he now veered off the youngest girls and determined ages beforehand.

Tiffany Dellapinto dearly missed her blond and bronzed surfie boyfriend but soon became entrenched in university culture. A sense of mingling with intelligent peers appealed to her thirst for academia. To her disappointment, she found experiments of sex with the bookish set lacking. Tiffany weighed each candidate against making love with Ethan and he had an unfair advantage of being her adored and trusted first lover. Without the comparisons, Tiffany would never have known just how damn good Ethan had been.

Tiffany was smart enough to know Ethan would be having other girls and her old school friend, Chantel, revelled in announcing the truth of that. If Tiffany allowed herself to dwell on Ethan, desolation sapped her focus on studies. On the other hand, taking fleeting lovers helped as distractions, and Tiffany was ambitious.

Isla kept paying rent on her own flat to maintain independence also giving Ethan the use of it as necessary. Aiden and Isla sensed Tiffany's absence was behind Ethan's very many brief trysts with other girls. Chantel tried her hardest to win him over but Ethan rejected her blatant advances. As Tiffany's best friend at school, he considered that one to be definitely off limits. There were so many others to choose from, so Chantel had no chance.

Aiden had no advice for his younger brother other than as before to practice safe sex. With Isla back in his life, Aiden no longer envied Ethan. Rather he worried that Ethan had no steady girl anymore. Ethan envied his older brother now, for having a stable and happy relationship.

The three at Birdwhistle Solutions continued to work together well and the private eye business thrived.

Having liquidated his home and content assets, Aiden thought about renovating the flat some more. Isla had been living between her own place and his, practically out of a suitcase, doing her laundry at her flat and bringing clean clothes to wear next day after spending the night. It wasn't an ideal arrangement in the longer term, though she didn't complain.

Aiden wasn't sure if Isla was ready to move in with him permanently. But as it was, they would be pushed for space unless he could come up with a way to add at least one more room to the flat. The subject came up for discussion while on a stake out with Ethan.

They'd been out to catch yet another compensation cheat. At the end of several fruitless hours, the brothers met for coffee, giving up on finding their target that day. They had at least located the man's car which had been modified for one man wheelchair access. The number plate confirmed his ownership.

Supposedly the man took a daily constitutional in his wheelchair along shoreline paths and parkways. Since he was nowhere to be found, they assumed he'd gone elsewhere that day, perhaps visiting at a private house. Aiden and Ethan consoled themselves with coffee, cake and conversation. Ethan asked:

"Tell me Aiden, now that you're out of that dream home, will you build another?"

"I don't think so. Been there done that. It would feel like going backwards. And I've come to like living in the flat now without the commute to the office. I realise happiness doesn't equate to bricks and mortar so much as the one you're with."

"I knew Isla would be good for you. Any plans to make it more permanent?"

"I've thought about extending the flat so we can live together properly." Aiden admitted.

"Wedding bells?"

"Not game to ask. Isla is an independent type. With everything going along beautifully now, I don't know if I want to upset the apple cart."

"She can only say no. But I get that marriage wasn't great for you the first time."

Aiden thought that was the understatement of the century.

"How about you? I know you must miss Tiffany. The age difference seems a lot less the older she gets. I mean, if you were to get together again." Aiden added.

"Slim chance of that I reckon." Ethan sighed.

"You never know."

Aiden tried to sound supportive but also thought it highly unlikely Tiffany and Ethan would rekindle.

"Pretty sure that ship has sailed. Tiff's out there exploring the world. She'll find another guy. Someone better educated with better options than a surf guard trying to be a private eye sleuth but who is really just a beach bum." Ethan said sorrowfully.

"Can't blame her for spreading her wings. You've been doing a fair bit of exploring yourself, little brother."

"Guilty as charged. I've lost count now. But I haven't met another like Tiff."

"She sure is one of a kind." Aiden laughed. "That time she asked Isla if she'd been gang raped!"

"I still cringe thinking of that. Tiff's a definite motor mouth. She'll actually make a good reporter or journo. She has no self-censorship and doesn't back down."

"Then the *feeling peckish* remark. That was a classic." Aiden laughed. "I wonder what she actually meant by that?"

"I am very sure you know." Ethan replied with an eye roll.

Aiden did know. He was trying to lighten the mood.

23

SOLUTIONS

Without asking Isla if she would move in with him permanently, Aiden speculated on how to make a comfortable home for her. Asking would be a whole lot easier if he already had somewhere nice for her to move into. Aiden knew from Ethan's description that Isla's flat was no palace.

When the hardware store next door to Birdwhistles had a closing down sale, Aiden perused the goods on offer wondering what he might pick up. He'd gotten to know the owner over the years and commiserated with the fate of small businesses against mega conglomerates taking over. The hardware shop owner said he saw the writing on the wall with a huge hardware franchise coming soon to the outskirts of town. He was getting out and taking early retirement.

The upshot of Aiden's hardware shop visit; He bought the entire building, lock stock and barrel.

The brick hardware shop, of similar age and style as Birdwhistle's, extended further back to encompass a double block of land with car park and delivery access at the rear.

Aiden stood across the road viewing his twin buildings and making plans to adapt the top story of the hardware shop. Aesthetically, he wanted to mirror the other side matching the verandahs and bi-fold doors. The former hardware shopfront would become a vestibule encasing a new internal staircase. The entire second story would be gutted and rebuilt as a residence. Under the new build, space would be divided into a wet room, undercover car accommodation and storage rooms.

The large rear car park area would be landscaped into a big back yard, incorporating trees and lawn. Aiden had always loved architecture and revelled in a new project to play around with.

As a former building inspector, Aiden knew what he might be able to achieve. His first port of call was to relevant council administrators to obtain permits and advice. He still had friends in that office so the visit combined business with social catch ups. No impediment prevented rezoning the hardware property as residential.

The project began to gel nicely so Aiden shared his excitement with Ethan and Isla.

"Gather around kiddies. Round table discussion." Aiden declared.

"We don't have a round table." Ethan pointed out.

"Figure of speech."

"So?"

"I bought the hardware store next door." Aiden announced.

"You what? Bought the whole kit and caboodle?" Ethan exclaimed.

"I did. I didn't want to say anything until I had council approval. But yeah. It's been re-zoned residential so I plan to make it into a home." Aiden smiled.

Isla and Ethan looked suitably impressed and wondered aloud why and how that change could affect everything else. Ethan was quick on the uptake.

"So can I have your old flat when you move?" he asked.

"Sure. Why not. You could stop paying rent at the beach house."

"What about Pebbles? And my surfboards?"

"I plan a big backyard. We'll make it so the poodle has access to either place. Maybe we'll get another pup as company eventually. Plenty of room for surfboards under the new build and there will be a wet room too."

"Sweet." Ethan said.

"What do you think Isla?" Aiden asked somewhat shyly.

"Sounds wonderful." She smiled. Not sure how she fitted in.

"You could stop paying rent on your flat as well." Aiden dared to suggest.

"You mean... move all my stuff in with you? Like living together. Permanently?"

"If you're willing." Aiden blushed.

Isla's heart soared.

"I'm willing." She replied.

Aiden's heart also soared.

"I witnessed that." Ethan said.

Aiden and Isla would celebrate together later. But for now, they returned to their work in hand, each unable to wipe elated smiles from their faces.

"OK. Moving right along. We've still got to nab the wheelchair bloke."

Ethan made an offer, thinking Aiden might like time alone with Isla.

"I can do it alone I think."

"That would be good actually Ethan. I've got a million calls to make to start up the building project."

"Might I go with Ethan then?" Isla asked.

She liked to get out of the office for a change.

"If you like." Aiden agreed.

It would be easier with two and he didn't want to seem like the jealous boyfriend. That nose tweak had hurt quite a lot. So Ethan and Isla set out on the wheelchair stake out. Luck was on their side as they soon spotted the target trundling his wheels along a paved pathway into a nature reserve. Isla said:

"I've got an idea. Quick Ethan. Let's run around the woods and get ahead of him."

They hid amongst the dense leafy undergrowth waiting for their quarry to appear. Ethan was to video while Isla set up a trick. As the wheelchair approached she began making loud suggestive screams of pleasure and threw scanty pieces of her clothing over the bushes.

She'd worn a loose mid length dress with short sleeves that day. Her pretty matching underwear of pink and white lace ideally suited her scheme. Isla managed to undo her bra and pull it through the armholes of her dress. She slipped out of her panties, while Ethan stood guard several feet away, ready to video the wheelchair man.

Isla's pink lacy underwear landed on the pathway in front of the wheelchair while she sung: "Yes Yes Yes" in the highest soprano voice she could muster. Ethan got into the swing of it and added some of his own sound effects in deep male baritone:

"Oh Ah Fecking Hell Go Babe."

It sounded like a couple indulged in wild sex amongst the bushes. The wheelchair faker wanted to have what they were having. Or at least a rattling good perv. Pausing to look about furtively, he jumped from the wheelchair and ran up a slight incline with agile swiftness to peer into the shrubbery. Ethan got it all on candid camera.

Isla and Ethan wandered out of the thicket together, tidying their hair and smoothing their clothing. Isla retrieved her underwear from the pathway and bunched the flimsy items into the large patch pockets of her dress.

The man pretended to be catching a snooze on the grassy bank. They ignored him and walked by his empty wheelchair, apparently engrossed with each other. The compo cheat had no idea he'd been filmed, caught shamming his disability for government payouts.

When he noticed the couple high-five as they strolled away it seemed to be for the success of their rendezvous. He was sorry to have just missed all the action. Maybe he would lie in wait for another day. It had definitely sounded worth a wait.

"Will we tell Aiden how that was done?"

Ethan asked because he now felt a bit nervous about it.

"He might wonder when he hears the sound effects." Isla said.

"Surely he wouldn't think..." Ethan began.

"No. He wouldn't. We've had that conversation." Isla smiled.

"Really?"

Ethan was intrigued but didn't dare ask how that came about.

"Let's see how it goes."

Isla and Ethan arrived back at the office with reports of a successful mission. Before showing the footage to Aiden, Isla pulled her lacy bra and panties from her pockets making sure he saw them. She said matter-of-factly:

"I almost lost these. I better go upstairs and put it all back on."

"Right. This is a set up." Aiden said. "Nice try Isla. I wasn't born yesterday."

"Huh?" Ethan was confused.

Aiden and Ethan viewed the video and were discomforted by the authentic sound effects. The film also caught Isla's underwear sailing over the bushes. Ethan blushed and gulped. What seemed badly over-acted at the time, sounded a lot realer and raunchier now.

"No wonder the bloke was lured in." Aiden said.

"I'd better mute the sound in the editing." Ethan replied.

"Yes. Do. And take out the flung clothes part."

"Sure. No reason to give away our methods. Actually it was all Isla's idea."

"Really? I'm shocked." Aiden said full of heavy sarcasm.

"She's good at this." Ethan allowed.

"She's good at a lot of things."

"You lucky bastard." Ethan said.

"I know."

Ethan missed Tiffany more than ever.

24

TIFFANY & ETHAN

Tiffany Dellapinto was driven to succeed. In her final two years of uni, she stopped socialising altogether to concentrate on getting ahead. After topping her grades, she landed a position as a junior reporter and presenter with a television news team. With her outgoing personality, uninhibited nature and dry humour, Tiffany soon became a popular television personality and minor celebrity.

Ethan caught her short story segments on the news at times. Knowing this smart young woman had been his ardent lover and he had been her first ever, pulled at his heart strings.

Tiffany now wore her dark auburn hair cut in a chic blunt bob. Her heavy spectacles were replaced with contacts when on screen although she still wore them at other times.

As time went by, Tiffany Dellapinto was promoted to appear on a morning talk show as one of its guests. Everyone tuned in to view it. Ethan watched on Aiden's big screen TV sitting beside his brother and Isla, sipping sodas in the spacious living room of the new build.

Tiffany came on early, ahead of better known and more famous guests. Professional make up highlighted contours of her high cheekbones and heavy black lashes glamorised her eyes. Tiffany Dellapinto looked absolutely stunning. Isla exclaimed:

"Oh goodness. Is that the same girl? She has matured so much. She's gorgeous."

"Absolutely." Aiden agreed.

"It actually hurts me to watch her now." Ethan admitted sadly.

Tiffany's interview was all about young people making it in the big hard world and how she had worked to achieve a foot in the door. It then went into her personal life. She spoke about her seaside home town and how she missed the simple pleasures of the beach and surf.

"So you've obviously made sacrifices to get ahead Tiffany."

"Yes. Of course that was unavoidable."

"And is there a special someone in the background for you Tiffany?"

"No one special. Not since high school."

"An old flame?"

"Not that old. Hi Ethan if you're watching." She waved at the camera.

"Oh God." Ethan spilt his drink. "Did she just do that? For real?"

"You've still got it." Aiden laughed.

"He never lost it." Isla added.

The show hosts jumped on the romantic interest:

"Ooh. A mystery man in Tiffany Dellapinto's past."

"Describe this special guy Tiffany."

"Sure. Ethan is the epitome of a tall blond bronzed Aussie iron man and lifeguard."

"Of course. He would have to be at least that." The show hosts laughed together.

Behind the scenes, the television show producers made notes to follow up on this mysterious surf lifesaver Tiffany named as Ethan.

"Why don't you phone her Ethan." Isla urged.

"I don't know....and what would I say?"

"Just say you saw her on the talk show looking beautiful." Aiden suggested.

"But she knows where I am and could phone me if she wanted to."

"I bet she'd rather you made that move." Isla said. "I speak from experience."

"She'll think I'm a klutz."

Ethan held off. For the first time in his life he felt unsure of himself with a girl.

The television people approached Tiffany about doing a catch-up interview on the beach with Ethan. Tiffany told them she and her first boyfriend had been out of touch for ages. That's ok, they said, even better, maybe do a surprise visit. Catch him on duty at the surf club. Tiffany levelled with them saying Ethan could be with another girl now.

"No worries Tiffany. Human interest. Another angle on all that you gave up for your career. It will be great. Trust me." The head producer said. "Be a boon for your resume of experience and achievements too. You can't have enough exposure in this industry."

He convinced Tiffany and she began to feel excited. Though she had her doubts about the method of surprise sitting well with Ethan, she yearned to see him again.

Chantel messaged Tiffany at times, saying Ethan had a different girl just about every week. Reading between the lines, Tiffany knew her old best friend from their school days was miffed. If Chantel ever got a turn with Ethan, she'd be shouting it from the rooftops.

Tiffany sent a short message to Chantel asking if much had changed at home, like, who still hang out at the beach? Were there any new lifeguards? The reply told her there was now a club mascot, a little dog that Ethan brought along every weekend while on duty at the surf club.

Chantel told what Tiffany what she needed to know without asking outright. Ethan still attended the surf club every weekend. Surf guard duties officially demanded a presence between 8am and 6pm in hot weather. Most of them, including Ethan, went much earlier to catch some waves before the beaches became crowded.

The short television feature was contrived to catch Ethan unawares, going about his normal day, as the element of surprise drove the narrative.

Tiffany wore an emerald green beach sarong, shining with gold embroidered seashells, for her enacted impromptu visit with Ethan. She wore a brief matching bikini underneath.

The meeting, early on a Saturday morning, was hardly a secret, with a director, cameraman, film crew and overhead mic carried in tow behind Tiffany. The entourage approached Ethan as he lifted Pebbles over the playpen fence. His back was to them as he spent a couple of minutes talking to the dog and settling him in with a meaty bone to chew on.

So Ethan was taken completely by surprise. Some other surf club members realised what was about to happen but only looked on grinning in anticipation and did not warn him.

"Good morning Ethan." Tiffany called brightly in her lilting voice.

Ethan spun around. Gobsmacked.

"Tiff. Is that really you?"

"In the flesh." She smiled. "Long time no see."

Ethan took in the media invasion and made no reply.

"So who is this little pup?"

Tiffany asked about the dog to cover the fraught moment. She knew Ethan was out of his depth and felt sorry for springing the segment on him. But it was what the show called for and insisted upon.

"He's called Pebbles now. I took him on."

"Oh. Alias Pitbull the peckish little guy who ate the…"

Ethan cut her short on that. Pebbles was gnawing his bone and giving out the evil eye in case anyone planned to take it from him.

"Yep. The poodle with an attitude."

"Are you surprised to see me?"

"I am. This is a massive surprise seeing you here Tiffany. Complete with a camera crew as well."

Tiffany had the grace to look guilty. Ethan would have been overjoyed to see Tiff but the very public circumstances spoilt that. He saw it for what it was: A promo opportunity.

The slight expressions of regret on both their faces could be interpreted to fit whatever the scene called for, perhaps enhanced with appropriate music in the final rehash. Cameras zoomed in lingering on Ethan's muscular tanned body and caught every quirk of the couple's mouths and flicker of their eyes in close-ups.

Tiffany waited in vain for a hug or a kiss that never came. Ethan, never shy with girls, was not about to perform for the television crew.

As the mini drama panned out, the director knew how he'd use the cool reserve between them. It worked well into the angle of Tiffany relinquishing her old life and fabulous boyfriend in exchange for her career. The director wanted to shoot the young couple walking towards the surf together as a fitting way to wind it up. A version of riding off into the sunset. Except it was early morning and into the ocean. Ethan wore nothing but board shorts, his long blond hair tied back at the nape, remained damp from his morning in the surf. He perfectly fitted Tiffany's description of the iconic blond tanned and fit Aussie surfer.

"Lose the sarong Tiffany." Was the instruction given to the starlet by the producer.

An assistant hurried to take the sarong from Tiffany and arrange the two pieces of her brief bikini to best advantage. Ethan flushed at seeing more of the graceful body that still coloured his dreams every night, regardless of who he took to bed as temporary stand in.

Tiffany spared a peek at Ethan's face and knew she must look pretty darn good. Both young people were glad to walk away and distance themselves from close scrutiny. They made a striking couple, Tiffany's slender figure beside Ethan's strong broad-shouldered form, as they ambled down the sandy beach, in the brightening morning sunshine.

Ethan did not take Tiffany's hand but walked beside her separated by almost an arms length. Tiffany tossed her shiny hair in the slight breeze and threw her arms wide to embrace the ocean. Her gestures served to disguise the stark rejection she felt by Ethan's lack of contact.

Out of earshot of the mic Tiffany quietly apologised to Ethan, saying she thought he would never have agreed to it if he'd known beforehand. That was a certainty but he didn't say so.

"It's part of my job Ethan. I hoped you'd understand." She pleaded.

"Yes. I did twig to that Tiff. OK. Let's give them something to talk about."

Ethan swept Tiffany up, her light weight easily carried in his muscular arms. She squealed in delight, pointing her toes, crossing her ankles and placing her arms about his neck as he waded into the sea. Ethan gazed at her face with a glint in his eye. Tiffany searched his handsome features, saying to herself: "I love him, I love him, I love him. Why have I stayed away for so long?"

Carrying Tiffany, Ethan walked into the surf up to his knees, paused a moment, then dumped her in it. Tiffany landed on her backside with her long shapely legs askew, up to her chin in foamy surf. She spluttered in rage and spat sea water from her mouth.

"You mongrel." She screamed. "I just bought this bikini and it isn't meant to get wet!"

Other lifeguards and onlookers could be heard guffawing. Pebbles began to yap as well.

"Go Ethan." The other lifeguards catcalled.

The television camera kept rolling. The director signalled not to stop. This was gold. Ethan took Tiffany by the hand and helped her up from her awkward position. She stood fuming at him.

"You look even better wet and angry." He grinned.

"I hate you Ethan Birdwhistle." She seethed.

"No you don't." He replied.

Ethan wrapped his arms about her slender waist and kissed her long and soundly. Tiffany tried to keep her arms straight down by her sides in protest. If not for the cameras she might have decked him. Instead, Tiffany yielded. Returning his ardour as his kiss worked its magic. But she would not be bested. Encircling his neck and on tiptoe, she grasped his wet blond ponytail and gave it a really good hard yank.

The audience cheered.

"Ouch. That bloody hurt." Ethan yelled in pain.

Tiffany leapt away and ran gleefully further along jumping through the water. Ethan chased after her while making dire threats. As the pair cavorted in the surf laughing and splashing, Ethan triumphantly waved her green bikini top above his head.

"Cut." The director called. "I said CUT." He called louder. His subjects ignored the call.

Tiffany emerged from the sea half naked but holding her head high, to more cheers from the onlookers. She was not ashamed of her bared perky boobs and in any case, needed both hands to keep the bottom half of her bikini up, which seemed the greater priority. The showy swimsuit really was not meant to get wet. The assistant ran to Tiffany with the sarong and quickly wrapped it to cover her nudity.

Ethan felt suddenly ashamed for pulling Tiffany's top off and hated that all the other guys had ogled her naked breasts. He presented the green strip of wet cloth to her in apology. Tiffany draped it around his neck and used it to draw him to her for another long kiss. Her bikini pants fell down around her ankles as she did so. Tiffany stepped free of the sodden bikini bottoms, and the long-suffering assistant whisked them away to more cheers from the surf club. It was difficult for Tiffany to feign anger since it was the most fun she'd had since leaving home for uni. Ethan shared the sentiment. No words were needed to confirm it.

"Let's get out of here." Ethan whispered in her ear.

"Where can we go?"

"I've got Aiden's old flat now at the office building."

"Perfect. And you still taste so good." She teased.

"Don't start. Not yet." Ethan blushed.

Ethan went back to the club house where his mates were still gawking. He collected Pebbles for return to Aiden's backyard as he hoped not to get back to the beach that day.

"Change of plans fellas." He told the other clubhouse members.

"Yeah. We can see that something has come up." One of the wags commented.

Ethan wrapped a beach towel around his waist. Tiffany grabbed her bag from the crew vehicle and told them she'd be back by Monday.

"Don't you want to see the proofs? It might go on tonight you know."

"I'm torn." She laughed, rolling her eyes.

"Half your luck." Her female assistant drawled.

The episode was aired on television that Saturday night as a 'feel good' news story. A news anchor narrated the voice over. Producers allowed a tag of 'Tiff Does It Tuff' but disallowed 'Tuff Titty'. Given the time slot, Tiffany's nude bits were blurred but left little to the imagination. Aiden and Isla, at home relaxing, happened to catch the upbeat news story and were amazed to see Ethan with Tiffany on the beach. It was the first they knew of Tiffany's visit. Pebbles wandered in and demanded attention. Isla ran outside to peer across to the other verandah next door but could see or hear nothing. They had to be there as the bi-fold doors were open and Ethan always shut them if he was going out.

"She must be with Ethan at the flat."

"Explains why Pebbles is back here with us."

"Do you think we should invited them over?" Isla asked.

"Too soon. Maybe tomorrow. They won't welcome interruptions tonight."

"No. You're right. OK. Let's do that beef roast. I'll take it out of the freezer now. We could do it with a traditional Yorkshire pudding. And brown onion gravy." Isla planned.

"Roast vegetables, spuds, pumpkin and sweet potato. And steamed green beans." Aiden added, checking the pantry and 'fridge.

"Let's make jelly and custard for afters." Isla enthused.

They rarely entertained and looked forward to having the younger couple over for Sunday dinner. Aiden messaged his brother to let him know they were expected.

The following day, at Sunday dinner, Ethan and Tiffany exclaimed over how much trouble Aiden and Isla had gone to.

"Wow. This is wonderful." Tiffany said. "I haven't had a good home cooked meal like this for longer than I can recall."

"I'll do it justice that's for sure." Ethan said sitting in at the table.

"We figured you'd need the calories after a marathon." Aiden smiled artfully.

"Aha. You never forget." Ethan laughed.

"Huh?" Tiffany questioned it.

"Tell you later." Isla promised.

Tiffany had hardly arrived back in the city than she was hit with an almost $300 fine for wilful exposure. The television people made a big deal of it as the priceless publicity added to the value of their youngest personality. Tiffany Dellapinto rose to the status of hot property and welcomed a huge hike in salary as other offers came her way.

The resultant fine for her nudity went viral on social media. Although some 'clothes optional' beaches exist in Australia, Tiffany exposed her breasts on a family beach and in the one state that had no nudist beaches. Detractors complained that nudity attracted lewd behaviour. Some went so far as to use the kissing between Ethan and Tiffany as proof. However, the far greater majority laughed and ridiculed the wowsers. Aiden and Isla were suddenly glad they'd not run home naked after their gritty lovemaking session on the shore. They'd have no excuse if they'd been caught.

Ethan went public with the lie that Tiffany's top had come loose in the surf. Footage could not dispute this, as amongst all the splashing and waves, it was impossible to tell. Tiffany backed Ethan up saying she was grateful he'd managed to retrieve her green bikini bra as it was one of her favourites.

"Now we're partners in crime." Tiffany laughed.

"I'd like to be partners in everything." Ethan told her earnestly.

Tiffany's fine was converted to a caution and the unedited version of her 'lewd' act appeared on a late night program. Ethan recorded it and the couple watched it together during her next visit.

"Are my boobs bigger than you remember?" She had to ask.

"Nope. Much smaller." Ethan teased.

"They are not! They're a lot bigger. I've at least got a good handful now." Tiffany retorted.

"Then why did you ask? Is anything of mine bigger now?"

"Just your ego."

Ethan proposed to Tiffany on her third visit to his flat as they sat out on the verandah in the twilight, enjoying the cool of evening. He went down on one knee and was able to offer a fabulous diamond engagement ring. Since Ethan stopped paying rent on the beach house, he had saved heaps. Tiffany's eyes lit up as her dearest wish came true.

"Oh my god Ethan. Yes yes yes. I love you."

"I love you too."

Tears of happiness sparkled in their eyes.

Aiden and Isla came out onto their own verandah to sit in the sea breeze.

"Guess what?" Tiffany called over the short space between the twin buildings.

Isla nudged Aiden and said in a low voice:

"Pretend we don't know."

They'd been just coming outside with drinks when Ethan knelt and offered the ring. Quickly drawing back to give them privacy, Isla and Aiden peeped between curtains to be delighted by the outcome.

"I want what he's getting." Aiden whispered behind the curtains.

"Tiffany?"

"Very funny. Guess again."

"Well? Have you guessed?" Tiffany waved her left hand, flashing the diamond.

"You bought a new ring?" Aiden asked trying for an innocent tone.

"No. Ethan proposed and I said yes."

"Actually she said yes yes yes." Ethan beamed.

"I think I've heard her practising that. Sound carries on a still night." Isla whispered.

"That means they've heard us as well." Aiden whispered back.

"I'm not that loud. What? I am not. Ok from now on we close the bi-folds."

"I didn't say anything." Aiden grinned.

Aiden beckoned the younger couple over.

"Congratulations you two! Come over for a celebratory drink."

"I'll order pizza." Ethan said. "What sort do you fancy?"

"Pepperoni. Hawaiian. Margarita." Everyone wanted something different.

Ethan ordered them all. The brothers and their girls talked and joked into the night, drinking wine and eating pizza, knowing it didn't get much better than this.

25

WEDDINGS

Ethan and Tiffany expected to have an extended engagement due to her career and work commitments. She wanted to eventually move into the flat above the office permanently rather than anywhere else. The place was so convenient for Ethan and her city accommodation arrangements were temporary and nothing she would miss. The younger couple also liked having Aiden and Isla as close neighbours and the share of Pebbles as their family dog. In the interim, Aiden and Ethan worked out how to enlarge the flat to include another spacious bedroom with walk-in wardrobe for Tiffany's enormous array of clothing and shoes. Tiffany wanted to take Ethan's name when they married but would keep her personal Dellapinto brand of maiden name in public life. Lunching together one weekend, the four tabled surname variations. Hyphenated surnames were out as being too ostentatious. They all winced at Tiffany Dellapinto-Birdwhistle as a choice. Tiffany chortled:

"Ha ha. How about Isla Tickle-Birdwhistle. That isn't much better."

"Tiff, you can't speak for Isla." Ethan reminded quietly.

He was well aware of his brother's doubts. Tiffany retorted:

"Aiden and Isla are as good as married now. They're whatchamacallit. De facto. I'm saying that counts legally and morally. Of course, Aiden might not want to share the hallowed name of Birdwhistle."

Tiffany raised her eyebrows to her future brother-in-law. Aiden jumped in automatically:

"I'd love for Isla to take my name. If she were willing."

Aiden reddened. Aware he'd laid his cards on the table with his off-the-cuff reply. He knew the concept of freedom was paramount to Isla and she might baulk at being tied down, even figuratively. Isla spoke up to cover her own blushes:

"Why are you all talking about me as if I'm not here?"

Tiffany picked up on 'willing' and pushed in her pedantic way to pin Aiden down.

"Willing for what exactly Aiden?"

Ethan chided gently:

"Babe. Not so much of the in-depth interviewing. OK?"

Tiffany blew him a kiss with a wink.

Aiden had taken the initiative, bared his soul and put pressure on Isla. Just what he'd tried to avoid. Yet, he dearly wanted to put a ring on Isla's finger. Two rings in fact. On losing their parents, Aiden inherited a classic pair of family heirlooms, a vintage plain gold wedding band and a beautiful matching engagement ring set with a diamond and rubies. Nestled in a velvet case, they were kept in a bank safe deposit box. He knew the rings must be over 90 years old by now, but he had not looked at them in years. Aiden had once shown the rings to Jenni McKinstock before proposing marriage, but she deemed the design too old fashioned and outdated. Now, and at the time, Aiden was enormously relieved not to have made the mistake of offering the precious family jewellery to Jenni. Instead, he bought a huge diamond solitaire engagement ring for Jenni.

Aiden had no idea what his ex-wife ever did with all the jewellery he'd given her, and he didn't care. He'd swept it aside as collateral damage, all relegated to the unhappy messy past Aiden strove to forget. He had never visited Jenni again but heard from Dougall Grimslade that she was known to be in a lesbian relationship with the former librarian, Millicent Wendall. Aiden felt some ease of his own sadness that Jenni at least had someone in prison, while knowing he shouldn't have cared less, after the wretchedness she'd caused him.

On the opposite end of the scale, Isla brought immense joy into Aiden's life. He loved her and wanted to marry, but so far none of his hints had returned any response from Isla. Now Tiffany had put them both on the spot, once again finding an elephant in the room, prattling on undeterred:

"Well. I'm just wondering if Isla and Aiden will make it official."

Isla smiled. Tiffany represented the pesky little sister she'd always wanted.

"Tiff, I promise you'll be among the first to know."

"Don't worry about stealing our thunder Isla, we won't tie the knot for months. But hey! I just thought of a brilliant idea. What if we have a double wedding? It could be on the beach. We could wear bikinis Isla, and wedding veils. And have a celebrant who dresses up like Neptune."

Tiffany raved on and began pacing the room in her enthusiasm. Isla laughed. She loved the incorrigible way Tiffany always leapt in, madcap as ever.

"You have a great imagination Tiff. What would the guys wear at this hypothetical double beach wedding?"

"Um...I know...board shorts and bow ties. They'd go bare chested of course. Have to make the female population jealous don't we."

Aiden and Ethan preened and puffed out their chests.

"Me Tarzan." Ethan said.

"King of the apes." Aiden laughed.

Aiden felt encouraged that Isla did not discount the whole wedding idea out of hand. That night, neither brought up the wedding conversation as if that subject was taboo although it was foremost on both their minds. Isla felt elated when Aiden said he'd love her to take his name. She hoped he might seriously propose someday instead of merely hinting he wanted her forever. But Isla knew Aiden's hard first marriage took some getting over and she must never apply force. 'Let sleeping dogs lie' she cautioned herself with the old adage. Sleepless that night, Aiden decided to go to the bank next morning and retrieve the heirloom rings. The plan sent butterflies flitting about in his stomach. He got up and went for an antacid tablet.

"Are you alright?" Isla asked sleepily.

"Yes. Just a bit of indigestion. Too much pizza. Go back to sleep sweetheart."

The following morning, Ethan drove Tiffany back to the city and would spend a few nights there. Aiden and Isla could handle any urgent work and put off the rest until Ethan returned. The place now seemed unnaturally quiet without the younger couple.

While Isla took Pebbles for an afternoon walk, Aiden prepared his best recipe again, the ginger flavoured stir fry with seafood, vegetables and steamed white rice. A bottle of Sauvignon Blanc chilled in the fridge. He set a romantic table with candles. Isla bustled in with Pebbles ready to prepare his night feed. She stopped in surprise at the nice dining table Aiden had set and the food preparations he was busily working at.

"Am I being spoilt tonight?" She smiled.

"I hope in a good way." Aiden replied.

Isla smiled to herself with the notion Aiden must be feeling up for some intense loving later. She happily went about feeding Pebbles and fluffing up his bedding in the dog basket. The poodle had pet door access to the backyard but slept indoors in the foyer under the staircase. Isla showered, spritzed some perfume on the nape of her neck and put on a slinky negligee. When she emerged, Aiden tossed the stir fry ingredients into a hot wok. He was fussy about not overcooking it.

"Wow. You look lovely. It won't be long. Why don't you pour the wine?"

"This is like the first time you cooked for me. Same delicious food. Same wine."

Aiden had planned it that way. He had the heirloom engagement ring in his pocket. Having tried in on his own little finger, he was sure it would slip easily onto Isla's ring finger.

Reminded of the first time Aiden cooked for her, Isla reminisced to herself that she'd seduced him for the first time that night. Oh what a night. A dreamy smile flirted about her lips. She had an inkling Aiden was angling for a replay and chose some romantic background music. They enjoyed the meal in peace and Isla thanked him for it as they both cleared the table.

"Shall we finish the wine out on the verandah?" Isla asked.

"I'd rather sit on the sofa. The moon is rising. I hope that's a good omen."

"You're being fanciful tonight. That moon is setting a very romantic scene."

"I ordered it especially. I'd love to give you the moon and the stars Isla."

That was a curiously whimsical statement from Aiden who had already given her so much. Isla wondered if his emotion stemmed from insecurity and did her best to reassure him, saying seriously:

"All I want is you Aiden. You are my moon and my stars."

In a now or never moment, Aiden knelt on both knees before Isla and took her left hand. Isla held her breath as he slipped the vintage diamond and ruby ring on her finger. Isla didn't know what to make of the surprise. Was he giving her a gift of jewellery? She was afraid to imagine Aiden meant to propose marriage. But he had placed the ring on the proper finger.

"Isla, this ring is a precious family heirloom. It's been in my family for generations. I would be honoured if you accept it as a symbol of my love."

"Oh my god. It's absolutely beautiful... Are you sure I'm worthy to wear it?"

"Of course you are. More than worthy Isla. Meeting you saved my miserable life. I was sinking fast before you came along. Now I couldn't imagine living without you. And now that I've burdened you with all that responsibility, maybe you won't turn me down when I tell you there is a matching gold wedding band to that engagement ring."

Isla felt her heart almost burst as hope dawned.

"Please say you will marry me Isla."

"Oh Aiden. Yes. A million times yes my darling. Oh I didn't expect this. You've made all my dreams come true."

They hugged and cried and kissed. They sat up talking for hours, too excited for bed. Isla let the reality sink in:

"Wow. I'm going to be a Mrs. Birdwhistle. Isla Birdwhistle. IB. I lose my IT status. I know it doesn't change that much about our lifestyle, but I feel like I've finally become a grown up."

"Then let's do what grown-ups do to celebrate." Aiden replied. "Time for bed."

26

BESIDE THE SEA

When told of Isla and Aiden becoming engaged, Tiffany screamed in delight and Ethan grinned from ear to ear. The sudden relief and joy Ethan felt for his brother, underscored the worry he had long kept inside. Before Isla came along, Ethan had been terrified of what Aiden might do as a result of his deep bouts of depression.

Tiffany was to take up a position as weather girl on a nearby regional station. At the same time, she was hired for a role in a chic flick soapie that largely relied on bikini girls and surfer boys with little necessity for acting experience. The show was to be mainly filmed on a beach just a little further down the coast. This production meant Tiffany could move in with Ethan much sooner than expected. Tiffany exclaimed:

"Will we do the double wedding thing? On the beach?"

Isla tried to be practical:

"I don't know. What would your parent's think? Won't they want all the traditional thing? And won't you be up for a celebrity wedding as well?"

Tiffany laughed off Isla's concerns:

"Our wedding is our call, and we don't want a lot of expense or fuss and publicity. And believe me, my parents will be happy to see me married off in any way especially after the naked titties episode. And they love Ethan.

Always have. Of course they didn't know he nailed me at fifteen while I was still in school."

Ethan exonerated himself:

"Hey! I didn't know you were only fifteen at the time. You looked at least eighteen. And let's be accurate. I think you were the one who did all the seducing Tiffany."

Tiffany smiled reminiscently.

"You were so easy Ethan; I don't recall much resistance. Was Aiden easy Isla?"

"Yep. Candy from a baby." Isla grinned.

"Hey! Stop talking about me like I'm not here." Aiden blushed repeating one of Isla's retorts.

Isla and Tiffany high fived and giggled together like naughty sisters.

"Come on. What do you all think about a double beach wedding?" Tiffany pushed.

Aiden replied looking at Isla with eyebrows raised in question. He didn't care how they did it and he certainly wasn't averse to a fun wedding.

"Well. We all love the beach."

Isla replied:

"I wouldn't want a church wedding. And the beach would be far nicer than a registry office. But do you two really want to share your special day?"

"We'd love to make it a family thing." Ethan assured her.

Ethan really did want Isla to be included as much as possible. He would also like the moral support of taking the leap of faith beside Aiden.

"I reckon the surf club might let us use the function room for a party after."

"So are we on for it?" Tiffany clapped her hands.

Isla thought about it and admitted:

"I'm just not too sure about me going in a bikini. Or the Neptune outfit idea."

"OK. No drama. Lose the Neptune outfit. That would be up to whoever we get as celebrant anyway."

Aiden piped up:

"I actually know a lady wedding celebrant. And before anyone asks, she did not do my first marriage. If she had I would never suggest her."

"Who is she?"

"Pebble's breeder. The lady who called him Frou Frou. Her name is Francis Funicular. So she calls all her pups with F names."

"You called Pebbles an F name too Aiden, when he chewed up your sneaker."

"Beside the point."

Tiffany intervened, she began organising and taking notes.

"OK. Aiden gets the celebrant. Now let's talk about outfits."

"I loved the beach sarong outfit you wore that time." Isla said.

"That's a great idea. Beachy without being too immodest. What do you guys want to wear?"

"I'm easy." Ethan shrugged. "So am I." Aiden agreed.

"We've established that." Tiffany laughed. "Both absolute pushovers."

Isla and Tiffany made a meal of the joke but neither Aiden nor Ethan minded. They were pushovers for their sweetheart fiancés and glad to know they were desirable and loved.

Complementary wedding outfits were decided upon without being exactly the same. The guys would wear lightweight summer suits with open necked shirts to match their bride's sarong. Isla chose cool mint green and Tiffany opted for sunny yellow. They bought three each of the sarongs and had the guys' shirts made out of the spares.

Instead of veils, circular wedding crowns with greenery and Frangipani flowers suited both outfits and the girls loved them. They all liked the idea of going barefoot and the girls were going shopping to look for shell anklets.

There would be no one else in the wedding party, the rings would be in the guys' jacket pockets. Tiffany's father, a keen camera buff, would be happily occupied snapping photographs. No one said it, but giving Tiffany away in the traditional wedding sense, would be like shutting the stable door after the horse had escaped. They all agreed on including the poodle.

"We could put Pebbles in some sort of little jacket or special collar. Aiden can you ask his breeder about that when you see her?"

"Sure. And I'll take Pebbles with me for the visit. He was three months old when I bought him so he might remember Francis."

And so they went ahead and made wedding day plans. Pouring over long-range weather forecasts, they arrived at a suitable date and agreed to time it to begin early, around nine in the morning, knowing the breeze usually picked up after then and might kick up stinging sand flurries. Being a public beach, a crowd of onlookers would probably gather but they felt confident people would respect the occasion and not intrude or misbehave.

"How about we make it to be no gifts but donations to Surf Life Saving Australia welcome?" Ethan suggested.

"I'm happy for that" Aiden agreed and so did the girls.

"I know my parents will give us something." Tiffany said. "But I'll explain so it can be separate and private. Not on the day or at least not at the venue."

"Sorted." Ethan said. "Who said wedding planning was difficult and expensive?"

"We should be right for enough photographs." Aiden said.

"Yes. Believe me, there will be plenty of photos with the TV crew and newspapers. Also, I know my dad will be in his glory using the excuse to dust off his beloved Nikon. We can ask some of the club members to take happy snaps as well." Tiffany suggested.

"I'm sure they will anyway." Ethan replied.

The surf club agreed to use of the function room for a private luncheon after the ceremonies, with catering done by the club as a fund raiser. The wedding breakfast would be by invitation but only Tiffany had any close family. Aiden had a tricky question for Isla:

"Isla. Just say no if you're uncomfortable with this...but I'd like to invite Dougall Grimslade and his wife of course."

"I'm over all that Aiden. Of course you must invite the Grimslades."

Isla wasn't altogether over it all but knew Aiden saw the detective as a kind of father figure and could never deny him that. Isla had another couple in mind to invite:

"Actually, I would like to invite Dulcy Vestige and her other half as well. She spent a lot of time with me in hospital, far beyond what duty demanded, more like a friend. Since Dougall is invited, I think Dulcy should be as well."

"Good idea." Aiden and the others agreed.

Isla and Tiffany poured over wedding invitation styles and made lists. None of Ethan's club members could be left out, so with their plus ones, the venue would be packed. They decided on a mixed grill menu with a variety of salads. The loose seating arrangement had the four newlyweds and Tiffany's parents together at one table with a tiered wedding cake as centrepiece.

Tiffany's mother had long dreamed of making the cake and had vats of dried fruits already steeping in rum at home in her kitchen. Other guests could choose their own places at the long trestle tables, in a party style atmosphere. Speeches to be informal, anyone invited to contribute, humour and ribaldry likely, knowing the surf club company.

Tasked with engaging the celebrant, Aiden went back to the poodle breeder, Francis Funicular, taking Pebbles for a visit as well.

Francis, a large and jolly lady, was absolutely delighted to be chosen as celebrant for a double wedding on the beach. Surprisingly, she seemed to know Pebbles right away even though the silver poodle had been jet black as a baby. Possibly the lady remembered Aiden and the puppy he'd chosen for his first wife. Tactfully, Francis did not query the second marriage or what had happened to Aiden's first wife.

People and their shifting relationships did not concern Francis greatly. The poodle she bred, raised and carefully placed at three months old, held her avid attention.

"Frou Frou! Oh my darling baby boy."

Francis gathered Pebbles to her ample bosom. Pebbles wriggled ecstatically and licked his breeder's face with his little pink tongue.

"I think he remembers you."

Aiden exclaimed in surprise. Or, he thought, perhaps the poodle just knew a true dog lover when he met one.

"Of course he does. Don't you Frou Frou? Poodles are very smart you know."

Aiden declined telling Francis that Frou Frou had been call-named Pitbull. He imagined she wouldn't think much of that tag.

Within a few days, Francis came to the beach to survey the location and how the ceremony might be best orchestrated. With all four participants present, they decided on separate short vow rituals with Aiden and Isla, as the older pair, going first. Then they would stand aside for Ethan and Tiffany. Each pair would be pronounced man and wife after taking their vows, then 'You May Kiss Your Brides' done together in a joint celebration.

The celebrant wanted to be holding Frou Frou Pebbles during the kissing part to be sure her homebred poodle was foremost in the photo shoots. She loved that he would be shared as a family dog between the two couples, as neighbours in their twin buildings.

Francis preferred wearing a flowing ceremonial cape to add drama to her role. She would remove the cape later to reveal a colourful Hawaiian style muumuu dress in keeping with the beach theme. The celebrant used a large portable gazebo at dog shows and suggested it for the beach weddings, to define the space. Out of a large selection of coats in the breeder's dog wardrobe, a little doggy t-shirt in a tuxedo design was found most suitable for poodle wedding wear. So nitty-gritty details for celebrations began to gel nicely.

It was impossible to keep the weddings secret. Tiffany had to advise her superiors of her upcoming nuptials. Following the surprise beach segment of Tiffany meeting Ethan again and how that turned out, the national news channel scheduled in their wedding day. They planned to recap with the original story and eke it out to conclude with a happy ever after marriage on the same beach. A double wedding made it even more newsworthy. In terms of feel-good news, it was gripping stuff.

Local newspaper reporters planned to be present, learning of the occasion when the Shire Council approved requests for media vehicles to park on the beach, for the one-time event.

A TV preview repeated footage of Ethan dropping Tiffany into the surf and began airing with a swatch patched in, of the celebrant walking the beach with the two couples as they made plans.

27

FLIPPED

Inside prison walls, inmates caught the double wedding promotion on a communal television set. It was of very little interest to anyone except Jenni McKinstock and Millicent Wendall.

Jenni choked on the fact that Aiden chose Isla as his second wife. Knowing Troy had once relished having Isla, she hated 'that bitch' with an insane passion. Jenni held no fondness for Ethan either. To her mind, her ex-brother-in-law was another pathetic drip since he'd ignored her sexual advances in his teen years. She could have taught Ethan a thing or two. *His loss.* Jenni told herself the lack of talent must run in families, and it was her misfortune to be saddled with the Birdwhistles during her best years.

Tiffany did not escape hatred; she represented all that Millicent despised. The girl had been one of her gum-chewing past pupils in high school and the loudest, most rudely vocal about standing up for student rights.

"That stinking little creep Tiffany Dellapinto. Trust her to make good. Probably slept her way to the top." Millicent seethed.

"We've got four weeks before their weddings to work this out. I'd rather go out with a bang than spend years in this place." Jenni McKinstock told her prison mate.

Millicent Wendall agreed. She adored being sheltered under Jenni's wing when other inmates avoided the scar faced woman. Most were in fear of Jenni's evil eyed stares.

As the alpha in the relationship, Jenni used a series of mental manipulations that led Millicent ever deeper under her control. When Millicent consented to having her head shaved, Jenni knew she had the older woman totally enthralled in their cult of two.

Millicent bloated up with weight gain in prison. She disgusted Jenni. Nevertheless, the librarian could be put to use when necessary so Jenni tolerated her clinging neediness.

Prison guards overlooked lesbian behaviour as long as it did no harm to others. Jenni and Millicent were careful to obey rules and cause no trouble, in order to be deemed as low risk inmates. The pair frequently worked side by side outside prison walls, in community programs aligned with the Women's Correctional Centre. It wasn't impossible to abscond, and Jenni and Millicent did so when the time was right.

The prisoners' escape went unnoticed for more than an hour. Jenni had previously convinced three other women to run away at the same time, to spread efforts of police to track them. The other three split up. One jumped on a freight train at a siding and was never seen again, another hotwired a car and took off towards the outback only to be caught by a traffic cop. The third escapee hitched a ride with a truck driver who exacted the popular payment method at an overnight truck stop and decided to keep the desperate young female for a while. She was never recaptured but stayed with the old truckie and had several children by him.

The librarian's vehicle had been left with her sixty-nine-year-old mother, who, if she drove it at all, would only be for local shopping. The small SUV was kept in a garage and Millicent knew her mother always hid keys on a ledge above.

Millicent was certain her mother wouldn't hear her drive out and not even notice the car missing until next pension day. All this information had been discussed with Jenni in formulating their elaborate plans. Millicent took the car in broad daylight as well as a couple of her mother's baggy house dresses from the clothesline. She spied her mother through the sitting room window, knitting in her lap, asleep in front of some daytime soapie on television. Millicent had to shake off a fleeting nostalgia for her carefree childhood.

Compelled by her worshipped companion and craving revenge on Tiffany, Millicent overcame her moment of weakness. She drove the car out and picked Jenni up along the way, where she had hidden in a public toilet block.

Jenni insisted that Millicent do all the driving and directed her to a remote camping grounds in the wooded hinterland hills high above the beach. The location was not far from the estate where Aiden built their luxury home.

Darkness had fallen by the time the women arrived at the site. Only a few campfires glowed some distance away near a flowing creek. Jenni surmised they were probably fishing parties or drinking parties. The two pastimes often went hand in hand.

The fugitives had hidden food from their prison lunches amongst their clothing and rationed this between themselves, keeping a couple of bread rolls for breakfast. Jenni had planned the location knowing drinking water and public amenities were nearby.

It was a stroke of luck that Millicent thought of snatching her mother's dresses. They changed in case anyone noticed their government issue clothing but no one came near them. They found slivers of soap left in the showers, refreshed themselves and used the prison garb to towel off, later hiding it in the car. They were cagey enough not to leave the prison clothing where searchers might discover it. Having so little, nothing would be discarded in case it came in useful again.

They would sleep in the vehicle without too much discomfort as the backs on the rear seats folded down flat into the cargo space. Millicent's mother had draped hand crocheted afghan rugs over the car seats. The hinterland nights grew cool under dense mists that rolled in from the ocean, and the woollen rugs were appreciated.

Sunglasses and a scarf were found in the glove box along with a few dollars in spare change. The next day, when the double beach wedding was scheduled to take place, Millicent would cover her shaved head with the scarf and Jenni would wear the sunglasses.

News reports had described in detail how the weddings would take place on the beach below the surf club. Jenni knew the area very well. She felt empowered with a manic notion that the scheme to run down the wedding party was *meant to be*. The idea arose from Millicent's attempt to ram the schoolkids at the bus stop. The librarian obsessed over how she would time it better given a second chance and not miss a next time. Now a chance to demonstrate what she could do, was to be granted.

The desperados aimed to kill or severely injure the wedding couples and speed away in the aftershock of wreaking so much havoc. Any sane person would see holes in their plan to escape during the mayhem, but rational thought was not a strong point of the obsessive and vindictive pair.

The utter convenience of having the four despised marks all together outdoors on the beach boosted Jenni's mania. When fate provided Millicent Wendall and her vehicle complete with roo bar as tools, Jenni was convinced either some god or the devil were on her side. She didn't mind which.

As the driver, Millicent would shoulder most blame if they were caught. At very least, in that worst case scenario they'd have the satisfaction of revenge and really be no worse off than before. Back in prison. Same old same old.

Jenni felt destined to succeed and did not seriously contemplate failure. She planned to ditch Millicent and her car immediately after fleeing the beach. Jenni counted her chances going alone as far better, even quite good. So easy when you had the smarts and the know-how, she thought smugly.

It would definitely be a great relief to be rid of her loyal follower's cloying dependence and disgusting body. Jenni knew stupid Millicent would be easily apprehended in an ensuing car chase.

Jenni could double back though the hinterland scrub and break into homes in her old neighbourhood where most residents were retired seniors. Jenni knew, at any given time, a few houses were likely to be unoccupied with the owners away on their endless cruises, making the most of their golden years.

28

BEACH WEDDINGS

S unrise burnt the sea mist away and the wedding morning broke to perfect weather, fine and calm, not too humid just a few snowy white clouds streaked the clear blue sky on high.

Very early, Aiden and Ethan set up Francis's white canopied shade gazebo by the shore, the legs weighted with water filled base pods. Sea grass matting covered the floor area, and a small heavy table and chair furnished the space for Francis to use while waiting for the two wedding couples.

The lady celebrant arrived well ahead of time, draped some decorative tulle and greenery around the gazebo frame and covered the table with a white and gold cloth, weighted at the corners, although the morning was calm and still. The humble gazebo soon morphed into a charming bower to receive the brides and grooms.

As her duties commanded, all paperwork and licences had been taken care of by the celebrant. Unless parties asked for a bible, Francis used a white covered folder with a gold tassel to read from as a prop with the couples' chosen vows printed out in case her memory needed jogging. Though Francis Funicular rehearsed her performance well and had yet to make errors in her wedding orations.

Almost time, a handful of guests waited under the shade of Pandanus palms or sat on benches under the surf club verandah amongst the lifeguards. The poodle had been clipped and shampooed at the dog groomers and dressed in his lightweight tux t-shirt. He was being minded in his usual surf club playpen, to be led down to Francis as the couples arrived.

The two couples arrived together, waved cheerily to everyone, and walked hand in hand towards Francis who now stood ready under the gazebo. Tiffany's best school friend, Chantel, carried the poodle to Francis who looped his leash over her arm. Chantel went back to join the other guests and Frou Frou Pebbles sat happily on the sea grass matting, beside his breeder, apparently enjoying his role as a guest of honour.

A few utility 4WD vehicles parked on the beach, well back, had media cameras set inside the open tubs to afford advantage shots over the heads of curious onlookers.

Francis began the ceremony with a short introductory speech before Aiden and Isla stepped forward to take their vows and be pronounced man and wife. Everyone including the beach going onlookers, clapped. Then Ethan and Tiffany stepped forward and the ritual was repeated to another round of applause.

Francis declared 'You May Kiss Your Brides' and both couples obliged, the guys lifting their brides off their feet. The ocean provided a crescendo, a fitting adjunct at this point as louder cheers, whistles and clapping, were accompanied by a sudden surging surf.

Pebbles did not like being close to the rougher crashing waves that spattered them all with flecks of foam. Francis picked him up and snuggled him under her cape.

All eyes were on the happy couples. No one noticed the insidious SUV creeping slowly in behind the media vehicles. Jenni could hardly contain her excitement:

"Buckle up. This might be bumpy."

"This is it. I love you Jenni." Millicent proclaimed sincerely.

Jenni came up with a reply meant to encourage Millicent:

"Then give it your best shot, Wonder Woman."

Millicent was overcome. Jenni had never called her Wonder Woman before. She gritted her teeth, revved the motor and lined up set to torpedo the gazebo.

Just as the happy newlyweds turned to face their audience, hands joined and arms raised together in jubilation, the small 4x4 gunned across the hard wet sand heading straight for them. People gasped and screamed as it seemed the five under the gazebo would certainly all be run down and crushed.

"Stop! Look out!"

Francis impulsively stepped in front of the four young people and held up her hand in a stop signal. Not that it could have prevented the disaster but with that attempt, the poodle wriggled free from Francis's cape.

Frou Frou Pitbull Pebbles dropped to the sand, yapping aggressively at the onslaught. In the final split second before impact, Jenni caught sight of her beloved dog.

"NO!"

Jenni shrieked, face contorted, stretching her scar tissue. She wrenched the steering wheel hard aside from Millicent's white knuckled grasp and the deadly mission was aborted.

The vehicle slewed sideways and wallowed into a patch of softer sand slurry where children had been digging a moat around a sandcastle the day before. Teetering on an invisible axis, momentum versus gravity flipped the car over to land upside down in knee deep backwash, the wheels still spinning.

Steam rose from the car as waves broke over it. The angry ocean threw huge breakers that splashed over the vehicle. Despite the car windows being wound tightly up, seawater infiltrated the cabin. The occupants could be made out through the foam washed windscreen. Alive.

Upside down, Jenni and Millicent found themselves helplessly trapped by seat belts as salty water rose to cover their wide screaming mouths and their eyes bulging in fear. As water level increased covering their noses and mouths, the women flailed their arms about to no avail. Panicked, neither were able to release their seat belts.

Ethan and Aiden were first to rush into the sea but found it impossible to open the car doors. Isla ran into the surf with Francis's heavy chair above her head and smashed the windscreen before being knocked over by strengthening waves. With access through the broken windscreen, Ethan and Aiden immediately set about unclipping the seat belts.

Tiffany ran to Isla's aid but both brides were dumped by big breakers, tumbling them over and over before their bridegrooms pulled them to safety.   A number of lifeguards who had sped down the beach to help, pulled the car driver and passenger, coughing and choking up onto the beach.

"Shit." Ethan panted. "How on earth?"

"It's Jenni." Aiden rasped.

"I know. I recognised her."

Dougall Grimslade and Dulcy Vestige hurried down across the expanse of sand as the wedding couples collapsed, wet and bedraggled, on the beach, their wedding finery ruined.

Dougall had already called it in. Sounds of distant sirens heralded the imminent arrival of police and ambulances. A tow truck got there before them.

"One of them is Jenni. I don't know the other one." Aiden told Dougall and Dulcy.

"She looks a bit like grumpy old Millicent my old school teacher." Tiffany offered.

Ethan said:

"Could she be the librarian? She looks different to how I remember her."

Dougall Grimslade confirmed:

"It is Millicent Wendall. The chewing gum nutter. We knew those two escaped custody yesterday but did not expect them to turn up here. Are you all ok?"

Aiden replied:

"I think so. I can't believe Jenni is still haunting me. I am so very sorry Isla. And Tiff and Ethan. Your day is ruined too."

Tiffany put a positive edge to it:

"Be some interesting photos from this wedding that's for sure."

The others were quick to assure Aiden it was not his fault. Isla squeezed his hand and shrugged with a smile to lighten the regret. He raised her hand and kissed the matching gold heirloom rings he felt so proud to have her wear. The rings were a perfect fit for Isla, so fortunately had not come off to be lost in the wild surf.

"Hello you." He smiled. "My beautiful wife."

"Hello yourself my handsome husband. I must look like a ship-wreck."

"Never. More like a beautiful mermaid. You've even got a piece of seaweed in your hair."

Everyone watched as ambulances arrived and medicos rushed to the aid of the stricken women stretched out on the sand, surrounded by lifeguards and police.

"They might have drowned but for Isla's quick thinking with the chair." Dulcy said.

"So Isla saved Jenni. Fate mocks me. But well done my Mrs. Birdwhistle."

Aiden put an arm around Isla.

"And well done the younger Mrs. Birdwhistle, thanks for helping me Tiff."

Isla and Tiffany shared a grin.

"I wasn't much use. But hey, this will make wedding history."

"Fame. It's a burden." Ethan shrugged.

At least they could see an upside that their wedding day wasn't marred by worse outcomes. Had the attack ended in drowning Jenni and the librarian, their deaths would forever blacken the wedding day memories. Dougall commented:

"It was a close call and nearly a multiple tragedy. Wendall was behind the wheel, she must have lost her nerve at the last."

Aiden had his own interpretation. He knew his ex-wife far better than anyone.

Tiffany insisted she was fine, but her parents and Ethan half carried her back to the flat to shower and change into dry clothes. Dougall went back to liaise with police who would escort the ambulances. Francis took Frou Frou Pebbles back to the safety of his playpen and accepted a large brandy for herself.

Following procedure, police taped the section of beach off as a crime scene, not that there was anything further to investigate. With the entire wedding and botched attack caught on several cameras, the media fraternity already had the first 'breaking news' sensation screening nationally.

Dulcy Vestige sat with Isla on the beach while Aiden helped other men to heave the stranded vehicle over upright. The rollover was assisted by strengthening incoming swells, the ocean seemed keen to spit the invader out. Salt water streamed from every orifice of the SUV as the tow truck winched it further up the beach. Dulcy predicted the ram raid vehicle would be a rust bucket before too long.

"You'll need to change into something dry, Isla. Do you want me to take you back home?"

"No. I'm ok. But thanks Dulcy. I'll wait and go with Aiden and see you soon at the wedding breakfast. Surely that will go a little more smoothly. Ha ha."

"You're all very brave." Dulcy patted Isla's back. "My husband is looking forward to meeting you."

"Have you been married long Dulcy?"

"Four years. Dave is in the army so we haven't actually spent the whole time together. Still, absence makes the heart grow fonder."

"I can sort of relate to that. Thanks for your support Dulcy."

"Anytime. Someday we'll all get together and laugh about this."

"That's a promise. Now go and join your husband before one of the beach belles nabs him."

"A friendly girl was keeping him entertained. I think she said her name is Chantel."

"Oh no. Not the dreaded Chantel. She's the worst!"

"I'll see about that!" Dulcy exclaimed with a laugh.

The policewoman left with a wink and Isla felt as if she'd gained more family, with Dulcy as a surrogate big sister.

Isla remained sitting on the beach admiring Aiden in the sea as he helped out, despite this auspicious day and his sodden trousers. Bare chested, he had shed his jacket and shirt. A small cut, probably from the shattered windscreen, stung Isla's foot. Aiden returned as Isla inspected her slight injury. He made her lie back on her elbows, while he knelt at her feet, grasped her ankle and kissed the sole of her cut foot.

They knew a horde of people would be watching so when Isla felt his tongue give a sneaky lick, she threw her head back, laughing wholeheartedly at his daring.

"Did you just taste my foot? Are you feeling peckish?"

"I'm famished." He admitted.

"Then you will really enjoy the wedding breakfast."

That became the iconic image of the day. The pair soaked through, hair mussed up, Isla's sarong clinging to her shapely curves and her new husband kissing her hurt foot to make it better.

After quick showers and changes of clothes, Aiden and Isla presented themselves at their wedding breakfast alongside Ethan and Tiffany. They were all introduced to Bella, Dougall's wife and Dulcy's husband Dave for the first time.

Aiden recalled Dougall describing his wife as a rough diamond and the good lady did look a little rough at that moment. Bella Grimslade appeared pale and shaky.

Bella Grimslade clutched her husband's arm. Dougall asked for a cup of sweet tea for his wife, saying she skipped breakfast and was feeling wobbly.

Isla surmised that if his wife skipped breakfast, then Dougall probably had as well. She ordered them to sit down while she went for tea and rustled up the caterers to bring them sustenance. Aiden smiled appreciating Isla making an effort with the detective. Once again, he marvelled at the way Isla faced her demons head on.

The media went wild for the sensational outcome of that double wedding even without fully knowing the back story, which was bound to surface over time.

Jenni McKinstock and Millicent Wendall were reassessed as dangerous and put away for a very long time without recourse to parole. In the long run, neither woman ever went free.

Later going over the large amount of video evidence, it became apparent that Jenni had yanked the wheel, averting the collision. Aiden had already guessed the only reason Jenni would abort killing them all, was her dog. He grudgingly accepted that a tiny spark of goodness dwelt in his first wife's dark soul. Over a drink with Dougall, he explained:

"Jenni saw her dog and couldn't hurt him."

"That wee dog played quite a part in all the ructions." The detective concluded.

Francis Funicular was nominated for an award after footage showed her stepping protectively in front of the younger set. In due course, the lady became the proud recipient of a medal for bravery. Meanwhile, the poodle breeder happily minded Frou Frou Pebbles while the newlyweds went on their separate honeymoon holidays.

Ethan and Tiffany headed for the city to take in the latest shows. Isla wanted to tour the high country and experience some really cold weather, so she and Aiden went on a road trip around the Snowy Mountain regions.

Francis very seldom boarded dogs for others but had taken in a young fawn whippet for a sick friend, who later passed away. Pebbles and Noodle the whippet shared a yard and formed a friendly attachment to one and other. Francis made sure to impress on Aiden that the two dogs had bonded, when he came to pick the poodle up.

During their first outing together, at the work dinner meeting, Aiden recalled Miss Isla Tickle saying sighthounds to be her favourite dogs, and she hoped to have a dog of her own someday. In fact, Aiden remembered everything about the down-to-earth woman he fell in love with and loved completely as his new wife.

As a member of the sighthound family, the whippet fit the bill as a breed of dog Isla might like. So, serendipity and Francis Funicular both decreed Aiden should take Noodle home with Pebbles.

Aiden climbed upstairs with the two dogs when he arrived back from Francis's kennels. He called a greeting to Isla:

"Honey I'm home. With Pebbles. And a poor little mutt Francis talked me into."

Isla hurried down the hall to meet them.

"Oh my goodness. Why did Francis want you to take this one?"

"Because Pebbles likes him as a friend. She says they have bonded. The whippet's name is Noodle. His owner passed away, so he needs lots of TLC. You can have the skinny kid for your own. That is, if you're willing to take him on."

"I'm willing."

Isla knelt beside the Bambi-like whippet and introduced herself. Soon Noodle smooched up to Isla for a cuddle. On seeing Isla's tears well up, Aiden knew he'd done the right thing.

"Francis says to return him if he doesn't fit right in."

"Oh no. I am definitely willing to take him on." Isla confirmed.

Francis Funicular knew the whippet would never be returned. She was happy to have placed him in a loving forever home and felt certain the former owner would approve.

29

WE ARE FAMILY

After the wedding excitement and honeymoons, everyone shuffled back into their various work routines. The dogs integrated into the two households and the couples went about their everyday business.

One day, out of the blue, not long after the honeymoon trip, Dougall Grimslade asked Aiden if he could meet him privately one afternoon, for a serious talk, saying:

"Please let it be just between you and me for now."

"Is anything wrong?" Aiden asked.

"No. Well not exactly. But I'll explain when I see you."

Aiden was mystified. He suggested meeting further up the beach in a secluded cove. He brought a cold bag with a couple of light beers to share. Isla and Ethan had both been occupied in the office and did not question why Aiden had to go out for a while.

Dougall sat in his car until Aiden drove in to park beside him, then they walked down a sandy path to the inlet and sat on a couple of smooth rocks by the shore. Dougall appeared uneasy. Aiden wondered what the hell was bothering him. For the first time he noticed a few silver hairs threaded through his older friend's dark hair. Dougall said:

"I'm not sure how to start. I suppose I should go a long way back. Right back to the beginning, if I'm to make sense of it to you."

"OK. I'm intrigued." Aiden said.

"Alright. Back in my misbegotten very early twenties, I sang in a rock band."

"My god! You were a pop star?"

"Not even close. We were bloody terrible. However, we somehow attracted a handful of teeny bopper fans."

"It's a long way to the top if you wanna rock'n'roll." Aiden quoted the AC/DC lyric.

"Got to love a rock band that uses bagpipes." Dougall said.

Aiden agreed and asked Dougall to tell him more.

"So anyway, one night after our final gig at a teen disco, I found a girl leaning against my car, waiting for me. She was one of the young fans. I had my eye on her for a while. The way she danced...and moved...you know."

Aiden got the picture.

"We, me and the other band members that is, actually called the bunch of groupies band molls. I know that's crude, and I wince over it now. They were just fun-loving girls with awful tastes in music."

"Is this some sort of confession Dougall?"

"It is. Yes. So the girl wanted a lift home. I stopped off at a quiet bushland park on the way and gave her what she really wanted. What we both really wanted I should say. I only realised she was a virgin when it was too late. Anyway that freaked me out. For some reason I felt annoyed at her for making me responsible as her first. So I didn't kiss her goodnight when I dropped her off home. She gave me her number and asked me to ring her. I said I would. But I never did."

"Did you see her again?"

"Not for a long time. The band had broken up. I'd been accepted into the force and was going away for training. Then a few years later,

I participated in a raid on a squat where a bunch of adolescents were getting into marijuana and other drugs. The girl was one of them and we recognised each other."

Aiden wondered where this was leading. He cracked a can and gave one to Dougall. They both swigged beer and sat looking out to sea before Dougall continued:

"I bestowed my judgement on that girl and asked how she'd sunk so low. I held the moral high ground being the clean upright officer in uniform and she the downtrodden miscreant. She says: 'Well we made our choices Dougall. I can see how yours went. As for mine, I didn't have many options.' "

"The girl blamed you?"

"She did and I blamed myself as well. See, I got her pregnant but left no trace for her to find me. Her parents were so strict and religious she ran away before they found out. What came as the biggest shock to me was learning I had deflowered a fourteen year old. Fourteen! A child! Ten years younger than myself. Seems I joined the ranks of utter bastards before I joined the ranks of the police force."

"Bloody hell Dougall. But I know teenaged girls can seem a lot older."

Aiden wondered if this was to do with Ethan nailing Tiffany under the age of consent...but surely that didn't matter now they were married.

Aiden prompted Dougall to continue:

"This fourteen-year-old had your baby?"

"Yes she did. And all alone. Of course she had to give it up. I guess you know where this is heading now, hey Aiden?"

Aiden replied truthfully feeling he should know but had no idea.

"Sorry. You've lost me Dougall. What happened to the young girl?"

"I married her. We fell in love over the months of me visiting her in rehab."

"So... the girl was Bella?"

"Still is." Dougall replied.

Dougall drained his beer. He'd gone this far and there was no turning back. Despite the many difficulties he'd faced as a policeman and later as a detective this thing felt hardest.

"What is it Dougall? Why are you telling me all this?"

"I'm Isla's father." Dougall confessed at last.

"WHAT!?" Aiden fell off his rock. "Are you sure? How can you know that?"

Dougall waited for it to sink in as Aiden picked himself up and began to work it out.

"So...you're saying...?"

"Yes. Me and Bella. We are Isla's parents and don't know how to tell her. She'll wonder why we didn't find her. We tried but ran into a brick wall with authorities and their privacy rules. Then we assumed she'd be adopted into a good home. We accepted we had no right to disrupt her life. We decided the best we could do for her was to stay out of it."

Aiden could think of nothing to say. For moments he just stared a Dougall, trying to take it in. Isla once spoke of a wish to know why she'd been abandoned at birth, no matter how bad the reason might be. She'd supposed it most likely that her mother had been a drug addict, maybe a prostitute. Now Aiden was being told Isla's mother had been a frightened fourteen-year-old child runaway.

"I'm gobsmacked. But are you absolutely sure Isla is your daughter? How could you know after all this time? She always yearned for permanent family. So she must not be told this unless it's an absolute certainty. It would be too cruel if it isn't true."

"Of course I'd never say until I knew for sure. But I felt she had to be from the first time I laid eyes on her. I've waited because of the dramas with her abduction and the fact Isla obviously doesn't like me." Dougall said.

Aiden knew Isla hadn't cared much for Dougall but refrained from confirming it.

"What made you think Isla might be the one?"

"She's the spitting image of Bella at the same age. Her face, her figure, even her voice and her feisty manner. Above all, it was the look of mutiny that passed over her face when I first interviewed her. I knew she was dying to tick me off for staring at her during that interview. She's Bella all over. I couldn't stop gaping at her."

"Isla did say she felt unnerved by the way you stared her down."

"I used police resources to research Isla's past. Her date of birth fit. Then I learnt she'd been abandoned. Left in a box in a church and brought up in an institution. Bella never filled me in on exactly how she managed the birth and handing over the baby. I always imagined something like a nunnery with a midwife. I'm guilty of avoiding asking Bella too much about it as well. And she's lived with her own guilt for abandoning the baby that way..."

"Isla told me she was found in a box at a church."

"Did she? So she knows that much. I also learnt the minister's wife had been trying to lure a stray cat in out of the cold. She put the cardboard carton lined with some old linen just inside the vestibule. The baby... our baby was found in it with a short note disowning the child."

"Isla has that note. She was given it when she left the orphanage. It's pretty sad I have to tell you. But can it be proven? You say you now know for sure Dougall?"

"During Isla's abduction recovery, at the hospital, I pulled out a few strands of her hair while she was under sedation. I put it in an evidence envelope and later had it DNA'd. It matches with me and Bella. So I've known for some time Isla is definitely our daughter."

"But why now? Why have you waited this long? I mean, I guess you have your reasons."

"Only that I didn't know how to tell Bella without breaking her heart again. But, as it turned out, Bella realised the truth by herself."

"How?"

"The first time Bella saw Isla was at your wedding. Somehow she knew and almost keeled over. I don't know how she could have known. Unless she saw herself in Isla, like I did. That night I had to confirm the DNA proof and Bella has cried and cried ever since."

"Jesus." Aiden couldn't get over it. "Your wife reminded me of Isla at the time as well. I recalled you saying she was your rough diamond and I also thought of Isla as such."

"Bella is short for Isabella, it even sounds a little like Isla... Did Isla ever tell you how she got her name?"

"No. I only know she was brought up as an orphan and almost forced to take the supermarket job as a guilt trip of gratitude to the home. How did she get the name?"

"Off the Tickles Thousand Island Dressing carton she was found in."

"The poor little mite. And the poor young mother too. I wonder why Isla was never adopted."

"Apparently our Isla was an outrageously wild and unruly child."

"Why doesn't that surprise me?" Aiden had to laugh.

"I wasn't amazed either. Knowing her mother." Dougall admitted.

Aiden and Dougall shared a fond smile for their bad girls.

"So now we have this dilemma. Of course Isla has a right to be told. And I'm sure your Bella wants to get to know her." Aiden summed up.

"I've mentioned to Bella that Isla doesn't like me. She wants to reveal our parentage but is afraid of rejection. Says she wouldn't blame Isla."

"I don't think Isla would do that." Aiden said. "She has a good kind heart and would absolutely understand about the whole underage aspect...we've had some experience of that with um...some others we know."

"You mean your brother and his young wife? I summed that up early on." Dougall said.

"How?"

"I'm a detective."

"You're also my father-in-law."

"You want to call me Dad?"

"Nah. I like Doogie for you better."

"Thank Christ for that. It's what Bella calls me too. Unless she's in a mood."

"I guess I'm the one to break it to Isla. Any ideas on how I go about it?"

"Up to you. You know her best of all. Just make it soon if possible. Bella can be rash. She might take it into her head to barge in to get it over with. But I reckon Isla needs to digest the news before we meet as her parents. Assuming she's willing to accept us."

Dougall couldn't hide how anxious he felt.

"I'll tell her tonight. Somehow. I'll have to think of an easy way to break it to her."

"Good luck son. Let me know how it goes as soon as you can. I'd better go get some take-away meals. I don't think Bella will be up for cooking tonight."

Aiden followed suit and texted Isla to say he'd bring home take-away and what did she fancy. She texted back saying anything would do but sweet and sour pork with noodles would be nice. He knew it had better be exactly that. Isla had the table set and Aiden presented the designated meal on cue.

"Do you want a glass of wine with it?" Isla asked.

"Let's save it for after. I want to talk to you about something."

"Uh oh. What have I done?"

"Nothing. All good. Don't worry."

So Isla did worry. She kept looking at Aiden's face throughout the meal. He seemed nervous. What had he done? They took their wine to the sofa and sat together.

"You were out for quite a while this afternoon." Isla ventured.

"I met with Dougall Grimslade."

"Really? He's become a good friend for you hasn't he."

"More than that." Aiden replied.

Isla's mind boggled. What on earth? Aiden took her wine glass and put it on the coffee table before taking both her hands in his.

"More than a good friend..?" Isla queried the description.

"He's my father-in-law." Aiden blurted out.

He kicked himself for the dumb disclosure, blaming it on nerves.

"What? Dougall is Jenni's father?"

"No. No. No. Isla, Dougall Grimslade is your father."

"Are you nuts? How does that work? You can't be serious."

"I am serious. I wracked my brains over what to say. And I've botched this. But yes my darling. Your birth parents have been found and confirmed."

Isla reeled with the news. Surely Aiden wouldn't make such a bad joke. She stared at him and shook her head in denial. This couldn't be true. Aiden tried for an embrace, but she shrugged him off, jumped up from the sofa and walked outside to the verandah, hugging her arms about her own body. It was the first time Isla had ever rejected his touch, so Aiden knew the degree of impact this had on her.

"I've messed this up. Sorry Isla. I know it's a great shock. It was to me as well when Dougall told me this afternoon. I even fell off my rock."

"You mean off your rocker! Why would that man make this up? That's what I don't understand." Isla exclaimed angrily.

"He didn't make it up. Isla, it's true. He even has DNA proof. And he and his wife are terrified of your reaction. That's why he got me to tell you."

"His wife? I scare her as well?"

"Bella is your birth mother Isla. The Grimslades are your blood parents."

Isla's legs went to jelly and she fell to her knees. Aiden picked her up.

"It's true? How could it be? That means....they...they dumped me?" Isla cried.

"No. Let me tell you how it happened."

Aiden half carried her back inside to the sofa while he related the entire story as Dougall told it. In the end, Isla's face swam with tears.

"Bella hasn't stopped crying either." Aiden told her. "When she saw you at the wedding breakfast, somehow she knew. Even before being told."

"There was something about her...then I got her a cup of tea...I got my mother a cup of tea."

Isla suddenly jumped up and grabbed her bag.

"I'm going to see them right now."

"Isla. No. You can't."

"I can. And you can't stop me Aiden."

"I mean we don't know where they live." Aiden explained gently.

Isla swore in frustration then ordered Aiden to find out.

"Ring Dougall and get the address."

"It's late. Why don't we sleep on it and go tomorrow?" Aiden tried.

"How could I sleep? If you won't help then I'm going for a walk on the beach."

"Not alone. I'll come with you."

"No. And don't follow me."

"I will follow you. And you can't stop me either, Isla."

Aiden's voice broke on the words. Isla heard the wretchedness in Aiden's tone. She looked at her good man and felt mean for taking it out on him. His parents were lost forever. Hers had been found. She put her bag down.

"I love you Aiden. I shouldn't take it out on you. What would I do without you?"

"Take it out on your Mum and Dad like any other brat would?"

Mum and Dad. Isla repeated the words in her mind. *My Mum and Dad.*

"Anyway. I'm tired and I need a shower." She said grudgingly.

"I'll soap your back if you do mine." He smiled.

"Deal."

Aiden phoned Dougall very early next morning.

"Mission accomplished." he said.

"How did she take it?"

"Refused to believe it at first. Then she was up for going to your place right away. Except we didn't have your address and I refused to phone you late at night. We had our first row. But all good now. I soaped her back."

"Knew you'd handle it."

"So. Now what?" Aiden asked.

"Let's have a picnic at that same cove again. If they play up we can always dunk them."

Aiden heard Bella comment in the background. "I know who'll dunk who."

Unperturbed Dougall said:

"Is today too soon? Weather looks fine for a dunking."

"Hold on. I'll just check with the trouble and strife."

Aiden came back on the line and confirmed for a picnic brunch at the cove that very day. He got busy making sandwiches and packing drinks.

Isla stressed over what to wear and decided on Indian harem pants with a cool white cotton t-shirt.

Isla and Aiden went early to the cove and set up some folding chairs under a big beach umbrella. They laid out a thick picnic blanket and put a couple of eskies in the shade. Then just waited for Isla's parents to get there.

The older couple arrived and made their way hand in hand across the sand. Dougall carried another esky which he set down as Isla walked over to greet them. Isla observed that Bella had also chosen to wear batik harem pants teamed with a white cheesecloth top reminiscent of the hippy era. Their outfits were almost identical. Bella wore her long brown hair twisted up in a roll, secured by a big hair clip. The women appeared more like sisters than mother and daughter.

Aiden stood back under the umbrella to give them some space. Isla spoke first.

"So. You're my parents. We meet at last." Her voice wobbled.

"My darling girl. Please believe me. I have thought of you every day of your life. And I am so sorry for the way I left you." Bella's voice also wobbled.

"You were only a child yourself."

Isla fixed Dougall momentarily with stern disapproval, at once giving a glimpse of himself in her heritage. Dougall's eyes pleaded for understanding but he had no answer. Bella stepped up and took Isla's face between her hands while Isla stood rigidly yet allowed her mother's touch.

"Let me look at you. Seeing you at your wedding was like looking at a younger me. Now I also see Dougall in your expressions."

"Win some. Lose some." Isla replied.

"He's not that bad when you get to know him. Trust me. I'm your mother." Bella mocked herself with an eye roll.

Isla relented and embraced Bella with a warm hug. They both sobbed and laughed at the same time. Dougall took his esky over to join Aiden under the umbrella.

"Could be worse." Dougall said.

"She'll come round." Aiden answered hoping he was right.

Isla and Bella walked to the shoreline, chatting together, picking up shells, putting them down again.   Isla learnt her mother was a dressmaker. Dougall had given her a sewing machine when they first married. She still used it and loved it. Isla told her Aiden had given her a whippet as her own dog.   Bella exclaimed that she loved those little sighthounds and couldn't wait to meet Noodle.

"We better get back to the guys before they eat all the goodies... Mum." Isla said at last.

"Thank you for that, Isla." Bella whispered.

Aiden and Dougall had set out some plates and helped themselves to light beers since the hour had passed noon.

"Aiden has been telling me how you both met." Dougall said to start the conversation.

"Yep. I was sprung being a bad girl." Isla laughed.

They proceeded to tell Bella all about Isla's matchmaking past.

"I was a bad girl as well." Bella admitted. "I sprung myself on poor Doogie and he had no idea I was so young."

"Huh. Bet he was easy." Isla said.

"Like candy from a baby." Bella laughed.

Aiden burst out with a loud guffaw, saying Isla told Tiffany the same thing about himself.

Coming to grips with the awkward meeting, the four talked and shared their picnics over the next few hours although Dougall felt the odd one out.

An afternoon breeze whipped up some flurries of sand. They would soon pack up for home. Finally, Isla's father faced up:

"Isla. I understand your feelings about the evidence tapes. But I made sure there are no longer any copies of the originals on file. What exists has you completely blurred out. And I want you to know, if those men hadn't died there, I'd be up for murder myself."

"Your father has your back Isla." Bella added seriously.

"Thanks. I do very appreciate knowing that. Of course, I still stress over the videos you and Dulcy told me about." Isla admitted.

"Forget about it. All destroyed when the yacht exploded." Dougall replied.

"Lucky there was no loss of life when that happened." Aiden put in.

"I made sure there was no one on board."

Dougall said it nonchalantly. He stood and gazed out towards the horizon, hands in his pockets. While Bella smiled and nodded. Aiden and Isla stared at the back of the stern police detective. They got the drift.

As the officer in charge of the case, it would cost Dougall Grimslade his job and his pension if it was ever discovered he had destroyed the yacht and all the evidence on board.

Dougall felt fully justified and was not sorry he'd broken the law to protect his daughter. Isla's expression softened. Bella gave her a nudge. Dougall didn't know if what he'd risked made much difference to how Isla felt about him as her father.

The gruff detective gave her an out:

"Isla. You can call me Doogie if you like. That's what Aiden and Bella call me."

Isla stood, wrapped her arms about her father and smooched a big kiss on his cheek.

"No way. You don't get off that easily. Dad."

A tear glimmered in detective Grimslade's eye. It might have been from sand thrown up in the sea breeze. Or not.

***

The End.

BOOKS BY

Jo Milanne

A FAIR CRACK – And a Walk-in Wardrobe
THE BRUISER – Bad to the Core
LEMON TANGO – It Takes Two
THE PECKISH – Hunger for Love

www.ingramcontent.com/pod-product-compliance
Lightning Source LLC
Chambersburg PA
CBHW051141190726
48290CB00006B/1947